RED FURY

FOLLOWING THE TRAGIC events that led the Blood Angels to the brink of civil war, the Chapter's strength has been badly depleted. The Blood Angels must act, and act quickly, before their enemies learn of their weakness and attack. Summoning their successor Chapters to Baal, their homeworld, the Blood Angels hope to replenish their numbers. Little do they realise that another, more desperate, plan is being enacted in secret. An old enemy plots against the Blood Angels, his machinations threatening Baal itself. With tempers flaring, and mutants running wild, can the Blood Angels and their successor Chapters put aside their rivalries and rebuild their forces before it is too late?

A WARHAMMER 40,000 NOVEL

BLOOD ANGELS

RED FURY

James Swallow

For Scott, Jane, William, Eliza and Annabelle.
Rock On!

A BLACK LIBRARY PUBLICATION

First published in Great Britain in 2008 by
BL Publishing,
Games Workshop Ltd.,
Willow Road, Nottingham,
NG7 2WS, UK.

10 9 8 7 6 5 4 3 2 1

Cover illustration by Adrian Smith.

A CIP record for this book is available from the British Library.

ISBN13: 978 1 84416 659 6
ISBN10: 1 84416 659 7

See the Black Library on the Internet at
www.blacklibrary.com

Find out more about Games Workshop
and the world of Warhammer 40,000 at
www.games-workshop.com

Printed and bound in the UK.

IT IS THE 41st millennium. For more than a hundred centuries the Emperor has sat immobile on the Golden Throne of Earth. He is the master of mankind by the will of the gods, and master of a million worlds by the might of his inexhaustible armies. He is a rotting carcass writhing invisibly with power from the Dark Age of Technology. He is the Carrion Lord of the Imperium for whom a thousand souls are sacrificed every day, so that he may never truly die.

YET EVEN IN his deathless state, the Emperor continues his eternal vigilance. Mighty battlefleets cross the daemon-infested miasma of the warp, the only route between distant stars, their way lit by the Astronomican, the psychic manifestation of the Emperor's will. Vast armies give battle in His name on uncounted worlds. Greatest amongst his soldiers are the Adeptus Astartes, the Space Marines, bio-engineered super-warriors. Their comrades in arms are legion: the Imperial Guard and countless planetary defence forces, the ever-vigilant Inquisition and the tech-priests of the Adeptus Mechanicus to name only a few. But for all their multitudes, they are barely enough to hold off the ever-present threat from aliens, heretics, mutants – and worse.

TO BE A man in such times is to be one amongst untold billions. It is to live in the cruellest and most bloody regime imaginable. These are the tales of those times. Forget the power of technology and science, for so much has been forgotten, never to be re-learned. Forget the promise of progress and understanding, for in the grim dark future there is only war. There is no peace amongst the stars, only an eternity of carnage and slaughter, and the laughter of thirsting gods.

CHAPTER ONE

SOME THINGS DO not die all at once.

Men. Daemons. Whole worlds. Sometimes, the fight bleeds them white and still they will not perish, moving as if they are alive, going through the motions of it, unaware that they are already ended. Such things are corpses, after a fashion, ashen and pallid, heavy with the musk of decay.

Eritaen was such a thing. An urbanised sprawl-planet, too far off the axis of the Imperium's prime trade routes to be thought of as a hive-world, it had at one time thrived in its own, limited manner. But the rebellion had made all of that go away.

The people had been weak; it was a lament repeated across the galaxy. They had been weak and allowed the taint into their society. And this was the reward they reaped, to die slowly in the ruins of the cities that had birthed them, dying but already dead.

Rafen dallied beneath the arching hood of an ornate atrium, the entrance to a public kinema. Shattered glass lay in drifts around the ticket vendor kiosk and the flame-blackened stanchions. Broken displays advertising pict-dramas and out-of-date newsreels glittered in the dimness. Like everything he had seen in the city, the debris had a fine layer of powdery, dun-coloured dust across it. The sandy fines were everywhere, billowing through the streets, hanging in great cloudy knots in the sky making the blue daylight muddy and bland. The dust left an unpleasant taste at the back of his throat, like bonemeal.

A flickering dash of fire danced in the depths of the open doors leading into the picture palace, and presently Turcio emerged from the darkness with his flamer at a casual ready in his augmetic fist, the pilot light in the muzzle hissing quietly to itself. The Space Marine went unhooded, his clenched fist of a face tight and severe. Absently, Rafen's eyes went to the penitent brand, laser-burned into Turcio's brow above his right eye, and the scars where his service studs had been removed. Other men might have gone about with their helmets locked tight and faces hidden, the better to conceal their shame, but not Brother Turcio. He wore the marks boldly, like a badge of honour.

'Anything?' Rafen asked.

The Astartes nodded to his commander. 'Brother-sergeant,' he began. 'The same as before. The structure is empty. I found signs of our kinsmen's presence, but they are long gone. I'd estimate a day, perhaps two.'

Rafen's lip curled in disappointment. 'This data they gave us is worthless.' He allowed himself to look up, along the long boulevard that stretched away to the north. The street was choked with rubble from fallen tower blocks and stalled vehicles abandoned in the madness of the rebellion. Like most of Eritaen's municipalities, this conurbation was built on a grid of kilometre-long roads that crosshatched the landscape of the planet. The buildings that sprouted from each city block were sheer-sided and narrow, rising fifty to seventy levels high. All that differentiated them were the colours of the stone and the odd architectural flourish; by and large, they had the uniform cast of buildings thrown up by the dogged and uninspired colonial administrators of the Munitorum. Rafen imagined that it would be easy to become lost in such a place, if one did not possess the perfect sense of direction granted to an Adeptus Astartes.

Still, the city made him uncomfortable. Acres of blast-blown windows gaped toward him, each one a dark pit that even his helmet optics struggled to penetrate. Any one of them could conceal a sniper behind a lascannon or a missile launcher. He would have preferred to range above the city in a shuttle, find their objective and proceed directly to it; but the rules of engagement for Eritaen had been impressed on the sergeant with no small amount of emphasis. This battle zone did not belong to him, and as such it was not his place to question how war was fought here. Rafen turned to find the rest of his squad waiting in half-cover behind an overturned omnibus, their crimson armour glittering dully in the afternoon haze. The Blood Angels were in this place as invited guests. This conflict was not theirs to prosecute nor comment upon.

He switched his vox to the general frequency and cut through the air with the blade of his hand. 'We move on,' he told them. 'They're not here.'

He heard the sneer in Ajir's words as the tactical trooper emerged from behind the burnt-out vehicle. 'Throne's sake! Are they playing some kind of game with us?' As always, the cocksure Space Marine was the first into the open, as if he were daring the city to take a shot at him.

Rafen's frown deepened. Ajir seemed to assume he was somehow indestructible, as if his bolter and a swagger in his step were all he needed to defend against the arch-enemy.

'It wouldn't surprise me,' offered Turcio. 'Our erstwhile cousins have never been ones to—'

'Enough,' Rafen silenced the other warrior with a shake of his head. 'We have our mission and our message. That will be our focus.'

'Aye, lord.' Turcio's head bobbed. 'Of course.'

He strode away, beckoning the largest of the squad toward him. The unit's designated heavy weapons operator, the Space Marine differed from his brethren by his blue-coloured helmet and the massive, slab-sided shape of a belt-fed heavy bolter in his grip. Brother Puluo stepped up and nodded. The thickset, broad warrior didn't seem to think that speaking was an important part of communication with his comrades, and for the most part that had proven to be true. Puluo brought new definition to the word 'taciturn', but Rafen had warmed to the silent man after he had been assigned to his squad. What he lacked in vocality he more than made up with martial prowess. 'Watch the windows,' he told him, in a low voice. 'I have an inkling...'

Puluo nodded again and thumbed off the bolter's safety, stepping past to find a better vantage point.

Behind them, young Kayne was hesitating, scrutinising the auspex in his gloved hand. 'No change in readings, sir. There's more cloud across this screen than a Secundus dust storm.' Kayne was the tallest of them, rail-thin and whipcord-strong in comparison to Puluo's densely muscled form. He also went bareheaded.

'Atomics.' Brother Corvus was the last to emerge, panning his bolter back and forth in a wary arc. 'Residual radiation from airburst detonations. It'll fog everything out beyond a half-kilometre.'

'Aye,' Kayne agreed, a sour tone in his voice, and he holstered the device, somewhat awkwardly. Rafen saw that Corvus noted the motion too, but neither said anything. The young Astartes was still finding his feet; only a scant few weeks ago, Kayne had been a Scout in the tenth company, and his promotion to the rank of full battle-brother was still fresh in his manner. The Mark VIII Imperator power armour he wore was new to him, and to the trained eye of a line warrior, it showed.

Rafen looked away. He had chosen the youth for the squad for several reasons, but largely because of his superlative marksmanship skills; however, in all truth the sergeant would have preferred to spend more time drilling and training his unit so that they meshed like finely-machined gears before they embarked on this sortie. Small things like Kayne's unease should have been smoothed out by now, along with the other, less obvious rough edges – he glanced at Turcio and Corvus, thinking again of the penitent marks that both men shared.

But the Will of the Emperor and the Chapter did not move to the clock of a mere brother-sergeant. Commander Dante had given him his orders, and he had left the home world the very same day, his small concerns paying no coin against the word of his sworn lord, the master of the Blood Angels. There had been time aboard the frigate that brought them to Eritaen, but not enough. Never enough. His gaze found Turcio once again; of all of them, only he had served with Rafen for any length of time, before the incident on Cybele and the madness that had followed afterward…

Rafen shook off the moment; that path of reverie would serve only to dilute his focus. Although the rebellion on Eritaen had been crushed, it would not do for the sergeant to have his thoughts elsewhere. The city-sprawls still contained pockets of resistance that might be foolish enough to prey upon a squad of Adeptus

Astartes, alone and unsupported. On some level, he hoped they might try; battle practice in the fortress monastery and aboard the frigate was fine as far as it went, but there was no substitute for the real thing.

The mission, though. The mission and the message came first.

They moved on, shifting into and out of the long, angular pools of shadow cast by the tower blocks. The glass, the dust-dulled shards of colour and light, lay everywhere. It was impossible to move without grinding them beneath their ceramite boots. At the base of some buildings, the glittering debris lay in mantles that were knee-deep even for the tall forms of the Space Marines. Once or twice, they caught the distant snarl of bolter fire, echoing and distorted down the concrete canyons of the city.

Rafen paused at an intersection, scanning the paths open to them. A hard, heavy breeze was moving east-to-west. It carried light debris in the air over their heads, scraps of paper, bits of torn cloth and the like; closer to the ground, it pushed the thick dust in sluggish waves that curled around their ankles. The sergeant dialled the filters on his breath grille to maximum and peered into the distance, watching for any sign of movement.

He found it.

'THERE,' SAID RAFEN, pointing with a gauntleted finger. 'Do you see?'

Ajir nodded. 'Aye. Someone inside the groundcar?' The Blood Angel frowned inside his helmet. 'I think… I think he's *waving* to us.'

At his side, Puluo made a grunting sound that was his equivalent of amusement. Kayne was sighting down the scope atop his bolter. 'I can't get a good angle from here. Brother-sergeant, perhaps I should find another vantage point?'

'No,' Rafen replied. 'It could be a ploy to draw us out.'

Ajir studied the intersection. Beneath the dust were the remains of what must have been a horrific road accident. Several groundcars, a cargo hauler and two rail-trams were snarled together in a mess of metal and plastic. The Space Marine imagined the component parts of the collision separating, mentally tracking them backward to their points of origin.

'The highway governance system's machine-spirit died,' said Corvus, clearly thinking along the same lines. 'The vehicles collided at high speed.'

'They were trying to flee the city,' offered Turcio. 'You agree?'

Ajir didn't meet the other warrior's gaze. 'I suppose so.' He found it difficult to converse with Turcio or Corvus and not see their penitent brands, not dwell on what they signified. For what must have been the hundredth time, Ajir found himself wondering what had possessed Brother-Sergeant Rafen to have the two men in his squad. They had proven themselves flawed, had they not? The very idea that the Blood Angels were in the business of giving those who failed the Emperor second chances was hard for him to swallow.

'Teardrop formation.' Rafen gave the order quickly and firmly. 'Watch your sightlines and be ready.'

'We approach?' said Kayne.

'We do,' said the sergeant. 'If it's a trap, then we'll trip it.'

BUT IN THE end, it was only the wind they found ranged against them. In the lee of the largest groundcar was the waving figure; the corpse of a man perhaps three or four days dead, fallen at an odd angle that let the hard gusts move him to and fro. The breeze gave the illusion of movement, of life.

'He's wearing remnants of a uniform,' noted Kayne, nudging the body with the toe of his boot. 'A local branch of enforcers, I'd warrant.'

'More here,' called Turcio, shifting a stalled vehicle with a shove of his shoulder. 'Civilians?'

Rafen's eyes narrowed behind his visor. 'Difficult to tell.' He came closer. The lay of the dead seemed incorrect. Bodies had a way about them when they fell in battle or from injury. He didn't see it with these. 'They weren't killed here.'

'Not in the accident, lord, no.' Turcio gestured to the vehicles. 'I would say they were executed elsewhere and then dumped here.'

'In the middle of a debris pile?' Ajir sniffed. 'To what end?'

Kayne spat on the highway. 'Who can fathom the purpose of anything the arch-enemy does?'

'True enough,' admitted Corvus.

Rafen's paid little heed to the words of his men. He knelt by the body of the enforcer and cradled the dead man's head in his palm. The corpse-flesh was so very white, almost a translucent colour against the bright crimson of his gauntlet. Eyes, sightless and cloudy, stared back up at him. The body felt strangely light.

With care, Rafen pinched a piece of flesh between the fingers of his glove.

Turcio followed his commander's scrutiny. 'What is it, brother-sergeant?'

Rafen let the dead man fall away. 'There's no blood. Look around, do you see any? Not a trace of it.'

Kayne sniffed the air. 'No... No, that's right. I didn't even notice...'

Corvus drew his auspex and spoke a quick invocation, setting it to a biological scan mode. He waved it over the body of another civilian, this one a woman. 'They have been exsanguinated,' he reported. 'All vitae taken from their bodies.'

Rafen pulled at the collar of the dead enforcer and found a large puncture mark just above his clavicle. 'Here. I imagine we'll find the same wound on all of them.'

Kayne spat again and made the sign of the aquila. 'Emperor protect their souls. It's not enough they were killed, but something did that to them.'

'The Emperor has no mercy for these fools,' said Corvus. He turned the dead woman's face so that they could all see the line of rings and arcs tattooed along her jaw line. '*Companitas*. The mark of the rebellion.'

The dissenter movement on Eritaen was not a product of that world alone. If anything, the Companitas were one of many minor factions that crawled and hid in the cracks of the Imperium's monolithic culture. Rafen knew only the surface details about them, only the information that was of tactical value. Outwardly the Companitas preached unity, freedom and comradeship between all men; behind closed doors they were said to engage in acts of wantonness that most decent folk would think shameful, if not utterly repugnant. The hand of Chaos was at their backs; Rafen did not doubt it. Perhaps not in the rank and file of misguided fools like these, but certainly elsewhere, in their upper echelons.

'Perhaps they did this to themselves,' offered Turcio. 'The Corrupted have been known to do the like.'

Kayne shifted. 'There may be other cause,' he said darkly. 'The taking of the blood… Perhaps it was a prize.' The young Astartes gestured toward the wreckage and the corpses. 'Perhaps we have come upon some sort of… warning. A message left here for the rebels.'

'Why take the blood, then?' demanded Ajir.

The younger warrior shot his commander a wary look, uncertain if he should speak further. 'You know where we are, on whose battleground we walk. We've all heard the stories,' he said, after a moment.

Rafen's men exchanged loaded glances, and he did not need the preternatural insight of a psyker to know the thoughts they were sharing at that moment. He drew himself up to his full height and spoke firmly, breaking the sudden, new tension. 'Whoever was the architect of this grisly scene, it matters nothing to us. They are long gone by now and lay outside our concerns.' He stepped away from the wreckage. 'We tarry too long in this place. Gather yourselves, we have a–'

His words trailed off, and the other men came instantly to alert. Rafen froze, staring down the roadway. Something was amiss.

'Sir?' said Turcio.

Puluo had seen it too. The heavy bolter's feed belt creaked as he turned the gun toward a building at the south-western point of the intersection.

'Auspex,' ordered Rafen.

Corvus still had the unit in his hand and studied it, tapping at the large keys on the surface, conjuring information from the device's machine-spirit. 'Motion detection read is inconclusive. You saw something?'

Puluo nodded gently toward the tower block. 'Movement,' he said.

'Rebels?' asked Ajir.

Rafen hefted his bolter. 'Likely.' From the corner of his eye, he had glimpsed the very smallest flicker of colour at one of the windows; the watery-blue daylight cast across something shiny and green, like an insect carapace. A man in combat armour. He had only the very quickest impression of shape and form, but hard-won experience had taught the sergeant to trust his instincts, to let the enhanced elements of his Astartes physiology bring the sense of his world to him, raw and unfiltered.

He raised the blade of his hand, opened the fingers; the battle sign command for *spread out*. The six Space Marines shifted away from the cover of the wrecks and moved swiftly toward the building, opening up into a fan, covering every possible angle of attack.

They came in, loping like hunter canines on the prowl, boots crunching softly on dull dust and chips of glass. Rafen saw that the building was a service tower, a layered structure of offices and Adminstratum facilities. Renditions of the noble Imperial eagle jutted from every corner, and across the main entrance a pair of towering figures in the robes of the Adeptus Terra flanked the space where the doors would have been. Some of the upper tiers had collapsed down into those below them, giving the building a stooped aspect. The sergeant noted this; the structure was probably unstable, which meant restricting the men to non-explosive weapons. The ill-considered use of a krak grenade here could conceivably bring the roof down upon them.

Kayne signalled to him, and pointed. Off to the side, the dusty road dropped into a shallow ramp leading toward the underlevels of the tower. An underground vehicle park, he realised. Rafen considered it for a moment. A good, defensible position, as tough as any fallout shelter or army bunker, concealed to the eyes of anything but a close-range inspection. A fair choice for a rebel seeking a bolt hole.

He hesitated. Once he gave the order to step inside, he would be venturing beyond the mission orders granted to him. Rafen's squad were to seek their objective, nothing more, nothing less. If he turned them all away and led them back down the highway, it would not be wrong to do so – but in all truth, the matter of the dead bodies had concerned him. He felt a building need to know more about what was going on here on Eritaen.

Rafen's brow furrowed. He decided to consider it an exercise. They had been prowling the streets of this maze for days. Some action would be a blessing.

He nodded to Kayne and gestured for him to take the point, all the better to give him something to focus on. The young warrior smiled thinly, pausing to replace his helmet before moving on.

THE UNDERLEVEL PARKING structure descended for several tiers beneath the service tower, dropping into sub-basements that ranged away into the dimness. The floor was canted downwards, each level a shallow ramp leading to the next. With the city's power grid long since smashed, the only light came from the sickly yellow-green glow of biolume pods along the rough ferrocrete walls. Rafen felt the familiar tensing sensation at the back of his eyes as his occulobe implant stirred to life, stimulating the cells of his optic nerves. The deeper they ventured inside, the more the chambers took on a flat, washed-out cast, his vision adjusting to the low levels of illumination.

He glanced at the sensor glyphs in the corner of his visor. The armour's integral atmosphere sensors were registering a slight build-up of monoxides in the atmosphere, but so little as to be beneath the notice of an Astartes. The ever-present powdery dust had not reached this far; only small curls of it lurked here and there, drooling from the grilles of ventilation shafts. Down here, the air tasted of stale hydrocarbons and spent batteries.

Turcio tap-tapped the side of his helmet, attracting the attention of the whole squad. 'More bodies.' There were perhaps fifty or sixty of them, piled in a long, low heap against a wall. 'These ones haven't been blooded.'

'Saved for later, maybe,' Kayne noted quietly.

Ajir bent closer. 'What are those?' He pointed to a strange contraption about the torso of the nearest figure. From Rafen's viewpoint, it resembled a metallic vest with racks of glassy tubes ranged down it, each one dark with some sort of oily liquid inside. His hearing detected a faint clicking sound. Every one of the bodies wore the same item; every one of them bore the Companitas insignia on their face.

'Touch nothing,' said Rafen. 'The corpses are likely to be booby-trapped.'

'We leave them here?' Ajir pressed.

'Aye,' he returned. 'Turcio will torch them when we've completed our sweep.'

They moved on. There were a few vehicles, mostly of the boxy, utilitarian kind pressed from the same Standard Template Construct pattern used on thousands of human worlds. Rafen imagined they had likely been abandoned in the rush to escape the city when the fighting finally spilled into the open.

'Still nothing,' offered Corvus, scrutinising the auspex.

'Not quite,' said Kayne, halting with his bolter at his shoulder.

Ahead of them, sitting cross-legged atop the bonnet of a low-slung cargo flatbed, was a figure partially clad in what appeared to be scraps of Imperial Guard-issue armour. It was a male, dirty and matted, hunched slightly forward. His shoulders were twitching and he paid the approach of the Space Marines no heed. Rafen's immediate impression was of someone silently weeping.

'He does not register...' said Corvus. 'I read no organic traces from him.'

Kayne had already drawn a bead, and the rest of the unit reacted as they were supposed to, spying to the corners of the parking space, looking for other threats.

Rafen took a step forward. 'Identify yourself,' he demanded. The Blood Angel was not in the business of being ignored.

The man looked up briefly, and it became clear he was not weeping, but laughing. He did it without uttering a sound, rocking back and forth as if the greatest comedy of all the universe had been revealed to him.

'I asked you a question, citizen.' Rafen's free hand drifted to the hilt of his power sword. 'Speak!'

Abruptly, the man slid off the vehicle and stumbled drunkenly toward them. 'The dust,' he gulped, gasping in air between quiet jags of hysteria. 'The dust is why it's… It's all that's left of them!'

'Stand back,' ordered Kayne, all hesitation gone from his voice.

'See,' said the man, offering something to them in his cupped hands. 'See.' It was a glass cylinder filled with thick fluid, identical to those mounted upon the metal vests. Closer now, and Rafen could see the laughing man was also wearing one beneath his dirt-slick jacket. 'Come to the dust,' he choked, and with a sudden motion, the ragged figure jammed the tube into his thigh.

A clicking noise sounded from the cylinder, and with a glugging cough the fluid inside discharged into the man's leg. He shuddered like a palsy victim and leapt at them, whooping.

Kayne's gun discharged and the flat *bang* of the shot echoed around them. The laughing man was slammed backward, his neck ending in a haze of pink mist.

'He tried to attack you.' Corvus was almost incredulous. 'Was he out of his mind?'

'Apparently,' opined Puluo.

Then from behind them, back up along the shallow rise of the slanting floor, a rattling chorus of clicking and hissing and chugging echoed off the walls. The pile of bodies writhed and slipped, figures falling off one another, dropping to the floor and rolling away. Others were stiff-legged, climbing slowly to their feet. Giggling. Mumbling. Empty glass ampoules fell from the ports in their vests and rolled down toward the Astartes.

'They were dead…' Corvus blinked.

'Yes,' noted Turcio. 'They *were*.'

'Remind them, then,' said Rafen, bringing up his gun as the figures swarmed toward them, each one injecting draughts of fluid into their twitching bodies.

PULUO UNLEASHED THE heavy bolter, and inside the confines of the vehicle park the noise of the weapon's discharge was a metallic bellow. A crucifix of muzzle flare split from the barrel as bullets the size of candlepins ripped into the advancing horde. Some of them were killed instantly as shots punched through the middle of their torsos, shattering them through hydrostatic shock; others lost limbs or hanks of flesh, spinning about as if they were taking part in some idiot dance.

The ones that did not die immediately showed no signs of fear, not the slightest jot of concern for their lives. They simply laughed and screamed, the meat of their faces bulging, puffed up with the surge of the dark fluid from the injectors.

They had poor weapons, but many of them. Stubber rifles, mostly, along with clubs of all kinds and countless blades. Ballistic rounds rattled off Rafen's chest plate, chipping at the red ceramite but gaining no purchase. He used his bolter to place single, pinpoint rounds into the head of any target that came his way.

The ones that had limbs blown out from under them did not appear to care. Rafen witnessed them reach for the ampules on their vests and fire fresh doses into their stomachs or necks. The Blood Angel was no stranger to combat drugs, although for the most part, his Chapter eschewed the used of chemical alterants to enhance battlefield ability, preferring to rely on the raw power of the bloodline of their primarch. But whatever it was that these rebels were using on themselves, it went beyond the scope of such things. The fluid was some kind of mutagen; he could actually see it altering the density of flesh or staunching the torrents of blood.

At the feet of the Astartes, the ferrocrete was quickly becoming damp and sticky with the vitae of their attackers. Through his breath grille, Rafen's nostrils twitched at the scent of the blood. It had a peculiar bouquet, the familiar coppery tang mingled with an almost sugary sweetness, like some succulent confection. He licked his lips automatically.

The attackers hurled themselves over the bodies of their fallen brethren with mad abandon, and abruptly the skirmish became a close quarter battle. Rafen's squad met the challenge with casual force. Such close-in fights were the very meat and drink of the Blood Angels. The sergeant let his bolter fall away on its sling and drew his power sword backhanded, bringing it about in a quick turn that beheaded a Companitas brandishing a drum-fed shotgun. The weapon discharged once, twice, as the headless corpse continued a little longer in the mad capering dance. Irritated, Rafen cut again, this time parting the abdomen. There was a slight resistance as the glowing blade sliced through the spinal column; he made a mental note to have the armoury serfs sharpen the edge and tune the sword's energy field when the squad had quit Eritaen.

Around him, the fight had contracted to a series of one-on-one combats. Puluo killed a man with the weight of his bolter, using the gun as a blunt instrument to crush his skull against the floor. Kayne buried his bayonet in the chest of a chattering swordsman. Turcio's flamer coughed out puffballs of yellow-orange promethium flame, turning his foes into screaming torches.

'Let's finish this and be gone,' said Corvus.

Ajir grunted with grim gallows humour. 'With all due respect, I think these fools may have other ideas. Do you not hear them?'

Rafen turned as the sound of clattering boots and chattering laughter reached his ears. There were more of the

Companitas emerging from beneath them, hundreds more, the bubbling rush of their hysteria echoing up from the sub-levels. He had wondered earlier where the enemy was hiding; it seemed that they had been hiding *here*.

'We've happened on a rat's nest.' Turcio's face was set. 'How many?'

'More than we have shells for,' Rafen replied. 'Draw back. If they bottle us up in here, we'll not see daylight again–'

Then without preamble, a new voice issued out over the general vox frequency, a gruff and resonant growl. 'Blood Angels. Exfiltrate now. You are in a fire zone.'

'Who speaks?' he demanded. 'Give your name and rank!'

'I will not warn you again, cousin,' came the terse reply, and the signal cut out.

Puluo turned to fire into ranks of the rebel reinforcements as the last of the first wave were dispatched. Kayne shot Rafen a look. 'Orders, lord?'

Rafen's expression soured. 'We go. Disengage and fall back!'

The squad reacted as one, Puluo and Corvus laying down cover fire as the Space Marines retreated back the way they had come. Rafen's grimace set hard; he knew full well who had spoken, and the arrogance of the words filled him with irritation; but to ignore what was said would be foolish.

Weak daylight glowed before them as they reached the uppermost level of the parking structure, and a faint sound reached his enhanced hearing; the shriek of multiple missile fire.

His rational mind barely had time to register the thought, questions springing to his lips; but instead he shouted out a warning. 'Incoming!'

They burst from the structure in rush. Somewhere above them, a barrage of rockets slammed into the flanks of the service tower and sent a shockwave hammering down through the sub-levels. Aged ferrocrete splintered, cracked, shattered, and down came the building around them in a torrent of stone.

Turcio felt the rain of rock rather than saw it. Dust blinded him and he cursed himself for going about without his helmet. Blinking, he glimpsed another figure in battle armour struggling to wade through the melee and instinctively reached out, tugging on an arm to help his comrade move through the landslide.

The arm was rudely snatched away. 'Look to your own welfare, penitent!' snarled Ajir, forcing his way through the choking clouds of powder.

Turcio scowled and said nothing, charging onward. He was aware of other men around him, the shifting, blurry shapes of red in amongst the falling rocks. Tiny stones clattered into his neck ring and ones the size of fists bounced across his skull, lighting sparks of pain. He almost stumbled, but a force propelled him forward. Puluo.

'Move,' snapped the Space Marine.

The blue sunshine turned grey as a haze of dust enveloped them.

CHAPTER TWO

THE FINAL, DYING fall of the stubby tower sent a ring of air rippling out around it, churning the ever-present dust and the smaller shards of broken glass. Rolling cords of bone-coloured powder rose in a wave, slowly to drift and settle anew across the wreckage of the intersection. The dust fell upon the armour of the warriors who stood ranged around the squat shape of the Whirlwind missile tank. Their wargear, usually a heavy, wine-dark crimson with black trim, was sullied from weeks of battle in among the cloying dust. The colours were dull and washed-out, as if sun-bleached. Only the sigil on their shoulder pads remained bright and starkly visible; a razor-toothed circular blade crested with a single droplet of blood in deep, arterial red.

Smoke curled from the mouth of the Whirlwind's rocket tubes as the commander of the unit glanced up at it. 'You didn't give them much warning,' noted one of his men.

'I gave them enough,' said the squad leader. 'Perhaps this experience will encourage them not to interfere where they are uninvited.'

'If any one of them is dead… There could be repercussions.'

'They'll live, if they're worth the name Astartes.' The squad leader pointed. Rubble was shifting and figures emerged from the debris, shaking off the effects of the concussion. 'You see? No harm done.' There was an edge of cruel amusement in his voice.

'Just to their pride,' added the other.

His commander smiled thinly. 'They can stand a wound or two to that.'

RAFEN KICKED FREE of the ruin and stepped out from the tangle of rebar and wreckage, casting one quick look over his shoulder to be sure that his men were all unhurt. He didn't wait for them to follow. He stormed out across the windblown intersection toward the tank, his fury building behind his chest. Rafen removed his helmet with an angry twist of his hands.

'Cousin,' said the voice from the vox. 'Well met.' Two figures in Mark VII Aquila armour advanced out to meet him. They wore the insignia of a trooper and a veteran sergeant, and as he watched the senior warrior mirrored his action, doffing his headgear.

Rafen saw a craggy face beneath, with close-cut dark hair and cold, lifeless eyes; and at that moment, more than anything, he wanted to backhand him for his recklessness.

But there was the mission. The mission and the message. Rafen bit down on the impulse and ignored the ritual greeting. 'I have often heard it said that the brothers of the Flesh Tearers Chapter are a savage and impulsive lot,' he said stiffly. 'And to think, I thought better of you.'

Rafen was rewarded by a small tic of annoyance in the other warrior's eye. 'We have a reputation to live down to,' said the Space Marine. 'The primarch, in his wisdom, did not see fit to bless us with the same gifts as our parent legion.' He nodded at Rafen's armour, at the winged blood droplet insignia upon its chest. 'But we have learned to play to the strengths we have.' The Astartes gave the slightest of bows. 'I am Brother-Sergeant Noxx. This is Battle-Brother Roan, my second-in-command.'

'Rafen,' he replied, his ill mood clipping his words. 'I await your apology, *cousin*.' He put a hard emphasis on the word.

Noxx returned a steady gaze. 'For what? For prosecuting a sortie in the battle that we have been ordered to win? If you have an issue, Blood Angel, I would suggest you take it up with my commander. It was on his orders we destroyed the target.' He gestured at the shattered building. 'Had it not been for him, we might not have known you were inside.'

'Orbital observation drones spotted your men entering the tower,' added Roan.

'Why were you in there?' said Noxx. 'Has there been a change of protocol that I was not aware of? Are the Blood Angels joining us at Eritaen to fight against the rebels? It was my understanding that you are here only as messengers.'

Rafen's jaw hardened. He refused to allow the Flesh Tearer to bait him. 'A target presented itself. I assumed you would appreciate our assistance in neutralising it.'

Noxx nodded once. 'Indeed. But as you can see, we have the matter well in hand.' He indicated the Whirlwind, and for the first time Rafen noticed that there were a group of civilians cowering in the shadow of the armoured vehicle.

'Collaborators,' explained Roan, sensing Rafen's question. 'One of them was supplying water to the

Companitas. When properly compelled, he revealed knowledge of this nest.'

'One?' Rafen repeated. 'You have a dozen people there. What are the others guilty of?'

'They lived in the same refuge. They sheltered the traitor.'

'You're certain of that?' he demanded.

Noxx turned away, signalling to another of his men. 'Can we really take the risk?'

Two Flesh Tearers turned toward the civilians and opened fire. In a brisk rattle of bolt shells, the group were gunned down.

Noxx looked back at Rafen, daring him to comment. 'Forgive me, cousin, if our methods are less refined than you might be used to. I'm sure they lack the elegance and purity of the Blood Angels.'

He matched the other man's challenging glare, unwilling to give an inch. 'You ought to drill your men more closely, Noxx. A Blood Angel would not have wasted so much ammunition on a dispatch.'

'Perhaps,' Noxx allowed. 'Next time, I'll have Roan here demonstrate the use of a flaying blade for you.' He tapped the wickedly barbed longknife at his waist.

'I imagine that would be very educational,' replied Rafen. Barely a minute in his presence, and the sergeant's patience with his opposite number was already running shallow; the days of aimless wandering in search of the Flesh Tearer forward command post, and then this blatant display of one-upmanship were grating on him. He glanced in the direction of his men and found them approaching warily. They walked in a combat profile, despite the fact that they were in the presence of what should have been considered their allies.

But then the Flesh Tearers were allies to no one, not the other Chapters of the Astartes, not even to those who shared a kinship to the primarch who gave them life and purpose, the Great Angel Sanguinius.

'Movement!' Turcio's shout cut through Rafen's musings and he spun around as sounds reached his ears; the rumble of shifting rock and a chorus of wailing voices, growing louder by the second.

The wreckage of the smoking tower trembled and moved, abruptly bursting open in a cloud of dust and fumes. A massive, headless humanoid form pressed itself out of the ruins. The wailing became screaming, the screaming became the maddened laughter they had heard inside the parking structure.

Rafen blinked through the smoke and saw the monstrosity clearly for the first time. It was no one being, but a mass of them. The form was an amalgam of the Companitas, hundreds of bodies all collected together, held in place by some arcane power; and all of them were hooting and chattering with their madness.

'Fire!' he shouted, and his squad opened up with their weapons. Noxx followed suit, bolt shells hazing the air around the collective creature.

Bodies were ripped apart and blown off in spiralling darts of blood, but the mass did not slow down. It seethed over the fractured stonework, one huge fist of flesh coming down like a hammer to crush a Flesh Tearer into a mess of ceramite and meat. When the fist came back up, the remains of the Space Marine were absorbed into the accumulation.

'This is the true face of the Companitas!' snarled Roan. 'This is the warp-cursed unity they promise! Chaos whelps!'

Noxx shouted orders to the Whirlwind crew, commanding them to reload; but the speed of the thing was too great. It would be upon them before they could retaliate.

'Blood Angels,' Rafen called into his vox. 'Grenades! Impact set!' He grabbed at the drum-shaped krak grenades clipped to his waist and thumbed the trigger from safe to armed, dialling the munitions to detonate when they struck their target. Around him, he saw Turcio, Puluo and the others doing the same. 'Ready! *Loose!*'

A rain of the small bombs arced through the air and struck the Companitas amalgam in the centre of its mass, a chain-fire of explosions rippling through it. The fusion-body screamed louder and tore itself apart, falling into smaller pieces, corpses tumbling away.

'Flamers!' Noxx bellowed. 'Forward and sweep! Nothing lives!'

A squad of Flesh Tearers advanced, casting whips of burning promethium over the writhing bodies. In moments, the intersection was a funeral pyre, tides of grey smoke billowing up between the towers.

Rafen shot a glare at the other sergeant.

Noxx ignored it. 'We require no assistance from any other Astartes,' he sniffed, in complete disregard to what had just occurred. 'My Chapter was ordered here to bring the Emperor's bloody retribution to Eritaen. That mission need not be diluted by the addition of any more forces.'

Rafen felt a slow rise of understanding. Noxx was labouring under a misapprehension. The sergeant's resentment for the most part stemmed from the age-old rivalry between the Blood Angels and their kindred, from the clash of methods between the blunt and brutal Flesh Tearers and the more studied way of Rafen's Chapter; but his anger was also at the threat of diminishment. The Tearers were one of the smallest Chapters in the Adeptus Astartes, and their harsh reactions to any perceived slight upon them – real or imagined – were well documented. They more than made up in ferocity what they lacked in numbers.

'We are not here to take this fight from you,' Rafen told him. 'The Blood Angels have no interest in the punishment of Eritaen.'

For the first time since laying eyes on him, Rafen saw something close to doubt in Noxx's expression. 'Then why in the Throne's name *are* you here?' All pretence at chill politeness dropped away and Noxx let his resentment show its colours. 'Come to remind your poor kinsmen of their betters?'

'I don't answer to you,' he replied. 'I carry a message for Seth, your Chapter Master. You will take me to him.' Rafen beckoned Kayne closer, and the youth produced a sealed metal scroll-tube, locked with sigil of Lord Dante himself. 'And by this authority, you will do it now.'

Noxx glared at the tube. The weight of a Chapter Master's word was an inviolate command for a line Astartes, and not even a Space Marine with the ingrained arrogance of the Flesh Tearers would dare to deny it.

After a moment, the veteran sergeant gave a slow, sullen nod. Without looking at the Blood Angels, he walked back toward the Whirlwind. 'This way, then. And try to keep up.'

THROUGH THE DUST, they followed behind the Whirlwind in silence for another hour before they arrived at the Flesh Tearers' field command post. At the point of the squad's teardrop formation, Brother Kayne studied the gutted structure they had taken as their temporary base.

It was a thing of steel buttresses and stone walls, missing a glass roof that had doubtless been obliterated in the early days of the Eritaen rebellion. A squat colonnade at one end of the old building ended in a tall, spindly antenna tower that reached into the sky; it was wilting, as if the metal had been twisted in some fearsome wind. The structure stood atop a shallow hill, giving it good lines of sight down all the highways around it. Kayne glanced at a fallen sign as they entered the courtyard, seeing a name, a designation. *Situa Alexandus Regina – Adeptus Telepathica*. Of course; the meaning of the strangely-barbed antenna became clear; this had been a communications temple, the nexus for planetbound signalling via machine-call vox and astropathic transfer.

He caught a familiar, stale scent on the wind – old blood. On the walls of the building he spotted dark brown spatter-patterns and metal impact rivets driven into splintered brick. Bodies had been crucified up there, at some point. He wondered if they might have been the staff of the complex; and then he wondered what had become of their corpses.

The Whirlwind peeled away from the group and grumbled to a halt near a knot of Chapter serfs, under the watchful eye of a Flesh Tearer Techmarine. There were only a handful of vehicles in the parking quadrant, and Kayne frowned at the condition of them. A Rhino, a Baal-pattern Predator tank, a pair of land speeders, all of them had a grubby and ill-maintained look to them, as if they were held together by little more than steel hull patches and prayers to their machine-spirits. But then Kayne considered for a moment; the Whirlwind they had followed also bore the same scars and rough aspect, and yet it had moved with swiftness and ready purpose. Perhaps it was not that the Flesh Tearers cared poorly for their machines, but simply that they cared little for their surface appearance.

The youth turned that thought over in his mind, his gaze moving across the other Astartes who paused in their devotions or tasks at hand to stop and watch the arrival of the Blood Angels. Their scrutiny was not kind, not indifferent, but wary, distrustful. He speculated on what they might think of Brother-Sergeant Rafen and his squad. Like their vehicles, the Flesh Tearers themselves did not display much in the way of ornamentation; the deep red of their armour, so dense that it strayed toward the purple, covered all except the helmet, backpack and shoulder pads. These were a hard, matt black that reflected no light. Kayne saw rank sigils, company badges and the like, but no decals or decoration beyond what was needed on the battlefield. In contrast, the red wargear of the Blood Angels sported fine filigree in gold across the wings on their chests, shimmering drops of ruby, elaborate votive chains and other symbology. The Space Marine felt overdressed alongside the successors. Some of the Tearers, the bolder ones, the veterans, arched an eyebrow and looked away. Perhaps they thought the Blood Angels to be peacocks; even Puluo, the least fetching of their squad, would have been considered handsome when placed alongside these scarred and hatchet-faced men.

It was hard to believe these Astartes stemmed from the same noble gene-seed that gave rise to the Blood Angels, and yet the Flesh Tearers were as much a legacy of the primarch Sanguinius as Kayne and his battle-brothers. In the aftermath of the Horus Heresy ten millennia past, when the Emperor of Man ascended to the Golden Throne and the galaxy reeled from the newborn war with Chaos, the great Legions of the Adeptus Astartes had been split off into smaller successor Chapters, and the Blood Angels had been no exception. Among others, the Flesh Tearers were spawned from that great Second Founding, set loose to range to the edges of human space in order to punish worlds who had given loyalty to the Arch-traitor Horus; but it was said that they had taken something dark with them, some black and vicious skein previously buried deep in the Great Sanguinius's spirit. Their manners in battle were spoken of in the halls of Baal's fortress-monastery with censure and cold reproach.

Kayne wondered how much of the rumours about their cousins were true, and how much were myth and obfuscation. He knew full well that other Chapters, like the stoic Ultramarines or the Iron Hands, said similar things of the Blood Angels; but meeting the hard eyes of the Space Marines who watched them walk by, he found it difficult to be generous with this understanding.

Every Son of Sanguinius, no matter if his Chapter was from the First or the last of the Foundings, shared the same gene-taint, the twin maladies of the Black Rage and the Red Thirst. The psychic echo of the death of their liege-lord, the dark potential to lose one's mind to the berserker rage of bloodlust lurked in all of them. It was a curse the Blood Angels fought against each day of their lives; but so it was said, the blight of the Rage and the Thirst was something the Flesh Tearers *embraced*. Such a thought sickened Kayne. To tap into that wild fury during the melee of battle was one thing, but to surrender to it? That was to willingly allow oneself to become nothing more than an animal.

'Kayne,' Ajir said quietly, so his voice did not carry beyond them. 'I'd advise you not to stare at them so much. They may take it as prelude to a martial challenge.'

He bristled. 'Then let them. I am confident in my skills.'

He heard the grim amusement in his comrade's tone. 'That much is certain. But remember, this is not a combat mission. Mind yourself. There's no need to start fires where there are none.'

'I bow to your superior knowledge, brother.' Kayne nodded reluctantly. 'But I find it is best to treat every mission as a combat mission. It lessens the opportunity for unpleasant surprises.'

'Less talk,' snapped Puluo, as the group came to a halt before the building proper.

The Tearer sergeant was speaking to Rafen. 'Your men will remain here.'

Rafen nodded and glanced at Turcio. 'Stand down. I'll proceed alone.'

'Aye, lord.'

Without waiting to be asked, Kayne recovered his burden from the pouch on his belt and once more gave his commander the sealed scroll-tube. As the two Blood Angels moved closer, Kayne lowered his voice, the question that had been pressing upon him since the day they left Baal finally falling from his lips. 'Will that be enough, brother-sergeant?'

Rafen took the tube and the youth saw the shadow of a deep hurt pass over his squad leader's face. 'For Baal's sake, I hope so.' His fingers closed around the golden rod. 'Or else our Chapter may be lost.'

Noxx continued as he had before. He did not wait to see if the Blood Angel was following him, he simply walked away and expected Rafen to keep pace.

Inside the walls of the building there were no interior partitions, nothing but stanchions spaced at regular intervals holding up the broken frame of the roof. The wide, echoing space resembled an aircraft hangar, but for the stubs of felled walls and the sprawl of temporary tent habitats dotted around. Chapter serfs, servitors and the occasional Space Marine moved between them, intent on their duties. Rafen glanced up and saw adaptive camouflage netting ranged over everything. The watery blue sunlight was attenuated even more by the nets, casting hazy shadows everywhere. The dust was in here with them as well, gritty across the cracked marble flooring.

'Inside,' said Noxx, indicating a circular enclosure.

Rafen eyed the vac-slit door warily and pushed his way through, the tough cloth tugging at his wargear as he did so. Within, the tent had a lamp casting a warm yellow glow about the temporary shelter. A ragged battle standard sat furled in one corner, fixed in a stand next to a mobile shrine. By reflex, Rafen bowed slightly to the small brass idol of the Emperor within it and made the sign of the aquila over his chest. Behind him, Noxx did the same.

There was one other Astartes in the tent, his face lit from below by the colours of a hololithic chart table. Rafen glimpsed a tactical plot of the city, with shifting arrows floating in the air above it. The live feed from the orbital scrying drones mentioned by Noxx's second.

The Space Marine – a captain, by the rank tabs on his armour – sub-vocalised a command word and the battle data on the map dissolved, leaving only the bare framework of buildings and streets.

'*Ave Imperator*,' said the Blood Angel. 'I am Brother-Sergeant Rafen. I have come with a message for his Lordship Seth.'

'I know who you are. And why you are here.' The Flesh Tearer officer stepped around the table. 'I am Brother-Captain Gorn, adjutant to the Chapter Master.' He nodded to the scroll-tube. 'You will disclose your message to me and in due time I will present it to my Master for his consideration.'

Rafen stiffened. 'With respect, brother-captain, I will do no such thing. And this is not a matter to be dealt with "in due time". It comes directly from *my* Chapter Master.'

Gorn seemed unconcerned by Rafen's retort. He moved into the light and the Blood Angel got a better look at him. Like Noxx, he had a hard face and an aquiline jaw that betrayed the passage of a hundred battles.

'What is it?' he asked casually, moving to a cabinet in the corner. 'The message, the contents therein. What does it say?'

'I… I do not know.' Rafen held up the cylinder. 'These words are for the eyes of our Masters alone, lord. It is not my place, nor yours, to read them.'

'Of course,' Gorn allowed, removing a seal-bottle and a goblet. 'But I suspect you already know the scope of what the message will say, if not the letter of it. Perhaps you could illuminate me?' He opened the bottle and poured himself a half-glass.

Rafen's nostrils twitched as the scent of the liquid reached him. Coppery, with a sickly-sweet thickness. He swallowed, banishing the aroma of it.

Gorn went on. 'I find it hard to believe that Dante would–'

'*Lord* Dante,' Rafen corrected firmly.

'Of course, pardon my error. I find it hard to believe that Lord Dante would send a warrior out here, all the way from Baal to the edge of nowhere, and have him be little more than an ignorant errand boy.' He took a sip of the fluid, savoured it. 'Is that all you are, brother-sergeant?'

And once more, the voice at the back of Rafen's thoughts spoke the mantra that had kept him in line these past few weeks.

The mission. The mission first and foremost, Rafen. Mephiston had said those words to him, the hard and unyielding gaze of the Lord of Death burning into him. *There has never been a moment more deadly to our brother-hood than this one.*

'I will speak to Seth, Chapter Master of the Flesh Tearers, or I will not speak at all,' he told them, iron in his tone. 'Take me to the presence of your lord, or else I will find him myself.'

Gorn put down the goblet. 'How predictable of you, Blood Angel. How predictable of your master, to simply drop in upon us without invite or regard and expect your cousins to bend the knee and show obeisance.'

Rafen felt his temper rising again. 'We have done nothing of the sort. We only require the respect that one Chapter of the Astartes ought to show another, and as the Emperor is my witness–' He nodded toward the shrine, '–your men have given precious little of it, brother-captain!'

A feral smile split Gorn's face. 'Ah. Some fire in your blood. Perhaps you don't all have adamantium rods up your backsides, then.' The officer threw Noxx an amused look.

Belatedly, Rafen realised that he was being deliberately provoked. He ground out his next words between gritted teeth. 'Where is Lord Seth?'

'I am here,' said a careful voice from behind Gorn, as a new figure emerged from a concealed slit in the far side of the tent. Rafen caught the glitter of muted steel plate across a shorn scalp and a face tracked by great claw-scars. Stern, deep-set eyes fixed him with an unwavering stare, and at the corners of his sight he saw Noxx and Gorn instantly change in manner, heads bowed and all trace of cold humour gone. 'I am Seth,' said the Chapter Master, extending a hand. 'You have something for me.'

Rafen nodded, and bowed his head as well. 'Aye, lord.'

Seth took the rod and with a twist of his wrist, snapped it in two, discarding the casing on the floor and plucking the curl of photic parchment from inside. 'Shall we see what my cousin Dante has to say?'

TURCIO BENT AND gathered a thickness of the strange, ever-present dust between the thumb and forefinger of his glove. He rolled the granules back and forth; they crumbled still more, became a thin paste. A dry smell, the air of ancient museums and long-sealed tombs, came from his fingers. 'This sand is everywhere. Where does it come from? There are no deserts for hundreds of kilometres in any direction.'

A shadow fell across him and he looked up. 'Bones,' said the Flesh Tearer. 'This is all that's left of them.'

'This is… human remains?'

A nod. 'The Companitas led the populace who were foolish enough to defy them into rendering plants. Then they did the same with those who complied. The grindings of the bones, they set them into airburst warheads and exploded them over the cities. And so, the dust.' The one who had identified himself as Roan leaned closer, gesturing at the brand on Turcio's face; an Imperial aquila with its wings furled and downward-pointing. 'Why do you wear that?' The Flesh Tearer was standing deliberately close to the Blood Angel, invading his personal space.

Seated on a fallen stone buttress, Turcio displayed not the slightest hint of annoyance at the blunt question. 'It is mark of penitence, cousin,' he explained.

'Penitence?' Roan repeated. 'What failure did you commit to require such atonement? Were you a coward upon the field of battle?'

The words had barely left Roan's mouth before Corvus and Puluo were on their feet, the insult burning hard in their eyes. Kayne and Ajir warily moved to follow them, but Turcio waved them back. Still he did not seem angered; only weary. 'I made... an error of judgement. I believed in something that was revealed to be a lie.'

'Among my brethren, errors of judgement result in death.'

Turcio nodded. 'And in mine as well.' He glanced at Corvus and the other Space Marine gave an imperceptible nod. 'But by the Emperor's Grace, we have been granted forgiveness. Now I live my life in the will to be seen worthy of it.'

Something in Turcio's careful manner tempered the Flesh Tearer's aspect; a moment ago, he had been spoiling to goad them. Turcio's steady honesty made that will vanish. 'What... What did you believe?' Roan asked.

'Does it matter?' A lifetime of fatigue filled his reply.

After a moment, Roan gave a grudging smile. 'Huh. Despite your finery and airs, the Blood Angels are not so faultless after all. Who could have thought it?'

'No man is,' said Turcio. 'But in the striving, we seek the Emperor's path.'

'Then in that, cousin, we are not dissimilar.' Roan twisted the cuff of his right gauntlet and removed it. There, on the skin of his forearm, was a brand of similar dimension to Turcio's.

The Flesh Tearer threw him a nod and walked away.

'You should have struck the braggart to the ground for what he said,' Ajir fumed, his dusky skin darkening.

'And what would that have proven, brother?' Turcio turned to face the other Blood Angel. 'That the men of our Chapter have no more self-control than a Space Wolf?'

'Better that than to trumpet our failures before our successors.' Ajir shot a look at Corvus. 'At least have the decency to hide your shame.'

Corvus removed his helmet; his brow bore the same mark as Turcio's. 'I am not ashamed,' he retorted. Corvus's narrow, canine face was set hard. 'We have proven our fealty, twice over. The rites of penitence made our contrition plain.'

'Perhaps,' said Ajir. 'But I have yet to be convinced.'

'Ajir.' Puluo spoke his name and all of them turned to face him. 'What you think doesn't matter. Sergeant chose them. End of story.'

'I suppose it is.' But Ajir's tone did not match his words.

SETH READ THROUGH the first few paragraphs of the parchment before he released a thin sigh through his teeth and bunched it in his hands. 'My honoured cousin has lost none of his verbosity, it would seem.' The Chapter Master of the Flesh Tearers came forward, and Rafen found he could not look away. Seth's face was a chronicle of injuries so fearsome that it seemed a wonder he could still speak. The scars Rafen had observed before raked across him, right to left, doubtless where the claw of some primordial creature had struck. The Blood Angel had seen picts of the Flesh Tearer home world, a feral sphere called Cretacia that teemed with violent saurian wildlife; the Tearers were said to hunt the beasts there, unarmoured and weaponless, as some kind of sport. Seth sported a disc-shaped implant that covered a good quarter of his skull, some arcane form of augmetic fused to the naked bone. Here was a man who showed all he was upon the surface, with no artifice possible. The Chapter Master's presence was at once as dominating as Rafen's Lord Dante, but with an entirely different energy of self behind it.

'Rafen,' he said, 'We shall cut to the meat of this, you and I. Tell me what it is that Dante demands, in direct and simple terms. I do not wish to wade through a page of florid text to find it.'

'As you wish, Lord Seth,' said the sergeant. He took a breath. 'Commander Dante, Lord of the Blood Angels and Inheritor of the IX Legion Astartes, calls you to a conclave of the greatest and utmost moment.'

'A meeting?' Gorn frowned. 'He summons the Flesh Tearers? To what end?' New suspicion flashed behind his eyes. 'We are not at the beck and call of–'

Seth silenced him with a look. Rafen went on. 'To be clear, brother-captain, this is not a meeting but an assembly of the Sons of Sanguinius. A gathering of *all*, sir.'

The Chapter Master of the Flesh Tearers raised an eyebrow. 'Every successor?'

'As many as possible, lord. Even now as we speak, battle-brothers of my Chapter range to the points of the etheric compass, carrying the same message to the

Masters of the Angels Encarmine, the Blood Drinkers…
To each Chapter that holds a lineage to the Great Angel.'
He paused, dry-throated. The scope of Dante's intent
still struck him as audacious as it had when he first
learned of it.

Seth glanced at the parchment again. '*A representative
contingent,*' he read aloud, '*of men so empowered to make
policy that will be followed to the letter by their Chapter's
brethren.*' He smiled thinly. 'In other words, the Chapter
Masters or as near as damn it.'

'Aye,' repeated Rafen. 'As you know, we have a ship in
deep orbit, the *Tycho*. It is ready to accept you, lord, and
your party for our return voyage to Baal.'

'You'll take that voyage alone, brother-sergeant,' said
Seth, offering him the parchment. 'I have no intention
of answering to this summons. Dante ought to know
better.' He took in the hololithic screen and the charts
scattered over nearby tables. 'I am in the middle of prosecuting a war here. Eritaen may be at the arse-end of the
Emperor's Sight, but it is still an Imperial world and still
subject to Imperial law!' The Chapter Master's voice rose
into a growl. 'I won't disengage from a campaign simply
because my cousin wishes to hold a… A family reunion.'

'The conclave is much more than that,' Rafen replied.
'Forgive me, lord, but I fear you do not grasp the gravity
of the situation. A gathering of this nature has not been
called in my master's lifetime, not since the thirty-
seventh millennia and the Pact of Kursa.'

'I know my history,' Seth replied, dismissing him, 'just
as Dante knows his battle doctrine. Go now. Perhaps I
may be able to spare a party of men as a token representation.'

'It must be you,' insisted the Blood Angel. 'Those were
my orders and I will not return to Baal with them unful-
filled!'

'Is that so?' Gorn took a warning step toward him.

Seth waved Gorn away. 'Tell me, then, Brother Rafen. What is so damned important that Dante would send you to clutter my day, and have me drop all that I am doing?'

Rafen's throat went dry as he said the next words. 'The conclave will decide the future of the Blood Angels. What is spoken of there will determine if my Chapter survives to see the dawn of the next millennium.'

CHAPTER THREE

THROUGH THE GLASS eye of the frigate *Tycho*'s observatorium, Rafen watched as Eritaen turned and fell away to port as the ship broke orbit. Above and to starboard, the dark dagger of the strike cruiser *Brutus* watched them leave, the saw-tooth disc of silver across her flank catching the blue of the local star. Laser pennants on the other vessel flared briefly in salute; a marked contrast to the sullen disinterest the vessel's crew had shown on *Tycho*'s arrival a few days earlier.

Rafen heard Turcio enter the chamber behind him, but did not turn to greet his comrade. The Space Marine cleared his throat. 'Reporting,' he began.

'Go on,' Rafen prompted.

'Lord Seth and his delegation are secure on the accommodation deck. His officer, Gorn, has made some demands...'

'See to them all,' said the sergeant. 'They are our honoured guests now. They will be treated as such.'

'Aye, sir, as you command.' Turcio paused a moment. 'I also have word from the bridge. The shipmaster informs me our Navigators are in harness and preparing to make space for Baal. Much of what he said to me is beyond my ken, I will admit, but the gist is that the etheric currents this far out along the galactic plane are less cluttered than in toward the coreward planets. Once we enter the warp, we should make swift time to the home world.'

Rafen nodded. 'Good. The quicker we discharge our orders, the more comfortable I will be.' He took a long breath. The confrontation with Seth had troubled him more than he was willing to admit.

'Not a man among us would disagree,' noted Turcio. Once more, he paused, and Rafen could sense he was framing a question.

'You have something to ask?'

Turcio gestured with his augmetic limb. 'The matter of Lord Seth and the Flesh Tearers... In all honesty, brother-sergeant, I had believed that this entire mission was nought but a hiding to nothing, that we would meet him and return home without him. I assumed that Seth would deny Commander Dante's summons.'

'He did,' said Rafen. 'You were not wrong.'

'But yet he is here aboard this ship and we travel for Baal. How was he convinced otherwise?' Turcio's brow furrowed. 'If I may know it, what did you say to Seth that so swayed him?'

'I did as I was ordered,' Rafen replied, turning away from the window. 'I told him the full and complete truth.'

'Everything?'

Rafen nodded. 'Aye, brother. Every bloody moment.'

'Was he... angry?'

'No. If anything, I think Seth may have been saddened.' He shook his head. 'The man is of such dour character, I find it hard to read him.' After a moment, the sergeant looked up and met Turcio's gaze. 'Tell me, how is the character of *my* men at this moment?'

'At the ready, lord,' said the other Space Marine. 'As always.'

'Indeed? After we left the Flesh Tearer forward base, I thought I detected a… a tension in the air.'

Turcio took his time over the answer. 'I saw nothing of remark, sir.'

Rafen sensed there was more, but left it at that. 'Very well. You are dismissed.' The other warrior bowed slightly and exited, leaving the Blood Angel alone in the chamber once again. Rafen drifted back to the window and placed his hand upon the armourglass, losing himself in contemplation of the void beyond.

Soon they would be in the skies over Baal, and then walking the hallowed corridors of the fortress-monastery once again.

His thoughts darkened, and in his reverie Rafen remembered the arching walls of the monastery's audience chamber reaching up around him; and fresh in his thoughts was his name at Dante's command.

'BROTHER-SERGEANT RAFEN, you may enter,' said the Chapter Master, beckoning the Space Marine from the tall copper doors. Rafen gave a deep bow before he did so, his robes pooling on the stone floor beneath him. Aside from the men of the honour guard -- and of these there were only a pair, to satisfy protocol but little else -- every Blood Angel in the chamber was without his armour, dressed instead in the Chapter's devotional robes of red and black.

He had been here once before, soon after the wounded battle-barge *Europae* had made orbit, returning to lick her wounds at the orbital dock in the aftermath of the battle at the shrineworld, Sabien. On that day, he had felt a conflicted mix of emotion; anger and sadness, fear and elation, a torrent of senses that still echoed in his heart all these months later. This place, this chamber was not the most ornate or expansive of those in the halls of the monastery, and yet it had seen much history throughout the years of the Chapter's life. The death of Dante's predecessor, Chapter Master Kadeus; the breaking of the starbow; the exile of Leonatos; all these dramas and more had been played out in this room.

The far side of the hall was dominated by a raised stage carved out of ebon basaltic stone from the mines on Baal IX. Great golden chalices that mimicked the form of the sacred Red Grail, as tall as a Terminator, stood to either side, blood-red flames rumbling quietly in the cups. There was little other illumination, save for the sullen glow of a few biolume floaterglobes. The fires threw jumping shadows across the walls; outside it was night, but the two moons had yet to rise and cast their umber light through the stained glass windows in the walls.

Banners of varying antiquity hung from the rafters. Many of them were old war pennants from campaigns long since ended, others devotional in nature bearing script from the Imperial Credo or the Book of the Lords. Rafen resisted the temptation to look up and examine them in detail. He had duty here, and it was expected that he would be circumspect. That he was even allowed to be in the room to observe this meeting was a rarity. He did not wish to do anything that might throw doubt on his presence here, not even the tiniest breach in protocol.

A cluster of men stood in a loose semi-circle before the black stone stage. Above them, upon a tall-backed throne made from laser-cut rock of similar hue, sat the Chapter Master himself. He was leaning forward, one hand beneath his patrician chin, his flawless face set in deep thought. Dante's robes collected about him, and by way of adornment he had only a thick golden collar that fell to his sternum. A rendering of the Blood Angel sigil was picked out in platinum and red jade. For a brief moment, Dante's gaze met Rafen's and the Astartes found himself nodding to his lord, trying not to misstep. Eleven hundred years of experience lay behind those dark, lidded eyes. His cool wisdom seemed almost a palpable thing, as if it radiated off Dante. Rafen's mouth went dry; once again, here he was, a line warrior in the presence of some of the greatest of Sanguinius's sons. Dante was unquestionably the ultimate among them, but many of the men in this room were legends in their own right.

He glanced around. Upon the stage, at Dante's sides, sat Mephiston and Corbulo. The two of them were studies in opposites. Mephiston, the man they called the Lord of Death, Chief Librarian of the Chapter and a psyker of near-matchless power, was a tall and imposing figure. In this light, he appeared wraith-like, his angular face set in an inward focus. Mephiston sensed Rafen's scrutiny and gave him a slight nod, placing only a fraction of his diamond-hard gaze upon the Space Marine. Rafen returned the gesture, fighting down a sense of ill-ease. He had shared a battlefield with the Lord of Death on Sabien, and then as now, he could not escape the sense that Mephiston saw into him as easily as if he were spun from glass.

Rafen broke eye-contact first and glanced at Dante's other advisor; Corbulo of the Grail. The Apothecary's robes were a splash of stark contrast, the spotless white lined with trim of red. The highest of the Chapter's sanguinary priests, Corbulo presented a grim and lined aspect beneath a shock of straw-coloured hair. Rafen had never met him, but he knew him; every Blood Angel knew Corbulo, the bearer of the Red Grail. He alone had the honour of stewardship over that most sacred of relics, carrying it into battle on Dante's commands. The Red Grail carried in it a measure of the blood of the primarch himself, so the Chapter's mythos went, and in echo of Corbulo's charge every sanguinary priest of lower rank carried a simulacrum of the great cup, a symbol with which to rally troops upon the field of conflict.

These three were all aspects of the Blood Angels made flesh and bone. Wisdom and nobility, ferocity and strength, fealty and majesty. They were the spectrum of the blood that sang in Rafen's veins, and once again he was struck by the great privilege he had been done by the grant of access to their presence.

He found himself a place at the foot of a tattered banner praising the Liberation of the Nine Sisters and surveyed the other men in the gathering: the Chaplain Argastes; First Captain Lothan; Caecus, the Apothecae Majoris, and all the others. He was indeed in esteemed company here. Hidden in the sleeves of his robes, Rafen's hands bunched into fists. He felt as if he did not deserve to breathe the same air as such noble heroes and learned men.

Argastes led them all in a brief prayer to the Great Angel and the Emperor, asking both of them for clarity and fortitude in the days to come. Then Dante rose and every other warrior bowed. The assembly came to the ready as the Chapter Master bid them to their feet.

He glanced at Mephiston, and the psyker nodded back to his liege-lord. 'The psi-wards are in place, my lord. What we say and do in the room will not be sensed by any agent of the warp.'

'Just so,' said the Chapter Master. 'For what we speak of now may well be a matter of the greatest crisis to befall our legion since the murder of our primarch, the Emperor protect his soul.'

A mutter of concern crossed the chamber. Lothan's open, pale face registered uncertainty. 'The matter of the…' He shot a look at Rafen. 'The *insurrection* was dealt with, was it not? I had thought that threat passed.'

'We have only exchanged one threat for another,' noted Corbulo.

Dante gave a solemn nod. 'Aye. It is not the incident that we deal with now, kinsmen, but the shockwave from its passing. Like the wake of a razor-wind, the damage that lingers behind may kill us by inches where the maelstrom failed.'

Rafen felt ice in the pit of his gut. He wanted to speak, to offer up some sort of explanation or apology, but he found no words. *Insurrection.* The word tumbled about within his thoughts, hard-edged and leaden.

It was a damnation, a bladed curse, and Rafen felt shame to think he had been there to watch it unfurl. Not since the grim times of the Horus Heresy had brother turned against brother, and yet in recent months the Blood Angels had been pushed to the very brink of a civil war within their Chapter. It began on the cemetery world of Cybele, when the Blood Angels battle-barge *Bellus* had arrived to rescue Rafen and his company from an attack by the Traitor Marines of the Word Bearers Legion. *Bellus* had brought salvation and among the crew, Rafen's younger sibling Arkio; but the reunion hid a darker purpose. An inquisitor, the deceiver Ramius Stele, had engineered the whole matter in league with a daemon of the warp. He conceived a complex plan to split the Blood Angels asunder, and Rafen's sibling was his cat's-paw.

Even to think of it now, he shuddered at the horrible daring of the scheme. Stele twisted Arkio into a mirror's twin of the primarch Sanguinius and pressed the Astartes around him to believe the boy was the Great Angel's reincarnation; but all of it was a gambit to break the Chapter in two, to lead them down the bloody path towards Chaos and the Ruinous Powers that Stele called master.

Rafen found himself looking down at his hands. The hands that had briefly wielded the mighty archeotech weapon known as the Spear of Telesto, the hands that had taken the life of his fallen sibling in order to save Arkio's soul.

So much blood upon them, he told himself. *Yet none of it visible to the eye.* Rafen took a shuddering breath, fighting down the moment of powerful recall.

Arkio was dead, his body become ash upon the pyre Rafen built for his blood kin. The Spear that Stele had hoped to claim for himself was safe within the reclusia of the fortress-monastery, deep beneath the chamber where he now stood. And many, many brothers lay fallen in the fury that had spread from the schism Stele created. Righteous men, fine warriors. Rafen's mentor Koris, taken too soon by the madness of the Black Rage. Delos and Lucion, Sachiel and Alactus…

Alactus; an Astartes who had fought alongside Rafen for decades, who died at his hands when they had been forced into conflict. His bloodless hands.

So many dead. The cold irony of it was pitiable, that in ten thousand years, the greatest destruction wrought upon the Blood Angels could come not from an enemy, but from the battle they fought amongst themselves.

Doubt, recrimination and dark, potent regret threatened to well up and fill him, but Rafen forced himself to shake it off, pushing the black emotions away, returning to the moment.

Dante was speaking. 'What each of you knows is that our Chapter was wounded by the machinations of Ramius Stele and his daemonic masters. But what we have not disclosed to you is how deep that wound goes.'

'Lord,' said Argastes, 'I beg you, speak plainly.'

The Chapter Master frowned, and for a moment he seemed to show his great and venerable age in a single breath. 'My brothers, I have grave concerns about the future of our Chapter. The decimation stirred by Stele's perfidy and the false angel Arkio claimed the lives of many of our kinsmen.'

'How many?' demanded Lothan.

'Too many,' Corbulo grated. 'Dead, or lost to the Rage. Far too many.'

'These events have depleted our numbers beyond anything we have previously faced.' Dante stepped off the stage and came toward Lothan. 'Did you not sense it, brother-captain? On your return from campaign, on your arrival this day?' He gestured at the walls. 'The empty corridors. The silent arena.'

'I… I did,' Lothan admitted, 'but I did not suspect…'

'To maintain the illusion of normality, we have sent senior battle-brothers to wargrounds all across the galaxy,' explained Mephiston. 'The Imperium at large will see nothing unusual. For the moment, we may show the outside world a face that seems unchanged. But that mask will decay in time.'

'Unless a solution can be found, the IX Legion Astartes may find itself unable to recover. We may be forced to recluse ourselves. We will not be equal to the tasks the Emperor expects of us.' The Chapter Master's pronouncement was grim. 'New inductions of aspirants have been taken from Baal Secundus and Baal Primus, earlier than the tithe suggests, but it will not be enough.'

'And numbers alone are not the greatest threat,' added Mephiston. 'We have enemies both within the Imperium and without. Should they learn we are…' He paused, framing his thoughts. 'Diminished… they may be emboldened to move against us and take advantage of any vulnerability.'

'We are spread thin,' said Dante. 'And the fiction I have set in place will, as Brother Mephiston says, only last so long.'

Chaplain Argastes nodded. 'Aye. Agents of the Ordo Hereticus have already made overtures to Baal, asking questions about the death of that bastard Stele.'

'If they are asking overtly, we may be certain they are doing much more in clandestine realms,' noted Caecus, speaking for the first time. His hairless head was dull in the lamplight.

'Measures must be taken, and swiftly,' said Corbulo. 'May Sanguinius give us insight.'

Caecus drew himself up and licked his lips. 'If it pleases the High Priest, I believe he may have done so already.'

Dante turned to study the Apothecary. 'Speak,' he ordered. 'You have known the dimensions of this concern for some time, brother.'

He nodded. 'I have, lord. And in my works and research, I have uncovered a thread of hope, if you will indulge me.'

Rafen studied the Apothecary. Caecus was one of many of the sanguinary priests of the Blood Angels whose mission was less of the martial and more toward the ephemeral. Since the rise of the gene-curse in the Sons of Sanguinius, there had always been priests whose sole purpose had been to study the complex skeins of genetic material that made the Astartes who they were. Men whose battle was not against the enemies of the Emperor, but against the dormant bane of the Red Thirst and the Black Rage. Caecus worked at the Vitalis Citadel, a medicae complex hundreds of kilometres away, in the stark and icebound wilderness of Baal's polar region. Isolated there with a staff of brethren and serfs, the priest was over two hundred years into his service toward finding a cure.

'I have a solution to this circumstance, a radical one. I admit, it may not sit well with many of you. But I could not in good conscience let it go unremarked. We are in an extreme circumstance, are we not? And that calls for an extreme solution.'

'Explain, then,' said Corbulo, with clear and steady doubt upon his expression.

'There is a method, a *technology* that will allow us to recoup the losses to our Chapter in less than a solar year, if enough effort can be applied to it.' The Apothecary nodded to himself. 'My kinsmen, consider for a moment a point in history, when a similar fate to that which now faces the Blood Angels threatened another of the Legion Astartes. Ten millennia ago, after Horus's butchery on Istvaan V obliterated all but a small handful of the XIX Legion.'

'The Raven Guard,' Rafen found his voice. 'The Sons of Corax.'

'Aye. The very same. After the treachery of the Arch-traitor, the Emperor's light forsake him, the primarch Corax needed to swiftly rebuild his legion. I believe that the manner in which he did it can be opened to us.'

'Caecus,' said Argastes, the Chaplain's expression growing cold. 'I have heard the stories of the Raven Guard. I warn you to consider what you are about to utter in this esteemed company.'

The Apothecae Majoris seemed unconcerned by his battle-brother's caution. 'I have considered, kinsmen. I have considered it in great depth.'

'I would hear more,' offered Lothan, 'if it pleases the Master?'

Dante nodded. 'Continue, then.'

Caecus nodded. 'The Sons of Corax guard their secrets well, brothers, but some of their history has become known to me through my researches. It is said that the Lord of the Ravenspire went to books of ancient knowledge from the Age of Strife, intent on gleaning wisdom from the Emperor's own hand on the matter of the creation of Space Marines.'

Rafen listened intently. Every Astartes knew of the legacy they shared, from the very first of their kind created by the Emperor's gene-smiths to forge the army that united Terra and led it out of Old Night. Those warriors were the precursors to the Astartes of the Great Crusade and every generation that had followed.

'Corax saw a way to repopulate his forces in these tomes,' Caecus went on. 'Not through the process of induction, training and elevation that we practise in these times, but through a mastery of genetic duplication.'

'You speak of the old art of replicae,' said Corbulo. 'The science that man called cloning.'

'I do, priest, I do indeed.'

A sense of dismay shifted through the room, and Rafen's mouth went dry. The ways of the magos biologis were beyond him, but even he knew that the creation of a life from a synthetic mass of genetic matter seemed... somehow *improper*. It was said by some that beings spawned in such manner could not be considered human at all, that they were born without souls.

'I believe these methods could be called upon to forge new additions to our ranks, my lord.' Caecus addressed Dante directly, a thread of passion building beneath his words. 'Blood Angels, cut from the whole cloth of our legion, brought to maturity in a cycle of months instead of years.' He smiled slightly. 'A pure expression of the Adeptus Astartes Sanguinia.'

'Pure?' Chaplain Argastes echoed the word with grim severity. 'And tell us, brother, what of the rest of Corax's story? What of the dark tales spoken of in hushed whispers by the Sons of Russ?'

'What do you mean?' asked Lothan.

'Corax did indeed use the way of replicae to bring his legion back from the brink of dissolution,' said Argastes, 'but the road to it was not a smooth one. The Space Wolves speak of… of *creatures* that fought amid the Raven Guard's numbers. Things more beast than man. Throwbacks. Monstrous aberrations spawned in error by the very process you suggest we now employ.'

'Mutants?' One of Lothan's subordinates said the word with barely disguised repugnance, earning him a hard look from his commander.

Caecus coloured slightly. 'This is true. But that was ten millennia ago. The Imperium's grasp upon such sciences is stronger, now. And I would warrant that no Chapter beneath the Emperor's eternal gaze knows the nature of its own blood better than ours, Argastes! Corax was too hasty. He was unprepared. We are not. We can learn from the mistakes of the Raven Guard!' He glanced back at Dante.

'Your plan…' The Chapter Master dwelled on his thoughts for a moment. 'You did not exaggerate when you said it was radical, kinsman. To call it bold is an understatement.'

Rafen saw the Apothecary's hope soar. 'Then… You will grant me your approval, lord?'

'I will not.' Dante shook his head. 'I too know these stories of which Brother Argastes speaks. If mighty Corax, a primarch, a sibling of our liege-lord and a son of the Emperor, could not undertake this arcane art without error, then I ask you this, Caecus. What makes you think that you can succeed where he failed?'

The Chapter Master's steady, careful words made the Apothecary hesitate. 'I only wish to make the attempt. For our Chapter's sake.'

'I do not doubt your dedication to the Blood Angels and your great work, kinsman. Never think that. But this plan, the risk of it… I am not sure I can give my blessing to such an undertaking.'

Caecus glanced around the room, looking for support, but he did not find it.

Mephiston brought the matter to a close with a single question. 'Apothecary,' he began, 'you would not have brought this to us unless you had already made some attempt to echo Corax's work. What have you accomplished?'

With the searching eyes of the Lord of Death upon him, Caecus could hide nothing from the assembled Blood Angels. 'I have had only limited success to date.' The admission weighed down upon him.

'If not this route, then what others are open to us?' said Lothan. 'We have spoken already of the increase in tithes, and I will assume that many of the men in our Scout company may be advanced to the status of full battle-brother into the bargain?'

'Correct,' noted Corbulo, 'but still it will not be enough.'

Dante nodded once more. 'It will not. And to that end, I have made a decision. The issue we face at this moment cannot find its answers within the walls of this fortress,' he said, glancing up at the ceiling, 'indeed, not even within the boundaries of the worlds that orbit our red sun. We must go further, across the galaxy if need be, to find the solution elsewhere.'

Argastes frowned. 'Are you suggesting that we take secondary tithes from other planets, lord?'

'No, my friend.' The Chapter Master shook his head. 'I believe there is only one way in which we can find a healing to the wounds of the Arkio Insurrection. We will call together all our kindred and seek the answer among the many Sons of Sanguinius.'

'A conclave,' breathed Rafen. 'A gathering of the entire successor Chapters of the Blood Angels.'

'Aye,' Dante shot him a look of agreement. 'I will call my cousins to this place and in unity, find a path.'

Caecus's lips thinned. 'Unity has never been at the forefront of the character of our successors, lord. We are not the Ultramarines. There are those who will simply ignore such a summons. Others lost to distance that we may never reach in time.'

Lothan rubbed his chin, thinking. 'We'll gather all that we can.'

'Then it is so ordered,' said Mephiston, rising to his feet. 'First Captain? You will liaise with the shipmasters at the orbit dock and the astropaths. Have a deployment plan prepared for the Chapter Master by morning.' He bowed to Dante. 'Lord, with your permission, I will choose the cadres of men to serve as messengers for your summons.'

'Do so,' came the reply.

In short order, the meeting broke apart and the men left in groups, many of them quiet and introspective, musing on the great weight of what had been revealed. Rafen, alone as he was and of lower rank than all of them, stood back and allowed his seniors to leave first, out of respect.

Caecus caught his eye, as the Apothecae Majoris crossed the chamber, deep in his thoughts. He hid it well, but Rafen could see the stiffness in his gait, the narrowing of his eyes. Caecus was silently fuming at the Chapter Master's censure; to be put in one's place by Dante, no matter that it was with consideration and not from off-hand whim, clearly did not sit well with Caecus. Rafen imagined how he might have felt in the same place; but then he, like Caecus, was a Space Marine, a Blood Angel. Dante was their Lord Commander, and his word was second only to the edicts of the Emperor himself. If it was spoken by Dante, then it was to be done. There was no other condition. Caecus's pride was wounded, but he understood. The veteran Apothecary would not have lived this long or been granted the responsibility he had if he did not accept that.

'Rafen,' Mephiston said his name, catching his attention immediately. From the foot of the black stone stage, the Librarian beckoned him with a long finger. He approached, bowing slightly. Behind Mephiston, Dante was in quiet conversation with Corbulo.

'Sir,' Rafen began. 'If you will forgive me, but I have a question.'

'Why was I summoned to this meeting?' He smiled thinly. 'I need not exercise my abilities to see that concern written across your face, brother-sergeant. You are here because I believed it necessary. Leave it at that, eh?'

'As you wish.' Rafen decided not to press the issue.

'In point of fact, I have already decided to deploy you and your tactical squad as one of the messenger cadres we will send to our cousin Chapters.'

'May I ask which?'

Behind him, Lord Dante broke off from his conversation as Corbulo walked away. 'That choice is mine to make,' he said, stepping down to Rafen's level.

The Blood Angel bowed again. 'Lord, I am at your service. Task me.'

'There is a world called Eritaen, in the Tiber Marches. It has fallen from the light of the Emperor and a punishment in keeping with that crime has been delivered to its people. Our cousins are the hand that wields that punishment.' Dante eyed him. 'Tell me, Brother Rafen. What do you know of the Flesh Tearers?'

He smothered his immediate reaction of dismay within a heartbeat; Rafen had no doubt that Dante saw it, but the Chapter Master said nothing. He picked his words with care. 'They are of the Second Founding, a small Chapter of only four battle companies. The Tearers have a reputation for ferocity. They are... Proud and aggressive, my lord. As much an embodiment of the Great Angel's darker nature as we are of his nobility and bearing.'

To his surprise, the Lord Commander's face split in wry smile. 'A very politic answer, sergeant. Mephiston was correct when he suggested you for this mission.'

Rafen nodded. 'I will do my best to be worthy of his faith.'

Dante's smile vanished. 'You'll have to. Chapter Master Seth and his men will not brook an intrusion from one of us, know that. Your welcome will be icy at the very best. Mephiston suggested I give you this task because you will rise to the occasion, because of your potential. But I give it to you because of who you are. Who you *were.*'

Rafen tasted ashes in his mouth. 'The blood-brother of Arkio.'

A nod. 'Just so.' Dante considered him for a moment. 'Seth will be the most difficult of my cousins to persuade. More than any of our other successors, the Flesh Tearers have always walked their own path. They resent anything that seems like the hand of control upon their necks. He will deny my summons. There is no question he will deny it.'

'Then, my lord, how should I convince him to return with me?'

Dante turned away. 'Tell him the truth, Rafen. Every bloody moment.' The Lord of the Blood Angels walked away, leaving the Astartes and the psyker alone.

Rafen found Mephiston studying him with a cool, measuring stare. 'Seth's men will goad you. They will attempt to draw you into challenge. As much as they might deserve a beating, you will not engage them, do you understand?'

He nodded. 'As you command.'

'The mission,' intoned the psyker. 'The mission first and foremost, Rafen. There has never been a moment more deadly to our brotherhood than this one. You are granted a singular trust this day. I know you will prove worthy of it.'

Mephiston left then, and it was a long moment before Rafen looked up to find he was the only soul in the chamber.

Above him, carved from the walls, figures of the Emperor and Sanguinius looked down upon him and his duty yet to be fulfilled.

CHAPTER FOUR

THE SKIES OVER Baal were filled with crimson.

Dozens of warships ranging in size from small corvettes to massive grand cruisers lay in lines of stately repose, at high anchor over the desert world's equator. Each craft had its own packet of space to surround it, each ship positioned in the same orbital plane so that no one vessel was seen to be above or below the others, in order to satisfy protocol. Only one group of craft drifted higher, near the dry docks at cislunar positions; the warcraft of the Blood Angels themselves. This was only right and proper; Baal was the home world of the Chapter and they were its masters. Every other Astartes gathered here was an honoured guest – to be respected, indeed, but still a guest.

Rafen imagined that some of his cousins would chafe before such a display, and he understood the feeling. The role had been reversed only a short time before on Eritaen. But now the Flesh Tearers were the invited of his

Chapter, and it was upon them to tread carefully. *Not that they will. It isn't their way.*

He considered Seth once again, wondering if the Chapter Master was watching the same display from the *Tycho*'s staterooms three decks down. He was a curious one; Seth confounded Rafen's expectation of what he thought a Flesh Tearer would be. He had no outward show of the bloodthirsty arrogance that Gorn and Noxx displayed. Their Chapter Master was eternally dour, distant in thought, as if he were still fighting a battle in some far off place that only his sight could reach. Seth was the polar opposite to the charismatic Dante.

The *Tycho* moved with care into a pre-determined block of sky and came to a steady stop on spears of thrust, anchoring in a geostationary position. To the starboard floated a red frigate with yellow trim, with a plunging solar sail emerging from the ventral hull. Upon the shimmering panel, there was the silhouette of a great black grail and above it a dark falling droplet.

'Blood Drinkers,' said Kayne, half to himself, the young Space Marine approaching the viewing window where his commander stood. 'They came all the way from the Lethe Front, so I heard.'

Rafen nodded but said nothing. Beyond the Blood Drinker ship lay a battle cruiser whose prow was a gigantic bone-white skull. Ruby-coloured wings reached back from it down the length of the bow. He saw the maws of torpedo bays inside the huge, sightless eye sockets. The rest of the craft was rendered in only two colours; the starboard side from stem to stern all in rich red, the port a nightfall black. 'The Angels Sanguine,' he noted, breaking his silence to point out the vessel to the youth. 'And beyond them the ships of the Angels Vermillion.'

'I feel blessed to see this day,' Kayne was humbled by the sight. 'How many of our battle-brothers can say they witnessed such an august gathering as this one, sir?' He smiled slightly. 'I would give much to be in the chamber when all the elite of these Chapters meet. I imagine it would be… interesting to observe.'

Rafen's eyes narrowed and he shot the other Space Marine a hard look. 'This is not a game, Kayne. This conclave has been called to discuss matters of the utmost gravity. Remember that.'

The youth bowed his head, chastened. 'Of course, brother-sergeant. I meant no disrespect.' After a moment, he spoke again. 'Are we the last to arrive?'

'The shipmaster informs me that two more craft are behind us, to arrive within the hour, the *White of Eye* and the *Rapier*. Once they have taken their positions, it is my understanding the conclave will commence in earnest.'

Rafen's discussion with *Tycho's* shipmaster had tested his patience somewhat; not with the man himself, but with the orders the officer had been forced to relay to the Blood Angel. A complicated web of flight corridors had been set up so that Thunderhawks and Aquila shuttles from each of the assembled craft would not cross over one another in transit, and a rotation of landing patterns was in place so that each contingent would set foot upon Baal's surface in order of seniority and Founding. It ground on his mood to consider that some of his cousins would insist on such posturing and open display of rank; given the importance of the meeting, could they not dispense with it all and meet as equals?

Before he left Baal to find Seth, Rafen had asked that question of Corbulo. The steady-eyed sanguinary high priest had allowed a rare laugh to escape his careful demeanour. *Brother*, he had said, *for all the greatness the Emperor granted us, he also made us rivals to one another. Sigils, flags and honours are at the core of what we are. If we ignore our heraldry, we deny part of our natures.*

All too true. And yet, still Rafen's impatience wound tight.

'It's strange,' Kayne was speaking again. 'I look down there, lord, to the surface of Baal and I see the scope of the land.' He pointed toward geographical features visible through the thin clouds. 'The Chalice Mountains. The Great Chasm Rift and the Ruby Sea... I know this place as I would a brother.' The youth nodded at the other ships in orbit. 'But to them... What is Baal? A vague, abstract thing? A place they only know of from doctrine and myth?'

The planet turned slowly beneath their feet. The desolate rust-red sphere had a stark kind of beauty to it, the layers of radioactive dust in the upper atmosphere haloed by the glow of Baal's red giant star. Such a harsh and unforgiving world, and yet the sight of it moved both men in a manner that neither would have found easy to articulate.

Rafen glanced at his subordinate. 'You wonder if our cousins are as awed to be here as you are by their presence, perhaps?'

To his surprise, Kayne shook his head. 'No, sir. I wonder if they will revere Baal as much as I do.'

Rafen sensed the unspoken thought in the other man's mind. 'The Flesh Tearers are only one successor among many, Kayne. The character of the Sons of Sanguinius differs greatly from one to another.'

He got a slow nod in return. 'It will be an education to see those differences in the flesh.'

Rafen found himself returning the gesture, once more feeling the press of the days to come. 'Yes. That it will.'

'IT'S NOT WHAT I expected,' said Noxx. He stood at the stateroom's window, his helmet in the crook of his arm, staring down at the planet. 'I thought it would be more...'

'Impressive?' offered his commander. Captain Gorn's attention was elsewhere, as he used a small monocular to peer into the darkness, studying the other ships that surrounded them. 'When held in comparison to Cretacia, it does seem a sparse vista. No jungle-sprawls and swamplands, no wreathes of storm clouds.'

'I suppose, lord. Perhaps I was foolish to imagine that birthplace of the Great Angel, may the light find him, would be a glittering sphere made of gold and ruby.'

From behind them, their Chapter Master spoke without looking up from the business of polishing his armour. 'Remember your doctrine, Noxx. Do not be obtuse. You know as well as any of us, Baal is not his birthplace. Sanguinius rose on the second moon, Baal Secundus.'

'The moons cannot be seen from this orbital position,' noted Gorn, with a frown. 'We are over the dayside, our angle is too low.'

Noxx was quiet for a moment, framing a question. 'Do you think… Would we perhaps be allowed to go there? To Secundus and the Angel's Fall? The place where he lived as an infant…' As much as he might have wanted to disguise it, there was a strong reverence in the veteran sergeant's gruff voice.

Seth went on with his work. 'I would think not. The Blood Angels are very protective of their exalted First Founding status, brother-sergeant. I imagine they would not take kindly to the heavy boots of an Astartes of the Second Founding upon their hallowed ground.'

'Lord Dante would not dare to deny such a request,' said Gorn, 'not if you made it, master.'

'My cousin Dante dares to do many things, so it would seem,' Seth mused. 'That we are here is evidence of it.' He flicked the cloth in his hand with an irritated snap, signalling a change in the direction of the conversation. 'The ships, Gorn. Tell me what you see out there.'

'The Blood Angel Rafen spoke the truth. Many vessels are gathered here, from nearly every Founding of our kindred, so it would seem. I spy the Angels Encarmine. The Flesh Eaters.'

A slow smile formed on Seth's lips. 'Well, now. The Flesh Eaters. Still alive, are they? They have the warp's luck.'

'I imagine they say the same of us, lord,' noted Noxx.

In an eye's blink, Seth's cold humour vanished. 'You *imagine*, do you? And what else do you imagine our cousins say of us?' He was on his feet, the cloth fluttering to the deck, his mood darkening by the moment. 'We, whose small fleet is so mired in conflict that we could not even come to Baal aboard one of our own vessels?'

Both Noxx and Gorn fell silent. Seth's temper had been mercurial all through the journey from Eritaen; flashes of annoyance that grew more frequent the closer they got to their destination. Neither spoke, instead allowing their leader to vent the frustration that had been slowly building in him. He gestured sharply at the craft out beyond the armourglass window. 'Such pride they must have, our cousins, with their pretty ships. Such pity for us.' He stalked toward Noxx. 'I ask you, brother-sergeant, what kind of blood-cursed luck do we have?'

'I… have no answer for you, lord.'

Seth held his gaze for a long moment, then turned away. 'I shall tell you, then. We are cursed, brothers. Caught on the claws of our own savagery, ravaged by the thirst and the rage, the least numbered of the successors of Sanguinius.' He held up a spread hand, the thumb tucked away. 'Four. Four companies is all we number, and yet we instil such fear in our enemies that Chapters of twice our size cannot! But for all that, are we respected? Are we not judged by every Astartes who lays his eyes upon us?'

'It is so,' agreed Noxx.

'Dante brings us here to bemoan the wounds suffered by his legion, but never once have our cousins considered *our* wounds! Our pain!'

Captain Gorn swallowed hard and shifted his weight. 'Then… If I would be allowed to ask this… Why did you go against your first answer to the Blood Angel, Rafen? In Amit's name, my lord, why are we here?'

And at that, Seth's smile began a slow return. 'What Rafen spoke of gave me renewed faith, brother-captain. It reminded me that Emperor is good and just, that he places the reward for hubris upon those who deserve it. The Blood Angels are so very proud, Gorn. And that conceit rose up and bit them, down to the marrow! After ten thousand years, they are suddenly wanting. The threat of dissolution shrouds them. Now Dante and his kindred understand how we feel, do you see? They are learning the lesson that the Flesh Tearers have known for millennia.' His eyes glittered. 'That when one is clinging to the ragged edge…' He made claws of his hands. 'You will do everything you must not to fall into the abyss.'

'They want our help,' said Noxx.

'Yes,' said Seth, 'more than that, they need it like air to breathe. And when a warrior finds himself upon such a balance of need, he can… He *must* take advantage of it.'

Noxx folded his arms across his chest plate. 'So the question is no longer why, but how. How can the troubles of the Blood Angels be to the benefit of our Chapter?'

'Such talk might be seen by some as seditious,' noted Gorn.

Seth gave a humourless snort. 'We are Astartes. It is our nature to seek the tactical advantage in all situations, in war or elsewhere. Everything we do is in the Emperor's name. He has never been one to accept weakness, and neither shall we.'

'Have the Blood Angels become weak, my lord?'

'That is what we will learn, brother-captain.'

THE ARVUS-CLASS LIGHTER dropped quickly from the sky, the hard gusts of wind buffeting the boxy fuselage as it spiralled in toward the cracked, arctic escarpments below. The bleak wilderness of Baal's polar zone went to the horizon, the frozen ridges of snow and ice like motionless waves caught on a pict screen. The white vista was tinged with the slightest aura of pink, where rock dust from the planet's iron-rich mantle was infused with the glaciers.

The lighter pressed through a screeching windstorm and continued downward, the stabilator wings vibrating. Caecus glanced through the viewing slit next to his acceleration couch. He had made similar journeys more times than he could recall, back and forth across Baal, to every part of the home world, and to worlds beyond in service to his research. The hard flight of the trip's last leg was of no concern to him; it served to remind him that he would soon be back where he should be, with the work. This trip, out across to Baal Primus, had been of little value, as he had suspected it would be. A thin sigh escaped the Apothecae Majoris and his hand tapped absently on the case by his side; the genetic material he had sampled from the tribals on the first moon would doubtless prove as useless as all the others. The impurities, they were the problem. If only it were possible to find a sample uncontaminated by radiation, by biological drift...

The ground was rising up to meet them, and across the shield plains to the south-west Caecus made out a string of red dots, bright against the ice field like droplets of blood on a sheet of vellum.

Battle-brothers. The tiny points of vivid colour were Astartes undergoing a trial, men dropped in with no weapons, no supplies, nothing but an order to make their way to some nondescript frozen crag and survive there for a span of days. They were Scouts from the tenth company, some of them advanced to full rank out of schedule because of the current crisis in numbers. Caecus wondered if they would be ready. Deaths were not uncommon during such exercises, stemming from mishaps upon the punishing ice or attacks by the feral packbears that prowled through the snows.

'We cannot brook more losses.' It was a moment before the Apothecary realised he had spoken aloud; but alone in the lighter's cargo bay, there was no one to remark upon it. He shook his head as the Arvus began to turn to the east.

'Lord.' The flat, rote diction of the lighter's pilot-servitor issued out from a speaker grille on the bulkhead. 'We are about to land at the citadel. Prepare for touchdown.'

The craft swooped around a high ridge and Caecus saw the tower. A pillar of frost-rimed red stone, it was a rusty spike hammered into the white crest of ice and rock. The lines of the Vitalis Citadel were smooth and sheer, marred only by the shape of a bartizan emerging from the apex. The battlemented structure protruded from the side of the tower, the flat circular roof providing a landing stage for service craft. Forty levels high, the tower was only the visible marker for the compound that ranged beneath it. Many such satellite facilities were scattered across Baal's surface; as well as the citadel's medicae complex, there were the reliquaries at Sangre in the south and the great labworks of the Chapter's Tech-marines in the Regio Quinquaginta-Unus. These places were spread far apart so that any potential enemy attack could not strike them all at once – and also to minimize any fallout damage in the event of an emergency within their walls.

The circular section of the roof of the bartizan drew back in an iris and the Arvus settled into it, rocking as the winds nudged the craft. The lighter eased into a cradle with a jerk, and Caecus was out of his restraints before the hatchway was half-open, ducking low to avoid the rising panel of hull metal. Overhead, the iris was closing, but a few flakes of thick snow had followed them in, drifting in the steady, cool air of the citadel.

Fenn stood waiting for him at the foot of the landing cradle, with a servitor at his flank. The Chapter serf bowed. 'Majoris,' he began. 'Welcome back.'

Caecus handed the sample case to the servitor and the machine-helot clacked a binary-code reply, before limping away on piston-driven legs across the exhaust-stained decking. 'A wasted journey,' he told his subordinate.

Fenn frowned; that was to say, he frowned more than usual. Rail-thin and somewhat unkempt in aspect, the serf always exhibited an outward appearance of fretful worry, his hands finding each other to wring as he addressed problems or points of concern. His outward appearance belied a keen mind, though. Like most of the Chapter serfs in service to the Blood Angels, Fenn had been recruited from the tribes of the Blood on Baal Secundus. Judged too weak to endure the punishing rituals that would transform a normal man into a Space Marine, as Caecus's assistant, his intelligence still served the Chapter.

'I should have gone in your stead,' Fenn noted. 'The possibility of harvesting new data from Primus was always a marginal one, at the very best.'

Caecus nodded. 'True. But I needed an excuse to leave the laboratorium for a time. To remind myself that a galaxy still exists outside these walls.' He gestured at the citadel around them.

Fenn's fingers knotted. 'There has been no improvement in the latest test series,' he said, answering Caecus's question before he asked it. Fenn's ability to anticipate his master's thoughts was one of the reasons that Caecus had kept him in his service for so long, even to the point of granting the man juvenat treatments so that the serf might share in some small measure of a Blood Angel's longevity.

The Apothecary nodded, taking in his comments, as they walked to the heavy elevator car that would carry them to the lower levels. 'Did we receive any... visitors while I was off-world?'

'No one came, my lord.'

'As I expected.' For all the great gnashing of teeth and stern, earnest words about the great import of the work taking place in the citadel, their labours were largely ignored, the plaudits going instead to those who engaged in the many battles under the Blood Angels banner. There would never be honours given and portraits painted of the Apothecaries who toiled in this place. There were no decorations for discovering a new thread of research that might cure the Rage, no award for breaking ground on a theory that could one day stem the Thirst.

Fenn continued. 'With all the ships in orbit and the comings and goings at the fortress, I imagine the citadel could take off and fly away without being noticed.'

Caecus had seen the great fleet massing over Baal as he returned from the first moon; the berthing of the various warships had forced his pilot to make a wide detour and approach the polar zone from the night side. Part of him wondered how interesting it would be to have a conclave of his own, to draw in Apothecaries and sanguinary priests from all the successor Chapters and pool their knowledge. What secrets could he learn from his cousins, if only they would be open to share them? But that was not the way of the Adeptus Astartes. For a moment, his mind drifted; he recalled the stories he had heard of a successor Chapter from the Twenty-first Founding, the Lamenters. It was said that they had found a way to expunge the gene-flaws from their shared bloodline. If it were true... Caecus would have given much to meet such men and glean wisdom from them; but the Lamenters had not been heard of in decades, not since a tyranid force had decimated their numbers, and every messenger sent to find them returned empty-handed. He had little doubt they would not be represented at Dante's grand conclave. *A great pity*, he mused, *but not the matter at hand. There are other concerns to be addressed.*

The ornate brass elevator car accepted them and began a swift descent into the heart of the complex. Tier upon tier of the Vitalis Citadel flashed past them, endless levels of experimental facilities, gene-labs and workstations. The quest to understand the labyrinthine nature of the Blood Angels gene-seed was an ongoing work, and this was only one of several sites engaged in it. The mission to find the causes of and cures for the twin curses of the Black Rage and the Red Thirst were ceaseless. But there were other efforts under way here, experiments that were hidden in vaults that only Caecus and his staff were granted access to. It was toward one such compound that they travelled now, a wordless understanding between them.

The Apothecae Majoris sensed something else unspoken, however. After a moment, he gave the serf a measuring look. 'What is it that concerns you, Fenn?'

His assistant's fingers knotted. 'It... is of no consequence, lord.'

'Tell me,' he insisted. 'All matters that occur under this roof are of my concern.'

Fenn puffed. 'It is the *woman*, sir. Her manner continues to vex me. I believe she does it to amuse herself at my expense.'

Caecus frowned. 'I have told you before, on more than one occasion, to make your peace with her. Do not be in error, serf. Those words were not a request.'

'I have tried, my lord.' Fenn bowed his head slightly. 'But she diminishes me at every opportunity. Mocking my skills.' He paused. 'I do not like her.'

'Like? You are not required to *like* her. You are required to work with her. If you cannot do so—'

'No, no!' Fenn shook his head. 'Lord Caecus, you know my dedication to the Chapter and our endeavours is true! But the air of ill-feeling she brings to the place—'

'I will speak with her.' Caecus ended the discussion firmly. 'We are on the cusp of something magnificent, Fenn. I will not allow such trivial minutiae to cloud the issue.'

The serf said nothing, staring at the hex-grid deck as the lift continued to descend. Through the metal flooring, the chasm of the elevator shaft extended away into the depths of the mountainside.

THE GREAT BRASS gates opened and a stubby iron drawbridge dropped into place, allowing them to exit the elevator car. Fenn followed, as years of drilled-in discipline suggested, a step behind and to the right of his master. Lord Caecus walked past the gun-servitors caged upon the stone walls, letting their canine snouts take his scent. Satisfied, the guardians gave a hollow yowl of assent and their stubber cannons drooped. Steam hissing in hot gushes, the pistons holding the pressure doors shut over the laboratorium ratcheted out and the steel plates were pulled up and away. The motion reminded Fenn of a curtain drawing back from a theatre stage.

Venturing through the blue-lit tunnel where the machine-spirit sensors watched, the two of them allowed a fine mist of counter-infectives to haze the air about them; then the inner doors opened and they were in the chamber proper.

The colours of white and red dominated everything. Hard illumination from glowstrips in the walls threw stark, pitiless light on the benches where chemical rendering was underway. Centrifuges whirred and fractionating columns bubbled in a slow rhythm, giving the chamber an austere but somehow animate sense to it. Medicae servitors moved to and fro, working at repetitive tasks programmed into their brains by decks of golden punch cards.

The red was here and there in patches; on the smocks of the servitors, pooling in the blood gutters of the dissection tables, thick in vials that ranged in racks about the walls.

At one such rack, the woman stood, using a lenticular viewer made of pewter and crystal to conduct a deep examination of a particular blood sample. She looked up, the sharp lines of her face accented by the night-black hair bunched in a tight fist upon her head. Discreet mechadendrite cords trailed from a line of brass sockets that began at her temple and ended at the nape of her neck. Like Fenn, she wore a simple duty robe of bleached cloth; unlike him, however, on her it miraculously accented the firm and well-muscled shape of her body.

'Nyniq,' said Caecus, and she bowed to the Blood Angel by way of returning his greeting.

'You've returned at a timely moment, majoris.' Nyniq's voice had a quality to it that some ordinary men might have found charming, sultry even. Fenn considered it neither; her manner seemed oily and insincere to him. He had objected to the involvement of the tech-priestess from the very beginning, but Lord Caecus had dismissed his concerns. The matter of the woman's motives was secondary to the work at hand, so the Astartes had said. *The work, the work, always the work. That is what is most important.* His master's words rang hollow in his ears.

Certainly, it was undeniable that Nyniq brought a great intellect to the project, and indeed, Fenn found himself reluctantly admitting that her solutions to some problems had allowed them to advance their research by leaps and bounds. But that didn't make him dislike her any less. This work was a matter for Blood Angels and their Baalite kindred, not for some itinerant member of the magos biologis to simply drop into and begin interfering.

She had been here for months now. She never seemed to leave the laboratorium, always there when Fenn arrived after a rest period, always there when he left again to take sleep or sustenance. And then there was that habit she had, of cooing some peculiar wordless melody to herself whenever she worked. Fenn found it irritating.

He comforted himself with a thought; if she did turn out to have another agenda other than the course of pure research she claimed, her life would be forfeit in moments. Caecus had been direct in his words with her; while she toiled within the walls of the Vitalis Citadel, her life belonged to the Blood Angels. If she did anything to damage that trust, it would be her blood spilled upon the floors here.

Fenn followed his master after Nyniq, through the crossway door at the far end of the chamber and into the tank crèche beyond.

In there, the colour was the sea-green of the oceans that had once shone across Baal before the fall of Old Night. Liquid shimmers of reflected light cast patterns over the walls. Boots rang across the service gantry between the two long ranks of fogged, glassy capsules. Nyniq took them to a tank resting up on its armature, turned so that it stood upright next to the gantry. Built into the glass wall of the tank was a metal bulb festooned with indicator lights. The air in here was heavy with stringent chemicals.

'Series eight, iteration twelve,' noted the woman. 'If you will observe?'

Fenn immediately frowned. 'That one is still immature.'

'Quite so,' Nyniq allowed, 'but it is far enough along to illustrate my point.' She tapped out a sequence on a keypad and muttered a brief incantation.

Inside the tank, the milky fluid cleared to reveal a naked male, of similar proportion to a young Baalite tribal but lacking the pallid flesh and wiry build. The figure in the tank had skin toned a tanned red, with planes of hard muscle beneath. He would not have looked out of place in the armour of a Scout.

Caecus studied the youth, who drifted as if in a slumber, a line of thin bubbles trailing from his lips. 'Outward aspect is promising.' He said it warily.

Nyniq nodded. 'But as we have become aware over the last series of iterations, that is not a guarantee.' She tapped another control and the figure in the tank jerked, limbs going rigid.

His eyes snapped open and Fenn gasped as he looked directly at the serf. There was no pupil, iris or white of the eye; only a hard, baleful orb of dark ruby. Hands that bent into claws came up and scraped at the inside of the tank, scoring lines in the reinforced armourglass. And then the mouth opened. Within, there was an orchard of daggered fangs, row upon row.

Caecus's expression remained cold and aloof as the figure gurgled and frothed, beating at its confinement. 'Another failure, then.'

'Aye,' said Nyniq grimly. 'Despite our every effort, my lord, errors continue to creep into the structure of the gene-matrix. With each iteration they become more pronounced. The replication protocols are flawed at a level so primal, so inherent, that nothing we do can correct them.'

Caecus turned away. He waved a hand at the tank. 'Dispose of it.'

'As you wish.' The tech-priestess pressed another control and a boxy device dropped into the top of the tank on a frame: a modified boltgun. Fenn saw a moment of almost human emotion on the face of the specimen before the gun discharged with a muffled concussion. The milky fluid swirled with red.

Nyniq stepped back, and the base of the tank opened into a sluice, liquid, flesh and dead matter alike dropping away into a yawning vent beneath the companionway.

Fenn went after his master. 'My lord, there are no failures. There is only more data. We shall learn from this iteration and attempt again.'

'Is that wise?' asked Nyniq.

Both of them stopped and turned to face her. 'I will decide what is and is not wise,' Caecus said, a warning beneath his words.

She touched the platinum pendant around her neck. The shape of a repeating strand of DNA, it mirrored the red helix sigil that crested the shoulder pad of every Blood Angel apothecarion. 'Majoris, I offered my services to you after our first meeting because I was captured by the purity of your dedication. I did so because I believed that what you attempted here will be to the benefit of the Adeptus Astartes and the glory of the Emperor of Mankind. But now I must speak honestly to you. We have reached the limits of our skills. We can do no better.' Her head bowed. 'I thank you for this opportunity to be part of your work. But we must accept failure and move on.'

A nerve jerked in Caecus's jaw. 'I will do no such thing! I am a Blood Angel! We do not give up the cause at the first impediment we encounter! We carry our mission to the bitter end!'

'But this is not the first impediment, lord. Not the second, not the tenth or the fiftieth.' Nyniq's words became quiet, conspiratorial. 'My lord, I know that you have kept certain things from us. I know that the Chapter Master has not given his blessing for this research to proceed, and yet you have continued it.'

'Lord Dante did not order us to stop,' Fenn broke in. 'He... He did not use those words!'

'Semantics,' said Nyniq. 'I doubt he will be pleased to learn we went on regardless for all these months.'

'She is correct.' Caecus moved to another of the tanks, and studied his own reflection in the glass, his manner cooling. 'But I made the decision. Lord Dante is a great man, but he believes in that which he can hold in his hand. It is only the Emperor and the strength of his brethren he takes on faith. I am convinced... I am certain Dante will see the value of this work, if only I could show him proof instead of words.'

'The only *proof* we have are unfinished clones. Bestial mutants and freaks masquerading as Space Marines, no better than the spawn of the Corrupted.' Nyniq shook her head. 'We know that Corax of the Raven Guard took decades over this process, and even then his yield was one success for every hundred stillborn failures!'

'Perhaps... Perhaps you are right.'

Fenn's lip trembled as he saw a change come over his master. The certainty in Caecus's manner slipped away. It was as if a great weight had come upon him. The serf had the sudden, terrible awareness that he was seeing behind the mask of determination his lord usually wore, that this weary aspect was his true face. The face of someone worn down by years of dogged, fruitless toil toward a goal he might never reach. 'Master, no. there must be another way! Some avenue yet untried, some approach we have not seen.' He reached out and touched Caecus upon the gauntlet.

'And who would know it, old friend?' The Apothecary favoured Fenn with a look. 'You? Speak, if you have a solution. I would hear it.'

Nyniq made a noise in her throat, drawing their attention. She was still toying with the pendant. 'There is… Someone. A man of great knowledge. I know him, Lord Caecus. He was my patron at the magos biologis during my time as an initiate. He spoke of interest in Great Corax's research on more than one occasion.'

Fenn's brows knitted. 'You wish us to bring in *another* outsider?' He shot a look at his master. 'My lord, is not one enough?'

'We are all servants of the Emperor!' snapped Nyniq. 'And this man may represent the last hope for your plans to rebuild the Blood Angels!'

'His name, then,' said Caecus. 'Tell me his name.'

'The Tech-Lord Haran Serpens, majoris.'

The Apothecary nodded. 'His work is known to me. He forged a cure for the Haze Plagues on Farrakin.'

'The very same.'

After a moment, Fenn's master gave a nod. 'Summon him, then. Do it with care and stealth. I have no wish to make issue with Dante until I have something to show him.' He stalked away toward the doors.

Fenn ran to catch up with him. 'Lord! Are you certain this is the right course of action? Can we trust the magos?'

Caecus didn't look at him. 'We are all servants of the Emperor,' he repeated. 'And sometimes we must dally with those we do not wish to in order to bring about a greater victory.'

'I don't trust her!' he hissed.

'Trust is not required,' said Caecus, 'only obedience.'

CHAPTER FIVE

SET INTO THE grey marble floor of the Grand Annex, directly beneath the Solar Dome, there was a four-pointed star made of rust-coloured stone mined from the foot of the Chalice Mountains. Flecked with tiny chips of garnet, at high sun the red light that fell through the dome's glass apex made it glow. At the centre of the star, an oval of mosaic formed the shape of the Blood Angels sigil, the wings pointing to the east and west, the tip of the bloody teardrop between them to the north, the jewelled bead falling southwards.

The building had stood for millennia. Even to an Adeptus Astartes, a warrior who might live to go beyond the eleven hundred years of Lord Dante, such a span of time was barely conceivable. How many Blood Angels, in all those generations, might have walked upon these stones? How many men? How many lives, ended now, gone in service to the same ideals that Brother Rafen stood for? The thought of it was history, solid and stone.

He stood at the southern arm of the star, his right hand firmly coiled around the mast of the Standard of Signus. At the other three points, battle-brothers dressed as he was, in full power armour and dress honours, stood holding other banners symbolising the greatest of victories in their Chapter's history. The vast circular chamber was one of the largest open interior spaces in the fortress-monastery, with the exception of some of the training arenas. The scale of the annexe was made grander still by the fact that there were no supporting stanchions or crossbeams holding up the curving roof above them. The chamber could have accommodated a Titan at full height and still given the war machine room to move. Long, thin pennants, each detailed with the symbol of a successor Chapter, hung around the lip of the dome at equidistant points.

About him, rings of Adeptus Astartes stood in four broken semi-circles around the compass star, equal numbers of men shoulder to shoulder, facing inward. Their battle armours were a mixture of variants and sub-classes, with even a lone Dreadnought standing amid them, and together they were a spectrum of red. Crimson through to ruby, scarlet to claret, colours deep as blood and bright as flame. Unlike the fellow Blood Angels who stood beneath the venerable standards, these were Rafen's distant kindred, the brotherhoods of the successor Chapters; *his cousins*.

The quiet murmur of conversation moved among them, some battle-brothers reaffirming old friendships, others making wary gestures of respect between them, some as silent as statues. As much as their colours differed, so then did their characters and manners. Rafen did not turn his head too much, but he knew that to his immediate right stood the contingent of the Angels Sanguine, resplendent in their half-red, half-black wargear and gleaming, polished helms. To his left stood Gorn and Seth of the Flesh Tearers, and following the circuit around, the smoky crimson of the Angels Vermillion, the gold-trimmed armour of the Blood Drinkers, and others beyond them… He let his eyes sweep over the figures assembled there before him, marvelling at the moment. Servo-skulls hummed overhead on impellors, recording every second for posterity on pict tapes and data spools; but Rafen was actually here, experiencing the moment, being a part of it.

The legacy of Sanguinius was laid out in this room, with representatives of nigh on every Chapter that paid fealty to the Great Angel's bloodline gathered under one roof. Rafen's gaze moved from one to another, seeing Astartes from Chapters that, until now, had been to him only names upon the pages of warbooks. There, the Blood Legion, in diagonal tiger-stripes of red and lightning blue; the Angels Encarmine, mirrors of Rafen's own colours except for a blunt trim of cold black; the Red Wings in their panels of pale snow and ruby; the Blood Swords ashine in glossy crimson, the sigil of a weeping blade stark upon their shoulders. These and more, united in a unique kind of kinship.

And yet, as with the families of common men, the fraternity of the Sons of Sanguinius was not without its bad blood.

Rafen became aware of Brother-Captain Gorn watching the party of Angels Sanguine with undisguised interest. Most of the warriors in the contingents went unhooded, but only the Angels Sanguine were, to a man, hidden behind their bi-coloured helmets. It was a quirk of their Chapter, known to most, although the reason was shrouded in rumour and supposition. The brothers of the Angels Sanguine habitually went masked upon the battlefield and all places where they might catch the eyes of others. Only among themselves, where those of their kindred walked, would they remove their headgear, and even then they retreated into the depths of heavy hooded robes. As an initiate, Rafen had heard many lurid and fanciful tales of what the Angels Sanguine hid from the world, and dismissed them as idle chatter; but now he stood close to them, he could not help but recall those tales and silently wonder, just a little.

Gorn, however, had no such desire to keep his own counsel. 'Rydae?' he said, in a low voice that did not carry, looking steadily at an Angel Sanguine officer. 'Is that you under there?'

Rafen watched the other Astartes from the corner of his eye. The Angels Sanguine ignored the Flesh Tearer.

'It's hard to be sure,' Gorn continued. 'Hard to tell one of you from another.' A tension built in the air between them. 'Will you not acknowledge me, cousin? No?' The Flesh Tearer chuckled quietly; at his side, Gorn's Chapter Master paid no heed to the hushed conversation, as if Seth thought it beneath his interest. 'Ah, I see. You still bear me ill-will after our meeting on Zofor's World? Because of the defeat?'

For the first time, the Angels Sanguine captain's helmet turned slightly so that his emerald eye slits could sight directly at Gorn. 'There was no defeat,' The reply was loaded with ready menace. 'Only... interference on your part.'

Gorn gave a tight, false smile. 'It aggrieves me that you see it that way.'

The helmet turned away with mechanical precision. 'I care not for your delicate sensibilities,' Rydae husked. 'Nor your conversation.'

Rafen saw Gorn's hand tighten into a fist, and he knew that this had been allowed to go on too long. With a slight motion of his wrist, Rafen tapped the base of the standard's mast upon the marble floor and a sharp *clack* drew the attention of both Astartes.

'Esteemed brother-captains,' he said firmly. 'With all due respect, perhaps this is a matter better pursued in other circumstances.'

Rydae did not speak, but Gorn shot Rafen a brief, poisonous look. 'Of course,' he said quietly, after a moment. 'It is always the privilege of a Blood Angel to be correct.'

Any reply he might have given to that was forgotten as a voice, clear and powerful, sounded out across the Grand Annex.

'Kinsmen,' called Mephiston, 'be gathered.'

The chamber instantly fell silent. Footsteps echoed as men approached along the four directions of the compass star, two figures coming from each direction. From east and west came the sanguinary priest Corbulo and the psyker Mephiston, each accompanied by a veteran warrior cradling the gold helmet of an honour guard in the crook of his arm. From behind Rafen, two more Blood Angels, sharing between them another standard – this one showing Sanguinius himself in his oft-depicted pose, wings spread and head turned to the heavens, presenting his shroud and grail. And from the north, followed by the captain of his honour guard, came Dante.

The red rays of the sun caught him and bathed the Chapter Master in a halo of light. Lord Dante wore his ceremonial artificer armour, the golden sheathes of ceramite polished to a lustrous sheen. Inlaid wings of pearl, ruby and jade glittered and shone. His helmet was a static facade in the reflection of Sanguinius's death mask. Like each warrior here, he carried no weapons but a combat blade sheathed at his boot. For a brief instant, Rafen lost himself in the sight of the armoured figure, his memory caught on another moment, months before in a basement on the forge-world of Shenlong, a moment when the image of another golden warrior had stood before him. He blinked and shook his head slightly, pushing the reverie away. Rafen focused and found Mephiston looking at him, a hint of curiosity on his face. It was on the Chief Librarian's insistence that he had been granted the privilege of bearing one of the sacred Chapter banners. Some part of him wondered why the Lord of Death had done so; the other men carrying the standards this day were all of captain's rank, and Mephiston was not known to grant favours without good cause. But Rafen was only a sergeant and it was not his place to question the will of so senior a brother.

The new arrivals came together upon the oval of mosaic tiles. Corbulo nodded to the standard bearers and the honour guard, and they went down upon one knee, Rafen following the motion with immediate precision. Then Dante bowed to the Chapter banner and the representation of their primarch, every other Astartes in the great chamber doing the same.

'Frater Sanguinius,' said the Chapter Master, his voice carrying through the stillness of the chamber, amplified by the vox-caster in his helmet. 'Brothers of Blood. In the name of the Emperor of Mankind and the Great Angel, it is my honour and my pride to welcome you all to Baal, the cradle from which our Chapters draw their shared lineages.'

'For the Glory of Sanguinius and the Imperium of Man,' intoned Mephiston.

'*For the Glory of Sanguinius and the Imperium of Man.*' Every warrior in the chamber repeated the invocation, the dome casting the words into echoes.

Dante rose and the assemblage followed suit. Rafen chanced a sideways look at Rydae and Gorn; the attention of both men was now firmly set on the Chapter Master of the Blood Angels.

Dante reached up and removed the death-mask helmet, handing it to Corbulo. His steady, fatherly expression crossed the room, deliberately making eye contact with everyone there. 'Cousins and kinsmen. Blood of my blood. It swells my heart to see such a monumental gathering as this one, and I am humbled by the faces I see here before me this day. That you would come here at my request, answering a call knowing only that it came from Baal, fills me with such respect. No matter what world you now call home, no matter how many suns span the void between there and here, *this* is our spiritual birthplace.' He pointed a gold-sheathed hand into the air. 'And in this place, we will discuss a matter of the greatest import to the legacy of Sanguinius. To do so without you here would be wrong, and my only regret is that we could not assemble a voice from every cousin Chapter for this singular assembly.' He nodded at a cluster of pennants hanging alone, among them a chequered banner bearing the symbol of a bleeding heart.

Dante brought his hands to his chest and made the sign of the aquila over the ruby droplet upon his breast plate. 'Let us offer an invocation to the Emperor, may His gaze be eternal and unswerving, and the spirit of our liege-lord. Let us ask them to watch over us in the days ahead, to grant us their blessing and a measure of their great wisdom.'

Rafen did as all the other Astartes, bringing his hands to his chest across the standard. His gaze passed over Mephiston and held upon him. He saw the psyker's gaze turn inward, his nostrils tense as if a foul scent had reached his senses. Then in the next instant the Lord of Death blinked and the moment passed, leaving the shadow of a troubled expression on his face.

Movement caught Rafen's eye and he saw up above, in the watcher's gallery, the robed figures of many more senior Astartes. The magnification optics in his helmet lenses picked out First Captain Lothan, the great Chaplain Lemartes and the acerbic Argastes at his side. But as each warrior bowed his head to make entreaty,

Rafen found himself troubled by a sudden question as he searched the faces and found one conspicuous by his absence.

Where is the Apothecae Majoris? Where is Brother Caecus?

THE GREAT SLABS of the laboratorium door folded away and the stranger was suddenly there, white gusts of steam falling from the piston-locks to pool around his ankles. Fenn was startled, and he flinched, putting down the rack of test vials he was carrying before he dropped them. The man surveyed the chamber with an air of quiet interest, in the manner of someone viewing a piece of art in a gallery. Fenn caught his eye and the new arrival offered him a small smile from a face lined and tanned, like aged, careworn leather. Behind him, a dark, square-sided shape shifted, indistinct in the dim glow of the biolumes.

The serf turned at the sound of his master's booted feet, seeing Caecus approach with Nyniq at his side. The woman's expression changed to something Fenn had never seen before; happiness. 'My tech-lord,' she breathed, 'the Omnissiah protect you.'

'And you, my pupil.' The man's voice was metered and calm.

Nyniq bowed slightly and the stranger bent to place a chaste kiss upon the top of her head. He was far taller than a normal man.

'Haran Serpens, I presume?' said Caecus.

He got a shallow bow in return. 'Indeed, majoris. I thank you for your gracious invitation.'

'How did you get here with such speed?' Fenn said the words before he'd even thought about them, earning himself a sideways look from his master.

Serpens seemed unconcerned. 'We have our ways, Omnissiah be praised.' He tapped the Adeptus Mechanicus symbol of cogwheel and skull that fastened his cloak across his broad shoulders. 'Fortune allowed that I was close by when Nyniq's machine-call reached me. I found the content of her code-summons to be most interesting.' He glanced at the doorway. 'If it pleases you, majoris, may I enter?'

Caecus beckoned him in. 'Come, then, tech-lord. But understand, once you do so, there are certain stipulations to be adhered to.'

Serpens shared a look with the woman. 'Whatever directives you have, Blood Angel, I will submit to them. I am interested only in the work. Nyniq told me it is in my interest to be here, so here I am.' They shared a familial smile. 'I trust her implicitly.' He cocked his head. 'How would you have me help you serve our Emperor?'

Caecus ignored the question and posed one of his own. 'Where is your ship? It is important that your presence here be kept clandestine, for the interim. It would not do to have one of the other successor Chapter craft in orbit make issue with your vessel.'

'There is no need to be concerned,' Serpens noted, studying a vial of blood. 'My transportation has made itself scarce. No one but those in this chamber knows of my arrival here on Baal.' The magos scientist walked slowly about the perimeter of the room, taking it all in. With slow and steady steps came the thing that had waited behind him: a tall metal box of black steel on a jointed cluster of spidery legs. Upon one face of the container was a porcelain mask with green-lit sensors in the eye sockets and mouth. The machine-thing moved delicately, never straying more than a short span from Serpens's side.

'You must understand that the nature of our research here is of the utmost secrecy,' noted Caecus. 'Nyniq vouches for you as both a man of great learning and great discretion.'

'I endeavour to be so.' The tech-lord was nodding approvingly. 'Ah. I see you are using the Ylesia Protocols as an operating source for your bio-cultures. A fine, fine choice. I have worked with a modified version of that medium myself.' He smiled again. 'I think I begin to see some of the work you are about.'

As much as he wanted to, Fenn could not look away from the tech-lord. Beneath a thick winter coat of dun-coloured animal hide, Serpens wore a peculiar over-suit that seemed somewhere between the design of Adeptus Arbites combat armour and the restraining straps of a straightjacket. He was bedecked with overlapping waist-coats of varying cuts, each alike only in the numerous sealpockets across them. The magos scientist had a mane of straw-coloured hair that sat over his skull in tightly braided rows, extending away down his back in a snaking coil. But it was the size of the man that held his attention; Fenn had met members of the magos biologis and others of the Adeptus Mechanicus on several occasions, and never in all those times come across someone with this man's stature.

'I am not what you expected, am I?' He studied Fenn.

'You are not,' admitted the serf. 'You're the size of an Astartes.' He nodded toward Caecus, and saw that his master was dwelling on the same thought.

'Indeed,' Serpens agreed. 'Throughout my life I have attempted to model myself in small ways upon the Emperor's most perfect children, the Space Marines.' He glanced down at his own hands, gloved in black leather. 'I hope the majoris will forgive a mortal's hubris, but I have modified my flesh in many ways to share a fraction of the greatness you were gifted with.' Serpens bowed. 'You should consider it the sincerest form of flattery, sir.'

'I see,' Caecus said, with wary detachment.

Fenn imagined his master was thinking the same as he, however. *What could Serpens mean? Has he taken it upon himself to have his body implanted with artificial organs such as those of a Space Marine?* It would certainly go a long way toward explaining how a magos could be so changed from the form of a normal man. The thought made Fenn feel uncomfortable – as if he *needed* more to do so – but his master's expression shifted. Caecus had decided not to pursue the line of conversation any further, for the moment.

'And that?' The Blood Angel gestured at the metal box. 'Your servitor?'

'In a manner of speaking,' allowed Serpens. 'It is merely an autonomous conveyance for my most vital equipment. Chirurgery tools and the like.' He snapped his fingers in a quick code, so swiftly that Fenn couldn't register it, and the machine-thing wandered away to the corner of the room, the mechanical legs sighing and clattering.

Serpens halted and brought his hands together in a gesture of fealty. 'My esteemed Astartes, Lord Caecus. If I may be so bold, let me say the word. *Replicae*, yes?' He didn't wait for a reply. 'That is my speciality and these mechanisms hereabout are turned toward work upon that science. I will warrant that you require skills such as mine for a thorny problem the wild mix of biology has thrown to you.' He touched Nyniq's face gently. 'My pupil, as skilled as she is, would not have called to me otherwise. And I tell you here and now, if I am right, I would be honoured to join you in solving it.' His voice fell to a whisper. 'Will you let me? It has been my dream to work in lockstep with the master biologians of the Adeptus Astartes.'

'And what if this work requires you to place your loyalty to the magos biologis second to the needs of my Chapter?' Caecus stood eye to eye with him. 'What then?'

Serpens broke away first. 'Lord... May I confide a truth to you?'

'Go on.'

'The works under the name of Haran Serpens have become less and less a challenge in the years gone by. My last great victory was over the Haze Plague… And I have done nothing of note since. I am out to pasture, majoris. Marking time. I would relish the chance to do something of worth once more. I can see no better a service than to collaborate with the Sons of Sanguinius. My loyalty… is to Terra and the Emperor alone.' Fenn sensed the faint air of desperation in the tech-lord's voice.

'Nyniq has proven herself a valuable asset,' Caecus began. 'I do not doubt you would be any less. But I must be clear, Serpens. Once you agree to join us here in the citadel, you will not be allowed to communicate with the outside world. The secrets that will be confided to you must be kept upon pain of death. To speak of any of this before we have fruition would not be tolerated.'

Serpens nodded. 'Lord Caecus, already I have courted the displeasure of my masters by stealing away to come to Baal on my own. I will not turn back now.' He offered the Blood Angel his hand. 'I say this to you. *Task me.* Task me, and together we shall surmount all obstacles. We will show the Emperor such majesty.'

Fenn stiffened at the tech-lord's words. He had heard them once before, only a few months ago, in a meeting that progressed in much the same way that this one had. *We will show the Emperor such majesty.* He stared at Nyniq. Those words had come from her lips, the dull echo of them now sounding once more in the serf's memories. Fenn watched her bow and follow Serpens in servile fashion and his thoughts fell back to the first time he had laid eyes upon her.

THE LIBRARIA OF LXD-9768 were so vast that they covered three-fifths of the nondescript planet's surface. The dull stone world with its nitrogen-heavy atmosphere had been polished smooth by the actions of heavy surface storms and hurricanes induced by the complex motion of three captured asteroid moons. Those satellites were gone now, mined to fragments by the Adeptus Mechanicus, used to build the endless lines of blockhouses that went from horizon to horizon; chamber after chamber, annexe after annexe, each storage facility housing millions of books, scrolls, picts and other forms of data storage. Whole island continents were given over to certain kinds of media, even down to millennia-old devices of magnetic tape, encoded discs and solid-state memory rods.

Worlds like LXD-9768 were dotted across the breadth of the galactic disc, planets chosen for their sheer inertness, locations far distant from any suns approaching their death cycle, alien borders or other sources of potential harm. Many of them duplicated each other's records, with multiple redundant copies scattered a thousand fold over the light years; but they were not all the same. Since Old Night and the loss of Mankind's great technologies, the millennia that followed had seen in part a series of struggles to recover what was once known by all. The Adeptus Terra, in its infinite wisdom and incalculable patience, had decreed that such a fall to darkness was never to be permitted again.

Thus, the libraria. Planets given over to file stores as big as cities, duplicating and protecting information so that the loss of any one of them would not mean the destruction of humanity's knowledge base. Every fact recovered from the past, and every piece of data generated since, had a place here. Nothing was to be lost again.

But the reality did not marry with the vision. In the 41st millennium, true information retained the same power it had in earlier ages, and those who had it hoarded it like precious gems. Instead of the libraria becoming the home of all learning, they had turned into great dusty canyons of worthless data, collected by a bureaucracy that collated everything as if it were of the greatest import, no matter how trivial, how pointless. LXD-9768's stacks could not tell a man what words the Emperor said upon his assent to the Golden Throne; but it could give chapter and verse about the migratory patterns of extinct breeds of rodents in the underlevels of hive cities, from worlds that had not existed for centuries.

The libraria cranked on, gathering and assembling information as a cetacean might strain ocean waters for krill through its baleen. And sometimes, by pure chance, they took in data that actually had value.

IT HAD TAKEN Fenn six days to locate the correct annexe, in endless rounds of quibbling and arguments with the quillans and savants who stood as gatekeepers to the great oceans of data locked up in the libraria's stores. Finally, the correct permissions had been provided, on a fanfold of greasy cardboard stamped with a dozen signets and consent indents. The books were close by, in a sub-basement.

While Fenn worked, Lord Caecus had remained aboard their Aquila shuttle, meditating in the spartan cargo bay. He had not taken food nor sleep since they departed Baal, he had said little to the serf during the voyage aboard the transport ship and the shuttle flight to the surface of LXD-9768.

It was an understatement to say his master was troubled. Ever since he had returned to the Vitalis Citadel from his meeting with Lord Dante, he had been withdrawn. Caecus has taken such high hopes with him, fully believing that the Chapter Master would accept his option for rebuilding their forces. He, and Fenn with him, had not expected such a negative response. Perhaps they had been too close to the idea, too enamoured of the work to consider that others might find it objectionable.

Fenn waited for Caecus to order the laboratorium closed, the work halted. When the Apothecae Majoris did none of those things, the serf did not question it. He understood his lordship's thinking; Dante's criticism could be overturned, if the right combination of results could be created. It was Fenn's duty to aid his master in bringing that to pass; and so they were here, to follow upon a thin lead. Certain tomes had been tracked to this place. Allegedly copied by the monks of Ionai from records laid down by Brother Monedus, a senior Raven Guard apothecarion, the papers were said to carry much knowledge of the primarch Corax's experiments in accelerated zygote harvesting techniques. The tomes had eventually come to LXD-9768, rescued from the obliteration of a valetudinarium station somewhere in the Ultima Segmentum.

Caecus showed the first signs of interest in weeks; but when they reached the annexe, that swiftly turned to grim annoyance. The quillan at the bookgate seemed startled to see them; *you are not the first visitors this day*, said the scribe-priest. Such arrivals, it appeared, were unusual.

Nyniq was there, reading the Monedus papers with a repellor-field tool that let her turn the pages without actually touching them.

At first Fenn thought it was some cruel twist of fate, that this magos had arrived at the same prize his master sought on the same day; he learned that this was not true. Nyniq weathered veiled threats from Lord Caecus and by turns revealed she was here because she had learned of the Apothecae's search for tracts on the subject of cloning. It was, she explained, a line of research that she too was following. *We could make such leaps if we pooled our works*, she offered.

Fenn hated her on sight, of course. As arrogant as she was beautiful, twisting her words to dance upon the edge of his master's fury, piquing Caceus's interest with her considerable knowledge and then backing away, as another woman might tease a normal man with the promise of physical congress. And she was shrewd with it. Nyniq made airy suggestions that she might simply bring news of this meeting to Lord Dante and approach the Blood Angels directly, doubtless knowing all along of Caecus's desire for secrecy. The Apothecae later admitted to Fenn that he had even considered ending the troublesome woman's life to be done with her. But what consequences could such a deed have?

The serf watched her win the Blood Angel's trust little by little, feathering his curiosity, enticing him. Fenn knew the moment had come when Nyniq presented a complex skein of biologian formulae to his master, a paper of such intricacies which the Astartes could only begin to encompass in his thoughts.

The woman understood it all, though. The Monedus papers were missing pieces of a puzzle to her, and she was eager to bring them together with the works under Caecus's dominion.

Perhaps, if the pressures of time and the censure of Lord Dante had not been upon him, Caecus might have rejected Nyniq on the spot, taken what he needed and left her broken upon the storehouse's stone floor; but in truth, the Apothecae Majoris concealed a sullen desperation. Over Fenn's ignored words, he accepted her offer of assistance, in exchange for some degree of the fruits of this research.

We will show the Emperor such majesty, she said, *in his footsteps we will walk, and make demi-gods from the crude clay of mortal men.*

'WHAT BARGAINS HAVE we made?' Fenn said the words under his breath, his voice carrying no further than his lips. He looked at his own reflection on the glass cabinets ranged across the walls of the laboratorium.

It was a mistake. Just to form that statement in his mind, to go against his lord and master within the privacy of his own thoughts, even that tested the serf's reason. He had lived his life in service to Brother Caecus and his great works, to the Blood Angels and Sanguinius. But Nyniq's recruitment had been the setting in of the rot, and now this man, this Haran Serpens? His master's rush to be proven right was pushing him to make choices that were rash. Still, Fenn could not openly speak the doubts that crowded in upon him. He had already talked of his dislike of the woman and that had brought him nothing. His concerns about the two servants of the magos biologis were real and certain, and it was his duty to act on them.

But how? To decry them both based on nothing but a personal dislike was foolish. There was no evidence that Nyniq had ever done anything less than what she promised, to assist the work and integrate the research of Monedus.

He would need something firm. Something certain, evidence that the magos were manipulating Caecus's work to their own ends.

Fenn studied Serpens as he spoke with his master. Suspicion without proof is nothing, he told himself. I will make it my task to learn more about this tech-lord. I will find out what he and that wench really want, and then expose them both.

'Fenn,' snapped Caecus. 'Come here. Bring the genetor's report on the most recent iterations.'

The serf bowed low, hiding a narrowed gaze.

CHAPTER SIX

THE PARTY MOVED along the corridors of the high arcade, beneath the slanted arches of the red stone ceiling. The glow of photonic candles gave the corridor a warm, aged feel, and shadows jumped in the passageways that radiated off at every intersection.

Rafen glanced over his shoulder. 'This is one of the earliest structures of the fortress-monastery,' he explained to the men who walked behind him. 'These walls were laid down under the eye of the Great Angel himself.'

'Impressive,' said Brother-Captain Gorn, in a tone of voice that suggested he thought the sight far from it.

At Rafen's side, young Kayne bristled and his hands made fists in his wide sleeves. The two Blood Angels were in stark contrast, their duty robes of rust-coloured cloth against the deep burgundy worn by Gorn and his party. As with their wargear, the Flesh Tearer contingent had little in the way of adornment about their person. Gorn, the veteran sergeant Noxx and the honour guard

Roan were dressed in identical habits with the simple saw-blade sigil upon their shoulders. Their Chapter Master had declined the invitation to join them, citing his desire to prepare for the forthcoming conclave.

Rafen gave Kayne a hard look, but the youth didn't acknowledge it. He was beginning to regret bringing the younger Astartes along with him. Kayne was a good Space Marine, that was never in doubt, but he was unseasoned and quick to anger. Rafen knew that the Flesh Tearers saw that as well as he did. This duty that Mephiston had assigned him and his men, to serve as adjutants to their cousins from Cretacia, was not a task fit for a warrior; but then to give it to a Chapter serf would have been taken as a grave insult.

Gorn gestured down the long corridor. 'Are we to walk the length of this, then?' He glanced around. 'When Brother Corbulo suggested we be shown some of the treasures of the monastery, I had expected to see more than just… stonework.'

'There's much here to be lauded, sir,' Kayne broke in, without waiting for Rafen's permission to speak. 'Our Chapter's riches are in the stone as well as the gold.'

'Riches,' echoed Noxx, seizing on the word. 'How blessed the Blood Angels are to have such boons.' There was a forced bitterness in the sergeant's voice and Rafen frowned, unsure of where Noxx was taking the conversation.

Abruptly, Gorn shot out a hand and pointed into a branching corridor, where the lights were dimmer. 'There. What is down there?'

'One of the galleries.'

'A shooting gallery?' questioned Roan. 'A bolter range, up here? I hear no gunfire.'

'It is an art gallery, Brother,' Rafen corrected.

Noxx made a derisive noise. '*Art?*' He stepped away and walked swiftly into the corridor, the dim candles there growing brighter as they sensed his presence.

Rafen thought to call him back, but already the other Flesh Tearers were following him, peering owlishly at the works upon the walls and in the oval alcoves.

There was a thin sneer on Noxx's face. 'What are these?' He gestured at the mix of displays that crowded the walls. There were paintings in various media, sculptures of stone and carved woods, tapestries and fine pieces of worked metal. Many were devotional items fashioned to show the Emperor or Sanguinius in reverent aspect, others abstract things made for the sheer pleasure of it, or representative works depicting landscapes from a dozen worlds. 'Are they spoils from the planets your Chapter has brought into submission?'

'These are the works of our battle-brothers,' said Kayne. 'Each one was crafted by the hand of a Blood Angel.'

Noxx chuckled. 'You... paint?' The very idea amused him. 'You sketch and you chisel at bits of stone?'

'Is that not work for remembrancers?' offered Gorn.

'It is work for men of spirit. The Great Sanguinius granted the Blood Angels many things,' Rafen said tightly. 'Among them was a sense of the aesthetic. These works are the expression of that gift.'

Noxx focussed on Kayne; the young Space Marine's jaw was set hard. 'Which of these pretty things is yours, then? Show me, *artist*.'

'With respect, brother-sergeant,' Kayne was careful to meter his speech. 'I would ask you not to mock.'

'You would, eh?' Noxx shared his cold smile with Gorn. 'But I wonder if I can accommodate you, in the face of all this?' The sergeant gestured around. 'Is this what the Blood Angels do when they should be engaging the enemies of mankind or kneeling in prayer to the Golden Throne? They scribble and they sew?' He snatched up a piece of tapestry, upon which a fine golden web of threads depicted an image of Sanguinius.

'My brethren have no time for such things. We are too busy fighting and dying!'

'Everything here is a mark of devotion to the ideals of the Great Angel.' Kayne matched the Flesh Tearer's dead-eyed gaze and anger entered his tone. 'How can an Astartes fight to preserve all that is good and beautiful in the universe, if he has no appreciation of beauty? To be blind to these things is to be blind to the glory the Emperor brings us.'

'This boy lectures me on how to do battle, now?' Noxx growled, addressing his kinsmen. 'Should I dare to correct him upon his needlework?' He shook the cloth in his fist.

Rafen saw the incident unfolding and moved to step forward. Noxx was once again goading a Blood Angel, this time seeking the weaker link of Kayne's ill-concealed anger. Clearly, the warrior had come to understand he needed to look elsewhere to get a rise. 'Brother-sergeant,' he began, ready to defuse the building tension, but Gorn stepped in his path and stopped him. The Blood Angel halted, taking a breath.

'A moment, Rafen.' The Flesh Tearer captain retained a disinterested air, but there was a steel in his eyes that made his words an order. 'Let the men talk.'

He hesitated. Gorn was not his commander, but he was still a ranking Astartes. To defy him… The thought caught hard in Rafen's chest.

'War is not all there is to life.' Kayne was speaking, his face colouring with resentment. 'If you cannot appreciate the majesty of a sunrise, or the power of a great hymnal, then I feel sorry for you.'

Rafen chest tightened. *Wrong. The wrong words to say.* And as he knew would happen, Noxx growled out a reply.

'Do you? How high-handed, how typical of a Blood Angel whelp to scold his betters!'

'That's enough–' Rafen snapped, but neither cared to hear him.

'Don't provoke the boy anymore, sergeant' said Gorn mildly. 'He may paint an unflattering portrait of you.'

Noxx turned away, shaking his head. 'No wonder your Chapter is such a shambles if you are the best of their breed. Are you all peacocks and cloth-cutters?'

Rafen saw the flash of fury in Kayne's eyes and he knew he would not be able to stop what was coming next.

In a blur, the youth's combat blade swept out from its scabbard and came to a halt a hair's breadth from Noxx's throat. 'I do not cut cloth,' Kayne snarled, 'but I would happily cut your arrogance from you, *sir!*'

Impulsive fool! Rafen's teeth set in a snarl. The youth had played right into the other man's hands, allowing his anger to bring him to draw the weapon. 'Kayne!' He called out, Gorn's censure be damned. 'You forget yourself! Sheath your blade!'

A moment of doubt was all it took. Kayne wavered and Noxx flicked his head forward, deliberately catching his cheek on the knife edge.

'The boy cut me,' said the Flesh Tearer.

'Unfortunate,' agreed Gorn, turning away. 'That will make an issue of it. Shed blood.'

Rafen knew it would be useless to argue the point that Noxx had cut *himself*. It would be his word against that of a ranking warrior. He pushed past the Flesh Tearer captain and came to his warrior's side. Kayne's face was ashen, as too late he realised that he had been played, made a fool for the sport of the other Astartes.

'I'll want restitution,' Noxx said darkly. 'In the fighting pit.'

Rafen glared at the veteran sergeant. 'You pushed him to this. Why?'

Noxx's voice fell to a whisper. 'To see what you're made of.'

The Blood Angel hesitated, then opened his hand to Brother Kayne. 'Give me your knife, lad. And show me your fingers.'

The youth did as he was ordered. Without pause, Rafen took Kayne's fingers in his grip and folded them back the wrong way, snapping all four joints at once.

Kayne barked out a cry of pain. 'What…'

Rafen silenced him with a look. 'Go to the Apothecary. Have those re-set. They'll heal.' He turned about and glared at Noxx, Kayne's knife still in his hand. 'The boy's fighting grip is useless. He can't meet you in the pit. It would be unfair.'

'I could break the brother-sergeant's fingers,' offered Gorn, a tic of amusement at his lips. 'Would that make it even?'

'No,' replied Rafen. Mephiston's words, the psyker's orders not to rise to the Flesh Tearers' bait, echoed in his thoughts. *I will ask his forgiveness later; but this must be done now.* The sergeant's lips thinned. 'Kayne is a part of my squad, and my responsibility.' His eyes never left Noxx. 'I will take his place.'

FROM THE VIEWING balcony, the stone hemisphere of the fighting pit was an unadorned bowl of light-coloured bricks set into the floor. Black lines bisected the inverted space like the rings of latitude and longitude upon a planetary globe. A servitor replaced the polished steel grate over the blood drain in the centre, and, with care, it used long and spindly arms to pick its way back up toward the edge.

The lower balconies were filling, knots of men from every Chapter gathering here and there. The call to commencement was almost upon them. Dante watched, his eyes ranging over his kinsmen and cousins, taking the measure of the room.

'I knew something like this would happen.' Dante didn't need to look over his shoulder at Corbulo, where the Apothecary stood, arms folded and face set. He didn't need to look at him to know the expression of grim dismay the grail bearer wore. He could hear it in his words. Corbulo blew out a breath. 'Are the Sons of Sanguinius incapable of meeting across a table without drawing each other into a pointless dispute?'

'A matter of honour is never a pointless dispute,' noted Dante. 'Such things cannot go without address.' He turned and found Corbulo looking at him, his manner shifting to something more quizzical.

'You don't seem concerned by this.' The Apothecary paused, and Dante let him draw his own conclusions. 'You knew this would come to pass. A disagreement, something that would lead to Astartes meeting Astartes in the pit...' He gestured out at the arena.

'I did,' admitted the Chapter Master. 'As you said, there is an inevitability about such things.' He adjusted the cuff of his robes. 'We are all Sons of Sanguinius, aye. But we are a fractious family. Friction is only to be expected.'

'We are Space Marines,' replied Corbulo. 'We are meant to be above such things.'

'*Meant to*,' Dante repeated, with a cool smile. 'But we both know the reality is not the same as the ideal. Even the primarchs, in their magnificence, could not range above the emotions of men. The Heresy is ample proof of that. We can only strive to do so... But it would be foolish to pretend we are free of such things.'

Corbulo frowned again, and Dante saw understanding in his eyes. 'You... You let this happen.'

'Indeed.'

'And more than that, perhaps you even encouraged it.' The Apothecary shook his head. 'Lord, why?'

Dante held up his hand for silence as an Astartes from his honour guard entered the balcony and bowed low.

'My lord? Word from the master of the arena. The duel may commence at your command.'

He nodded. 'Thank you, Brother Garyth. Tell him they may proceed.'

'THIS WILL BE a single combat, a duel of prowess,' said the servitor, the grating mechanical vox speaking in a flat, emotionless voice. 'Fight to assent, show courage and honour. Edged weapons and firearms are prohibited. In the Emperor's name.'

'In the Emperor's name,' chorused Rafen and Noxx. Both men had stripped down to fighting tunics, suits of sand ox leather and cloth of the like that initiates often wore in the days of training. The servitor offered them both a wooden exercise blade; balanced to mimic the weight and heft of a light battle sword, the training weapons had no cutting edge to them.

Noxx eyed him, tracing a finger over the rapidly-healing scar across his cheek. 'A pity. I'd prefer a proper blade to these toys.' His voice was low.

'A warrior fights with whatever he has to hand,' Rafen retorted.

'How true,' Noxx grated, and threw him a mocking salute with the weapon.

'Commence,' said the servitor, and it trundled backwards into an alcove on brass wheels.

Rafen stepped up to the lip of the bowl-shaped fighting pit and sighted across at Noxx, taking a position directly opposite him. He wasted no time with showy motion or play at the Flesh Tearer's expense; Rafen stepped off the edge and slid down the steep incline of the arena wall, riding on the heels of his sandals.

Noxx bellowed a war cry and threw himself headfirst at the Blood Angel, leading with the training blade. The shout, loud enough that it would unman an ordinary soldier, did nothing but draw a sneer from Rafen. He pivoted and met the Flesh Tearer's weapon, batting it away.

Noxx landed hard and rolled, dodging a follow-up strike. Rafen skipped sideways across the curved stone blocks, over the black lines. He felt the vibrations of machinery through the soles of his feet, great cogs and rods at work beneath the floor of the arena.

The Flesh Tearer spun about and came at him again, fast and agile. Noxx rained blow after blow down upon Rafen, and the Blood Angel parried them all; but the attacks were so swift that he had barely a moment to consider a counter-strike of his own.

Then a lucky blow; Noxx scored a hit, the nub of the training blade's thick edge hitting hard across the dense muscle of Rafen's bicep. A lance of pain shot through him, startling the Blood Angel. He fell back, feeling an echo of the hurt tingle in his fingers. *Strange; but the blow did not draw blood, in fact it barely even bruised me...*

Noxx attacked again, and this time Rafen was slow. A second hit, and then a third, one to a spot above his clavicle and the other on his forearm. Each one made his skin twitch and tremble with a quick flash of palsy. Fighting through it, Rafen made a hard return and caught Noxx across the face with the flat of the blade, opening up the cut on his cheek again.

He moved to follow through, but the vibration in the floor became more violent. Abruptly, the stone blocks began to shift and the ground on which Rafen stood jerked and rose up. Other parts of the fighting pit pivoted or changed in height, the static surface becoming an unpredictable, disordered landscape to make the combat more challenging.

The Blood Angel caught a glimpse of the men watching the duel as the block on which he stood rose up above the lip of the arena; he spotted a grim-faced Kayne and the rest of his squad alongside a cadre of Blood

Drinkers, who called out and applauded; then in the
next second the block dropped away from under him
and he fell into a controlled tumble. Fangs bared, Noxx
dived to meet him and he pushed away – too slow to
avoid another blow across his shoulder.

This time the impact bared his teeth and sent his muscles tensing all down his flank. *Nerve points. He's
attacking the clusters of nerves beneath the surface of my
flesh.* To an observer caught up in the pitch and moment
of the duel, Noxx's blows would have seemed random,
without order; but they were far from that. The correct
application of force in the right places, even through the
protective sub-dermal sheath of a Space Marine's black
carapace, could be enough to deaden nerves, to slow a
fighting response. And if one were trained well enough,
the right blow, no matter if it were struck with an edge-
less training blade, would cause a seizure.

'Noxx FIGHTS WELL, for a barbarian,' noted Corbulo.

'That is the way of Seth's men,' agreed Dante, glancing
at the group of Flesh Tearers across the arena, in another
of the viewing balconies. 'They have always excelled in
making anger their weapon.' He looked back at the
Apothecary. 'And that, my friend, is why I allowed this to
come to pass.'

'My lord, I do not doubt your reasoning but I confess
I do not see it.' Corbulo folded his arms across his chest.

Dante opened his hands and took in the whole of the
arena. 'I knew from the moment I ordered the conclave
that tension and uncertainty would fill the monastery as
easily as smoke. For all the well met and noble greetings
between our successors, we are all still warriors,
Corbulo. It is in our nature to be guarded, to fall into
patterns of rivalry and challenge toward one another.
That tension had to be dissolved.' He nodded toward
Rafen and Noxx, as the Blood Angel landed a

particularly savage blow upon his adversary. 'This manner seemed the most direct.'

'Mephiston ordered Rafen not to allow himself to be goaded. Yet you set him up for just that.'

Dante nodded. 'I consider it a test of the lad's character. Mephiston speaks highly of Rafen, and I wanted to see the colour of his spirit for myself. How a warrior reacts to the unexpected, the extreme... It can be most revealing.' He stood back from the edge of the stone balcony. 'As for the Flesh Tearers, I already know them well enough.' He smiled thinly. 'If the blood of our primarch could be light through a prism, then we Blood Angels range toward one end and the Flesh Tearers are at the opposite. They are everything we are not, kinsman. And they are truly fearless, for they have nothing left to lose.'

Corbulo mused on this for a moment. 'That is why you placed Rafen with them.'

'Just so. To draw out the true intentions of Seth and his party.' He studied the other men in the various wargear and robes of the other successor Chapters. 'There are those among our cousins who will follow my lead because I am Lord of the Blood Angels, because we are the first chosen of Sanguinius. But there are others who cut their own path, who will resist what I will ask of them. None more so than the Sons of Cretacia.'

'They consider us to be decadent and irresolute. They've never made a secret of that.'

'It is important to disabuse them of such thoughts,' Dante replied, his tone hardening. 'And so Rafen becomes the object lesson. A reminder of what a Blood Angel is.'

He's trying to kill me. The realisation was hard in his thoughts, like diamond.

The duel was sanctioned as a fight to submission; the rules were adamant. While blood could be drawn, the battle between the two men could not go on beyond the point of a crippling injury, and certainly not to the death. But Rafen saw other intent in Noxx's dead eyes, watching the Flesh Tearer measure every blow against his flesh with all the care of a sniper picking off targets from a rooftop hide. It would be easy to argue the point after the fact; such 'accidents' in training were not uncommon among the Adeptus Astartes. And if Rafen was lost in this fight, what would be said then? That the Blood Angels, so wounded by their own mistakes, could not even stand up to a brief brawl with dulled blades in a fighting pit?

The stone floor clattered and shifted again, rearranging itself and both men moved with it. Noxx extended and hit him once more, and sparks of pain glittered across Rafen's vision. He felt his hand going slack around the grip of the training sword as the nerves in his fingers refused to answer to him. Another strike like that, perhaps two at the most, and Rafen would be slowed enough for the other sergeant to take him down at his leisure. He had to end this, and end it quickly.

The blade grip felt rubbery and limp in his hands, and with a snort he threw it aside, flexing his fingers into claws. Noxx's eyes flashed; the Flesh Tearer had not expected that.

If he had been fighting another Blood Angel, Rafen would have expected his foe to drop his weapon as well, as a gesture of respect so that they could battle on an even footing. It did not surprise him that the Flesh Tearer did no such thing. Noxx attacked, feinting a stab with the training weapon that swung about into a descending hammer-blow strike.

The dense wooden blade came at Rafen horizontally, at throat height. The veteran sergeant was putting every iota of his strength behind the stroke. Moving as quickly as he could, ignoring the spikes of pain from the deep-tissue welts left by the Tearer's earlier hits, Rafen dove into the attack, not away from it, cutting the distance between them. His arms shot out and he caught the edge of the heavy weapon in the open palms of his hands, the wood smacking bare skin with a hard impact. The reverberation of the blow went all the way to Rafen's shoulder blades.

The Blood Angel's fingers dug in, and twisted. The Flesh Tearer snarled and grimaced, jerking the weapon in a vain attempt to free it from the other warrior's grip. Rafen had purchase, however, and would not be shifted. Turning into Noxx's motion, he pulled the length of the blade against itself, and the dark lacquer shell protecting the weapon cracked and crazed.

Noxx suddenly understood what Rafen was doing, but he had overextended himself, and allowed his attack to be turned against him. The Blood Angel's face took on a feral cast; Rafen felt a familiar surge of anger-fuelled heat ignite inside him. The very edge of the fury; the shadow of the Black Rage.

With a yell, Rafen turned the blade the wrong way and the tough nalwood splintered and snapped. The weapon came apart with a snapping report of sound, the torsion of the sudden release knocking Noxx back a step.

The broken pieces of the blade still in his clawed hands, Rafen went after him and threw blows against the Flesh Tearer's forearms as they came up to guard his face. Then, with a grunt, he tossed the fragments away and attacked with bare hands tracked with deep, fresh scratches.

Rafen's fist struck Noxx's face and he felt the satisfying pressure of the blow landing. His knuckles came back filmed with blood – some of it belonging to his opponent, some of it belonging to him – and his nostrils twitched with the sudden immediacy of the scent. The sharp, acrid tang was welcoming.

Noxx staggered back, trying to shake off the violence of the punch. Rafen came on, and did not allow him to do so.

CORBULO'S EYES NARROWED as the watchers below applauded the display. 'How far shall we let this go, lord? They may end one another.'

Dante watched the fight carefully. 'It will not come to that.'

'Are you certain?'

The Chapter Master did not look up. 'All I am certain of is that any intervention on my part will do more harm than good. This must play out as it does.'

'You're putting your trust in someone whose sibling was a traitor,' the Apothecary retorted.

'I am putting my trust in a Blood Angel,' Dante replied firmly. 'Brother Rafen is that before all else.'

'I have my doubts,' Corbulo said, in a low voice.

'Of course you do,' said his master. 'That is why you are at my left hand – to keep me from becoming complacent.'

The Apothecary took a long, slow breath. 'Then, in that capacity, let me be candid, my lord.'

'I expect nothing less.'

Corbulo was silent for a long moment. 'This gathering... I fear it will not serve the purpose you wish it to. I look about the fortress-monastery and see all these unfamiliar faces, I see the absence of men dead and men sent afar to maintain the fiction we have spun. I am surrounded by strangers, lord, and I feel as if I am a ghost at my own wake.'

Dante nodded slowly. 'It is quite a thing to consider one's own mortality, is it not, my friend?'

Corbulo opened his mouth to answer, but his words were silenced by a sudden rumble of noise from the Astartes crowded beneath them.

* * *

THE COGWHEELS BENEATH the fighting pit clattered and spun, the flagstones moving once more, drawing space between the two combatants. Rafen found himself dropped downward while Noxx was elevated over him. The Flesh Tearer saw the opportunity and launched himself at the younger warrior, falling the distance with his teeth bared. Rafen accepted him and struck out with a double-handed sweep, knocking Noxx aside so the veteran's head bounced off one of the hissing piston rods supporting the raised blocks.

Rafen's teeth were grinding against one another, and suddenly all he wanted was the taste of blood in his mouth, the hot gush of vitae torn from this arrogant, contemptuous fool.

How dare these barbarians consider themselves the equal of the Blood Angels? The fury rumbled in his ears, his blood thudding through his veins. *How dare they sully this place with their presence?*

Every spiteful look, every arch word and conceit that the Flesh Tearers had turned toward Rafen and his men on Eritaen came back to him in that moment, and all he could feel was dark and potent anger at the slights of Noxx's brethren. Mephiston's words of censure were lost in amongst the growling wrath that tightened in his muscles. Rafen wanted only to strike the veteran sergeant again and again, to beat the arrogance out of him, to make him understand his place against a true Son of the Great Angel.

Noxx hit back, but the building Rage made each blow seem a distant, unimportant thing. Rafen landed another crippling punch, this time sensing the snap of a rib beneath the tanned-dark hide of the other man's torso. Noxx coughed and Rafen saw the glitter of emotion for the quickest of instants, a flash of surprise inside those dead eyes.

He moved without a conscious thought, sweeping his leg back beneath Noxx to knock the Flesh Tearer's feet out from under him. Rafen's hand shot forward and snared the front of the other warrior's leather jerkin, pressing him down, slamming him hard against the stone floor of the fighting pit.

Noxx let out a bark of pain as he hit. Rafen ignored the other man's sharp blows to his torso and forced the veteran's head back until it hung over the edge of a broad flagstone, into a cavity made by the action of the shifting pistons. Overhead, a suspended block reached its apex and the risers spat out a belch of steam. Without pause, it began a descent back into its place, falling down on the collapsing piston rod toward the empty space currently occupied by Noxx's skull.

The Flesh Tearer saw the dark shape dropping and thrashed against the Blood Angel's iron grip; unless Rafen released him, it would sever Noxx's head from his shoulders and mash it into a mess of bloody pulp.

Perhaps Rafen knew that on some level; but he was focused only on pressing the life out of his opponent, his fangs bared, the stink of spilled blood thick in his nostrils. Noxx tried to speak but his throat was choked with fluid that drooled from his lips. And still the stone fell, growing larger and larger in his vision.

'Rafen.' The name was a command, clear and unequivocal; but the Blood Angel did not seem to hear it, did not loosen his grip. Noxx's life would be spent in seconds, the falling guillotine of rock coming to end him.

'Rafen, *release him!*' Mephiston's words cut through the miasma of the great rage and with a jerk of motion the Blood Angel did as he was ordered to.

Noxx rolled away an instant before the stone slammed back into place and lay there, panting. Rafen glanced up at the rim of the pit and saw the Lord of Death watching him with a forbidding air.

'Fight to assent,' he told him, rebuke beneath his words, 'not to kill.' Mephiston looked up and took in the balconies arranged around him. 'This bout is concluded. The matter is settled and honour has been served. Let us hear no more about it.'

With a grinding hiss, the stone floor returned to its original configuration, settling the bowl back into shape. Above, the Space Marines in the observation galleries began to drift away in groups.

Rafen stood, saying nothing, the anger inside him ebbing but not vanishing. It drew back like a retreating tide, but remained on the edge of his thoughts, still churning.

The Flesh Tearer got to his feet with difficulty, and then spat out a fat gobbet of bloody spittle. He drew his hand over his torn cheek, wiping away a sheen of dark fluid. 'Pity,' he ventured, after a while. 'I'd have liked to take this as far as it could have gone. Don't you agree?'

Rafen shot him a baleful look. 'Then you would be corpse flesh now, *cousin*.'

With difficulty, Noxx chuckled. 'My death will be a long way from this place.'

The arrogance was unbelievable; only a moment ago Noxx had been moments from fatality at Rafen's hands, and now he behaved as if it were of no more concern than inclement weather. The fury briefly surged again, and for a moment Rafen wished he hadn't answered Mephiston's command to desist.

Noxx turned and walked up the incline of the pit's walls. Rafen watched, his hands balling into fists once again. He called out Noxx's name, unwilling to let that be an end to it. 'I beat you. I believe that means you owe me a spoil.'

The veteran turned and glared at him. 'I have little to give to one so rich as you,' he retorted.

'An answer to a question, then.' Rafen stepped after him. 'Why? Why did you force this duel? There was no point to it, nothing to be gained!'

Noxx hesitated, and glanced up toward where Gorn and the other Flesh Tearers waited. 'I did only what I was ordered to do.'

'Seth demanded it?' Rafen shook his head. 'To what end?'

The veteran nodded at him. 'Your Chapter has fallen from grace, lad. That begs the question that must be asked. How weak have the Blood Angels become?' Before Rafen could frame a reply, Noxx turned away once more and left him there in the pit.

He stood and looked down at his hands, still slick with Noxx's blood, and wondered. What kind of answer could he have given to that question?

CHAPTER SEVEN

THE PAGEANTRY AND ceremony of the last gathering inside the Grand Annex was gone now, along with all but the most senior Astartes from the various successor Chapters. Only two from each cadre of the Sons of Sanguinius had entered, with the towering doors to be sealed shut behind them. The chamber was unadorned, no pennants, no standards, only a ring of simple wooden benches set out across the open space. The absence of the mass of Space Marines made the vast hall seem even larger. Slanted rays of red sunlight pooled against one of the walls, beginning an inexorable journey across the grey marble floor.

Barring the single Dreadnought that stood among them like a silent ruby statue, none of the assembled warriors wore battle armour, only hooded robes or duty tunics. The austerity of their dress reflected the mood. The prayers and entreaty to their liege-lords now spoken and the matters of tradition satisfied, it was time to take the import of this conclave in hand.

With a leaden finality, the magnetic locks on the doors boomed as they set in place, and the footsteps died away as the last of the assembled Astartes approached the circle of men.

Dante greeted the arrival of the final representative with a nod of his head; the gesture was returned as Armis, First Lord of the Blood Legion, advanced into the circle. The Chapter Master ran a long-fingered hand through the silver-grey hair that ranged down to his shoulders. The question in the Space Marine's eyes was repeated on every face around him.

Correction. *Almost* every one.

Dante found Seth, hunched forward on one of the benches, watching him with those hooded, blank eyes. As if he took that glance for a permission, the Master of the Flesh Tearers got to his feet and sucked in a breath. 'And so finally, we are all gathered,' he said. 'Or at least as many as could be found.'

Armis nodded, a deceptive half-smile on his pale face. 'Aye. I'm glad I'm here. I imagine that whatever Dante has to speak of, it will be interesting.'

The Master of the Blood Angels threw a look at Mephiston. The psyker was staring into the middle distance, eyes down, intent on realms that only someone with his preternatural senses could see; but still he sensed his lord's attention and gave a slight nod. The psychic wards were still firmly in place; it was safe to speak.

'You have many questions,' Dante began. 'I will answer all of them as best I can.'

'Only one answer is needed, cousin,' said Master Orloc, the Commander of the Blood Drinkers. 'Your summons brought me across the warp from my temples on San Guisuga, without explanation, without account, with only decree. And I came, out of respect to you, Great Dante.' Orloc licked his lips; the Blood Drinker had the same perpetual air of aridity that characterised all in his Chapter. 'But I did not come to take part in pomp and spectacle, nor to be given a tour of this great edifice.'

'Indeed.' The synthetic voice issued from the vox-coder of a motionless crimson Dreadnought. Inside the towering armoured sarcophagus, the flesh and brain of an Astartes warrior lay preserved and forever wired into his machine-hulk body. 'The Blood Swords have battles to be fought. My brethren will brook no distraction from the Emperor's purposes without good cause.'

'As Lord Daggan speaks, so I agree,' Orloc continued. 'The question, then. Why am I here? Why are any of us here?'

Dante exhaled. 'You have come here to take part in a rescue, cousins. To save the lives of hundreds of your fellow Astartes, whose future hangs in the balance.' The Chapter Master felt as if a great weight was being laid across his shoulders, and for a moment, it was as if he could truly sense the measure of every day of his eleven hundred years of life; but he did not hesitate to speak his piece. 'I have brought you here to save the Blood Angels from dissolution and oblivion.'

Armis broke the silence that followed. 'The empty halls. The silent barracks.' He cast around, voicing thoughts that the other Chapter Masters had until now kept to themselves. 'You have tried to conceal it from us, but your brethren are thin upon the ground, Dante. At first I thought you might have over-committed your forces to some military adventure, but that is not the case, is it?'

'Your men are dead,' intoned Daggan.

'Some,' Dante replied. He sighed.

His face hidden deep in the shadows of his hood, Sentikan of the Angels Sanguine spoke for the first time. 'The cost of your insurrection must have been grave for you to seek our aid in this manner.'

Dante concealed a flash of shock; Sentikan and his men had not been given any prior knowledge of the Arkio incident, and yet the Angels Sanguine Lord was clearly aware of it. He glanced at Seth, wondering; but no, the Angels Sanguine and the Flesh Tearers did not speak on good terms. It was highly unlikely they had communicated with one another. The matter of what Sentikan knew would need to be addressed later, however; for now, the disclosure of the full facts was required.

Orloc folded his arms across his chest. 'What in Blood's Name are you talking about? What insurrection?'

'My Chapter has learned of certain truths,' Sentikan said quietly. 'I imagine not the complete dimensions of the events, but the core of them. There was a great battle on the shrineworld Sabien.' He glanced at Brother-Captain Rydae, who sat at his side. 'Many Blood Angels were committed to the field. Many of them were lost there.'

'Who was the foe?' demanded Armis.

'The Word Bearers,' offered Mephiston.

'*Chaos*,' snarled Orloc, his lip curling. 'And how was it the Cursed Sons of Lorgar, the Emperor blight his name, wounded you so deeply?'

Dante stiffened and felt Seth's eyes upon him. 'It was not the Word Bearers who wounded us, cousin. We did this to ourselves. In the name of Sanguinius Reborn.'

'THERE IS NEWS,' said Serpens, 'and it is good and bad in equal measure.' He had a pict slate in his hand and he gestured with it in a casual manner.

Caecus studied him over the top of the fractionator module. The glow of the device threw flickering light across the laboratorium, and cast peculiar shadows over the tech-lord's face. 'I have had little in the way of good news in recent days,' admitted the Apothecary. 'Tell me the best first, then.'

Serpens gave him an indulgent smile and handed the slate to Nyniq. He didn't seem to be aware of Fenn at a nearby console, making a poor attempt at pretending he wasn't listening to every word they said. 'It is my firm and honest belief that I can solve the errors creeping into your replication matrix.' He knitted his fingers together. 'It will not be a simple matter, by no means, but the way of it is well known to me. My own experiments have progressed along similar lines to yours, but further toward fruition. I can, as my pupil did, help you move more swiftly down that road. With our collective knowledge, we can avoid making the same mistakes.'

'And make new ones?' Fenn shot the comment across the room.

Caecus gave him a censorious look in return, and the serf turned back to his work.

Serpens spoke as if he had never heard Fenn speak. 'The mutations are the result of tainted genetic code in the base samples. If those errors can be reduced, the end result...' He nodded toward the zygote tanks. 'Well, shall I say, it would be a wine of a better vintage?'

'This I know,' said Caecus. 'But the way to fix the errors eludes me.'

'And Nyniq too,' agreed Serpens. 'But it does not elude *me*, my friend.' He tapped the loose fleshy wattles along his face. 'I have a methodology we can employ.'

'This is the good news. What is the bad?'

The magos allowed himself a sigh. 'Great science requires great sacrifice, Brother Caecus. I have made such forfeit to come here to Baal against the wishes of my masters and–'

The Blood Angel's retort was fiery. 'And you think I have not?' He shook his head, frowning. 'Already I have stepped across lines of ethics and honour in the pursuit of something I cannot even be sure is achievable!'

'But it is!' insisted Nyniq. 'We can rediscover the art of the replicae and make the Great Corax's dream a reality.'

'She is not wrong,' said Serpens. 'It can be done. But to progress beyond this point will require the most singular mind. I tell you this in candour as a colleague. We must be willing to take what some...' He shot a look at Fenn. 'Will consider to be extreme measures.'

Caecus lost himself in the shimmer and motion of the milky fluid of the zygote tanks. He could see the fluttering motion of an immature clone inside, the irregular jerk of a hand drifting against the inside of the armourglass. Would it be another disappointment, another mutant freak? How many more mistakes could there be before he admitted failure?

'We will do what must be done,' he said.

Serpens nodded eagerly, and beckoned Nyniq to them. The woman had a sanguinator gun in her hand. 'Then, if you please, I would take a measure of your vitae.'

'I was there,' said Mephiston, 'and I will tell you what happened on Sabien.' With a nod from his master, the Lord of Death walked to the centre of the chamber and unfolded the tragedy of Arkio and the Spear of Telesto, speaking without pause as the rays of light from Baal's sun marched across the marble floor. At times, the assembled warriors reacted to things he said, their emotions running the scale from cold deliberation on the part of Master Seth to barely-silenced anger from Master Armis; but none of them interrupted.

When he spoke at last about the battle on Sabien, of the psychic explosion of red fury that turned Blood Angel against Blood Angel, not an Astartes among them moved, all of them barely breathing, silently listening to his words. Each marked in the very blood that raced through their veins with the gene-curse of the Great

Angel, they had only respect for the horrific power of the Black Rage and the Red Thirst. Each of them knew only too well the dark power of the twin banes every Blood Angel and successor Astartes were forced to share. Each of them had seen kinsmen fall to the madness, the blood-hungry berserker frenzy that was the echo of their liege-lord's violent killing. Their shared primarch was ten millennia dead, and yet still the psychic shock of his death at the hands of the Arch-traitor Horus burned hard in all of them, the madness it conjured forever lurking beneath the veneer of civility in every Son of Sanguinius. Not a one thought to disturb him as Mephiston brought his report to a conclusion.

As he finished, he found Dante watching him, and his Chapter Master nodded, one comrade to another. It was a difficult thing for the psyker to address, the dark moments there on the shrineworld, as the Rage came to consume him. He had ventured down the Scarlet Path to madness once before, in the experience that made him the man he now was, trapped beneath the rubble of Hades Hive for days and nights, wrestling with his bestial id; ventured down it and returned reborn. But on Sabien… There had been a different colour to the darkness, and a part of him would forever wonder if he would have drowned in it, if not for Rafen's intervention.

He pushed the thought away. That was past; what mattered now was how the aftermath was dealt with.

Daggan was first to speak in reply, his flat, mechanical voice hissing with piques of annoyance. 'How was this allowed to happen? An ordos lackey, commanding an Astartes warship and a cohort of battle-brothers?'

'Stele assumed command when the *Bellus* was beyond our astropathic contact,' Dante noted. 'It is believed he engineered the death of my chosen agent, the Sanguinary High Priest Hekares, and then consolidated his influence over the crew.'

Orloc was ashen. 'That these corrupted bastards would dare to taint the memory of Sanguinius by making a cheap simulacra... It fills me with a revulsion I cannot find the words to express!'

'I concur,' offered Seth, 'but we should be thankful. Despite the errors of judgment made, the matter has been dealt with. Lord Dante's warriors have cleaned up the mess they made. And the Blood Angels paid the price for their laxity and hubris into the bargain.'

Mephiston's eyes narrowed at the open insult in the Flesh Tearer's words, but he saw that his commander did not react at all to them.

'It is right that you have granted us full disclosure of this, Dante,' said Armis. 'While some may consider it a matter for Blood Angels alone, it is far more than that. Sanguinius is father to us all, not just to the First Founding of Baal. An attack upon his glory is an attack upon his sons.'

'But that is not why we are gathered here,' said Sentikan. 'Our cousin Dante did not bring us to Baal so that he might speak of this, as some hive citizen would atone to a street-preacher.'

The other Chapter Master nodded. 'That is so.' Dante spread his hands, taking in all the Chapter Masters and representatives, those who had spoken and those who had not. 'The Blood Angels are the first among the Astartes. We carry a position of honour, we lead the way where all others follow. Each of you shares in that. We have a lineage that can be traced back beyond the Heresy and the Great Crusade, before even the birth of our primarch, to the beginning of the Age of the Imperium. That great legacy cannot be allowed to falter. The Blood Angels must survive. They must live on to be present when the day of mankind's ultimate victory dawns, so that the Emperor can lay his eyes upon us when he rises from the Golden Throne.'

'But your folly has left you open to attack, to diminishment,' said Daggan. 'If what you say is so, then the Blood Angels teeter on the brink–'

'And one swift push could be enough to make them extinct,' Seth broke in. The ghost of a cold smile crossed his lips. 'How does it taste, Dante? How does it feel for the inheritors of the great and noble IX Legion to be that close to annihilation?' He snorted. 'I'll warrant I am the only one here who knows.'

'The Blood Angels must survive,' repeated Dante. 'And *that*, cousins, is why you are here. I have an audacious request to make of you, in the name of our liege-lord and the bloodline of Baal.'

Sentikan's shadowed face was taut. 'Speak it.'

Dante drew himself up to his full height, and Mephiston watched him sweep his patrician gaze across every warrior in the chamber, making eye contact with each of them in turn. 'In order to return the Blood Angels to strength and stability, I have brought on new inductions of initiates and battle-brothers ahead of schedule, but I need more. And so, to that end, I ask this of you. The Blood Angels require a tithe of men from each successor Chapter, of your newest initiate warriors to swell our depleted ranks.' He opened his hands and offered them palm-up, in echo of the carvings of the Great Angel upon the annexe's walls. 'This I do in the name of Sanguinius.'

The Chapter Master's words faded away into silence; and then the room exploded with voices as every Astartes spoke at once.

NYNIQ CARRIED THE vial of Caecus's blood to the techlord's boxy servitor and fed it into the open lips of the mask upon its forward surface. The machine suckled greedily at the tube, quickly draining it. Fenn made a sour face, but the Blood Angel ignored him.

He glanced at Serpens. 'I have used my own vitae as a base pattern in previous iterations. The improvement it gave was only minor. Not enough to overcome the replication failure.'

'Perhaps so,' said the magos, 'but that was without the aid of the filtration and enhancement process I had developed.' He preened. 'I have formulated a counter-mutagen that blocks the degradation of cellular parity and recursive malformation. We will blend the two.'

Caecus accepted this with a nod. He knew such things were theoretically possible, but until now the science of it had been out of his reach. If Serpens was as good as his word... The Blood Angel frowned. What happened in the next few moments would be the acid test. He shot Fenn a look. They would soon know if his agreement to allow the magos into their circle was a mistake, or not.

The servitor-box gurgled and a melodic chime sounded from the lips of the mask. Nyniq placed her hand before the machine and it disgorged another vial. The fluid within it had a thick, syrupy flow to it, dark in colour. Serpens took it from her with some eagerness, holding it up to the light to examine its consistency. The scientist licked his lips, apparently unaware of the gesture. There was an expression on his face that Caecus had never seen before, at odds with the perpetually earnest air Serpens usually wore. *Need.*

'The blood, the blood is the key to it all,' said Serpens, half to himself. 'I have heard it said that in the rituals of consecration practised by your Chapter, each Baalite son is imbued with a tiny measure of blood from Sanguinius himself, is that not so?' He shook the vial, watching the motion of the liquid inside. 'This blood, your blood, Lord Caecus, has within it an iota of the primarch's. And the primarch is the gene-spawn son of the Emperor, so his blood contains an iota of the Lord of Mankind's.' He let out a breath between his teeth. 'This is the distillate of greatness, my friend. The essence of perfection, if only one could unlock it.' Serpens blinked, as if he suddenly remembered where he was, his manner shifting back to his usual easy smile. 'Shall we begin?'

Caecus gestured toward the zygote tanks. 'At your discretion.'

'My lord, we should go no further!' Fenn blurted out the words. 'We do not know what will happen!'

'Quite so,' noted Nyniq. 'But science is quest for knowledge, serf. If we allow ignorance to blind us, we willingly set ourselves toward a return to the Age of Strife and the darkness of Old Night!'

The serf's lips trembled and Caecus gave him a level stare. 'This is right, Fenn. It must be done.' He let out a breath and felt a conviction take hold in him. 'We cannot sway from this course of action. I hold it in my grasp to be the saviour of the Blood Angels. I cannot refuse that call.' He turned and nodded toward the magos. 'Proceed.'

'Emperor watch over this endeavour and grant it success,' said Serpens. The tech-lord inserted the vial into the complex snarl of machinery ringing one of the glass cylinders. 'Moment of truth, then,' he said lightly.

The fluid discharged into the festoon of tubules snaking away into the milky processor medium and with a sudden shock of movement, the clone inside began to thrash and hammer against the glass. Caecus heard a peculiar bubbling wail issue out from the tank.

A scream.

'I KNEW THE Blood Angels were conceited, but never had I dreamed that their master could show such towering arrogance as this!' Seth's voice was loudest, and it cut through the chorus of dissent in the chamber. 'You have excelled yourself, Dante! You lay down an edict as if you are the Emperor himself!'

Mephiston snarled at the Flesh Tearer's words, but his commander placed a warning hand on his arm. 'I would never dare to do such a thing. I have told you what is needed, nothing more.'

'It did not sound like a request to me,' Daggan grated. 'Your statement had the colour of a command, Lord Dante. Is that what it was?'

Armis shook his head. 'Is it necessary to make it so? I see only a brother Chapter in need and the opportunity among us to meet it.'

Seth gave Armis an arch look. 'It does not surprise me that the Master of the Blood Legion takes the side of a First Founding Chapter.'

'What are you implying?' demanded Armis. 'Are you questioning my loyalty, Flesh Tearer?'

Orloc raised his hands. 'Hold! This is a serious matter, and I will not see it descend into small matters of rivalry!' The Lord of the Blood Drinkers shook his head. 'This is not about "taking sides"! We are all kindred beneath the armour… A family, in as much as that term can be applied to the Adeptus Astartes.'

'Then you agree to this?' asked the Blood Swords Dreadnought.

'I did not say that,' Orloc replied. 'I say only that now is not the time for divisiveness! Clear heads and rational thoughts must carry the day.'

Seth walked forward, and his second, Brother-Captain Gorn, came with him. 'Forgive me, cousin, but I find it hard to remain *rational* in the face of this… this decree.' He swept his glare toward Dante. 'You want my men? The Blood Angels wish to gut my Chapter to patch up the wounds in their own. And then it will be the Flesh Tearers left with diminished numbers, our best and brightest taken away…' He bared his teeth. 'As if my Chapter is not lessened enough!'

'The tithe will be proportional,' said Dante. 'The numbers requested from each successor will reflect the size and disposition of that Chapter.'

Seth turned away. 'How magnanimous. You've thought of everything.'

'And what will happen to the men you take?' asked Sentikan. 'The recruits?'

'We will uplift them as Blood Angels,' explained the Chapter Master. 'They will be granted the implants and rituals in keeping with that status.'

'They will lose the identities they had,' Daggan grated.

Dante shook his head. 'As Lord Orloc said, we are all kindred beneath the armour.'

The room fell silent for a long moment; then Sentikan spoke again, in a quiet rasp. 'We are to take a vote upon this, then.'

Seth turned about and uttered a single world. '*No*.'

'You refuse to assist our parent Chapter?' said Armis.

'More than that,' Seth barked. 'I question the right of the Blood Angels to demand anything from us!'

'We are the First Founding,' said Dante, steel entering his voice. At last, the hidden challenge boiling away beneath Seth's manner was rising to the fore.

'I know what you are!' snapped the Flesh Tearer lord. 'I cannot be allowed to forget what you are, even if I wished it!' He shot a look at the other Chapter Masters and representatives. 'Are we to agree to this without even raising the question as to why?' Seth stabbed out a finger toward Dante. '*He* allowed this to happen. Under his stewardship the Blood Angels were taken to the very edge of the abyss, a fall that would have led to the gates of Chaos itself! If not for the Emperor's grace, we might have called this conclave to discuss the extermination of his Chapter, not the salvaging of it!'

Dante's words were stony. 'I know the full measure of my responsibility, Seth. I bear the shame of this without shirking from it. But I have led the Blood Angels to glory in the name of Terra for centuries. I fought against the black armies of the Ruinous Powers before you were born, *cousin.*'

Seth's fury ebbed and became cold. 'True enough. I do not dispute your elder status or the record of your victories. But I question your future, Dante. You are indeed among the longest-lived of the Astartes. And perhaps, with that in mind, you should consider your responsibility. Consider stepping down from your position in light of what you allowed to transpire.'

The Flesh Tearer's words brought a sharp intake of breath from the other Astartes; for Mephiston, it was one insult too many.

'You dare–' he began, stepping forward.

The Dreadnought Daggan moved swiftly to block the Librarian's path with a heavy steel footfall that echoed through the hall, turning with a speed unexpected for a form of such mass. 'He dares,' said the venerable warrior. 'He *must*. In this most grave of circumstances we cannot shy from even the hardest of questions.'

Dante kept his annoyance in check. 'All too true.' He took a breath. 'Seth. Do you challenge my judgement?'

'Do I need to?' returned the other Master, his tone mild. 'What has taken place speaks louder than any voice could.'

Armis shook his head. 'You go too far, Flesh Tearer.'

'That is my way,' he replied. Seth paused, taking the measure of the men around him. 'I make a counter to Lord Dante's demand with one of my own. If his judgement is indeed brought into question – and it must be so in the eyes of any sane man – then perhaps it is the Blood Angels themselves who must be called to account!' He smiled coldly. 'I advocate the reverse of my honoured cousin's demands. I suggest that we should not tithe our men to Dante, but that he should tithe his to us!'

'We cannot disband a First Founding Chapter!' Orloc was aghast.

'We know the history of the Astartes. It has happened before,' insisted Seth, 'we can take the men among the successors, spread equally. As you said, Lord Orloc, we are all kindred beneath the armour...'

Dante looked around him and saw the spread of emotion, clear on the faces of Seth and Armis, hidden under Sentikan's hood and behind the immobile mask of Daggan's sculpted facia; and a dozen other points across the spectrum in the manners of the men of the Angels Encarmine, the Red Wings, the Flesh Eaters and all the others assembled. He felt the moment slipping away from him. Seth's words were fragmenting his kindred, and to venture further along this path might force them to divide into lines both for and against. 'We must take pause,' he said quietly, almost to himself.

'Aye, lord,' Mephiston was at his side. 'If we force the hand of anyone here, it will mean discord.'

Dante gave a solemn nod. 'I must rely on their loyalty and honour. Seth plays only to their doubts.' He spoke again, louder this time, so all could hear him. 'We have much to think on. I call a recess so that we may all reflect on what has been said here.'

'My answer will not change,' said Seth.

Dante nodded again, keeping his voice even. 'And that, cousin, is your right.'

THE NOISE AND the disturbance inside the tank died away within moments, but Fenn could not take his eyes off the cylinder. He could make out the murky shadow of a man-shape inside the liquid, but he dared not wonder what it might look like if revealed in the hard, cold light of the laboratorium. The panoply of mutations he had seen throughout the many iterations of the replicae process – things without skins, mewling forms with multiple mouths, limbs twisted into tentacles, and worse – these were horrors that haunted his dreams. And yet he could not look away. He had to know what Serpens had wrought.

Nyniq was reading from a medicae auspex. 'The amalgam has taken, tech-lord. We have stability.'

'You're certain?' There was concern in Caceus's voice.

Serpens placed a hand upon the shoulder of Fenn's master. 'There is only one way to be certain.' He turned to the serf. 'Open it.'

Fenn shot his master a look. 'My lord?'

'Do as he says,' said Caecus. 'Decant the Bloodchild.'

'*Bloodchild*,' repeated Serpens, with an admiring nod. 'A fitting name.'

With shaking hands, the Chapter serf worked the controls and the milky fluid spiralled away as the tank split open, one half drawing up, the other falling away. A mass of flesh tipped forward and crashed to the gridded flooring; a man, his skin a smooth russet as if tanned by a hundred days beneath the sun.

Fenn backed away, his hands in front of him in a subconscious gesture of self-protection. The clone was shivering as he got to his feet. Wet and naked, the figure was carved as if from planes of nalwood, dense packs of muscle shifting beneath the surface of his flesh. A fine mane of blond hair coloured his scalp, and the flawless planes of his face were the ideal of a patrician Blood Angel countenance. Fenn saw the smallest reflection of his master's face in the duplicate's aspect, no doubt some artefact of the amalgam process.

Only the eyes seemed strange; they were blank and doll-like. No intelligence glittered behind them, only emptiness.

'Behold the future of the Blood Angels,' said Nyniq, with reverence.

Fenn took a wary step closer, and the clone watched him blankly, like a docile animal. 'Can… Can it understand us?'

'He has the mind of a newborn, in many respects,' said Serpens, smiling like a proud parent. 'Much of what he is remains locked in his brain through chains of genetic-memory. With the right stimuli, he will re-learn what he already knows.' He glanced away. 'Give me a month of indoctrination and hypnocordia, and you'll have a Space Marine fit for line duty.'

Caecus came closer, his face rapt with wonder. 'A success, after so long. I hardly dare to believe it is true.' He swung about in a flash of motion. 'I must bring this to Lord Dante immediately! One look at this creation and he will know that I was not wrong! He *will* acknowledge the rightness in my plan!'

'With respect, Lord Caecus, this is only an archetype,' said Nyniq. 'Perhaps we should run some more tests before we–'

'No,' snapped the Apothecae Majoris. 'I understand your intent, but you must know, time is of the essence! Even as we speak, Dante is in conclave with his fellow Chapter Masters… I must bring this to him before he makes a choice that he will later regret!'

Fenn blinked. His head was swimming; he couldn't find the words to express his swirling thoughts.

The serf watched Serpens nod thoughtfully. 'Lord Caecus is correct, Nyniq. This success must not be concealed. Go with him to the fortress-monastery, take the Bloodchild. Show the master of the Blood Angels the fruits of his kinsman's great work.'

The woman bowed low and Fenn's voice caught up to his thoughts. 'Lord, I will attend you–'

But Caecus shook his head. 'No, Fenn. I want you to remain at the citadel. Start the test series as Nyniq suggested, and prepare more iterations for infusion with the amalgam compound.' The Apothecary was already walking away, lost in thought.

Fenn felt his blood chill as he turned and found Serpens watching him intently. 'It will be a fine opportunity for us to work together,' said the magos.

BROTHER-CAPTAIN GORN FOLLOWED his master into the grounds beyond the Grand Annex, moving swiftly to keep pace with him over the ochre flagstones of the wide drilling quadrangle. He ignored the sideways looks from the Blood Angel guards who patrolled the edges of the open space.

Seth slowed as he crossed toward the towering statue of Sanguinius that stood in the centre of the quad, its presence dividing the space into four smaller areas. The Great Angel was depicted with his wings furled and his head turned down to those walking beneath him. Beneath his hands he held a great sword, the point toward the earth. 'He's watching us, Gorn,' said the Chapter Master. 'Do you see?'

The captain looked up; true enough, the eyes of the great carving seemed to follow him as he moved.

'He watches us and we must not be shown vulnerable in his sight.' Seth shook his head. 'Sanguinius wants strength, brother-captain. He would not have given us the gene-curse if he did not. He did that to test us. So he could be sure that his sons would be forever strong after his death.'

'It is so, lord,' Gorn offered. 'We will do whatever he asks of us.'

Seth stopped abruptly in the shadow of the statue. 'Will you? Here, beneath his gaze, can you swear to that?'

'I can,' Gorn spoke without hesitation. 'In the name of the Great Angel, you have my pledge, as you always have. My men and I will do whatever is needed of us to bring this matter to a close, even if that comes to measures of…' He faltered, unable to find the right words.

'Measures of an extreme nature?' suggested Seth.

'Aye. I heard the merit in your words today, lord, as did many others. Perhaps the sun has set on the supremacy of the Blood Angels.' He felt a thrill of excitement at speaking such a rebellious thing aloud. 'Perhaps a stronger, more vital Chapter would be better suited to be masters of Baal.'

'A Chapter like ours?' said Seth, without weight. He looked up once more at the statue; behind it, the sun turned the clouded sky a dark crimson the shade of a Flesh Tearer's armour. 'Wait, Gorn,' he said, after a moment. 'Be ready. But for now, just wait.'

CHAPTER EIGHT

THE DATA-SLATE WAS exactly where it was supposed to be, concealed beneath a careworn copy of the *Litergus Integritas*, under the fourth pew from the right.

Fenn threw a wary glance over his shoulder, and then bent to recover it. At this time of day, there would be no one else inside the devotional chapel; in fact, this small sub-chancel rarely saw more than one or two worshippers at a time. The majority of the staff in the Vitalis Citadel preferred to make the trip up to the larger temple on the upper tiers of the tower for vespers, where true daylight was cast through the windows. This minor chamber, beneath the surface of the frozen polar landscape, had only biolume simulators to match the passage of Baal's day-night cycle. The place had a perpetually musty, undisturbed air to it; precisely the reason that the serf had chosen it as a dead-drop.

A thin hum of antigravs momentarily drew his eye to the roof. In the dimness, he could just about make out the shape of a servo-skull making lazy circles in the air, a smoking censer rocking beneath it on a chain. Fenn made the sign of the aquila and pretended to pray, nodding towards the basalt statues at the altar. Sanguinius knelt before the Emperor, his father's hand upon his shoulder. Forgive my subterfuge, my Lords, he mouthed, but what I do here is in service to the Imperium.

When he was sure the servo-skull was far enough away not to surveillance him, Fenn raised the slate to his ear and ran his finger over the activation rune. He listened to the scratchy recording of the voice encoded there, the words of the contact he had cultivated in the citadel's communicant staff. When the serf's suspicions of Nyniq and Serpens had finally crystallised, it was to that man that Fenn went, bribing him with minor drugs from the medicae stores to see that an extra query was included in the machine-call message stack sent out toward the sector capital.

He had not expected to get a reply so soon; the signal had just been a shot in the dark, some vain attempt to feel as if he were doing something instead of sitting back and allowing the magos biologis to ride rough-shod over his master's work.

But here it was. *Proof.* With shaking hands, he wound the vox-spool back and played it again, to be certain he had not misheard.

'The message from the astropath is garbled, as they always are,' said the recording. 'but the meat of it is apparent. Quite why you require this datum is beyond me, but I will state it for the record.' Fenn felt sweat prickling on his arms as he waited to hear the words for a second time. 'The Tech-Lord Haran Serpens is listed in the rolls of the Adeptus Terra as missing presumed dead. His craft was reported lost in the deeps of the Segmentum Pacificus, beyond the Thoth system.'

Fenn stopped the playback and rocked on the pew. By the Emperor's sight, Thoth was clear across the galactic plane from Baal, hundreds of light-years distant. 'He's not the same man,' the words tumbled from the serf's lips and he looked up at the statue. 'In Terra's name, he cannot be the same man!'

He scrambled to his feet in a rush, dithering as he stepped into the aisle. What could he do? If he returned to the laboratorium, the impostor would be waiting there for him. Fenn gripped the data-slate hard. How could he face the magos – or whoever he was – like this? The serf had never had the skill to conceal his emotions; the pretender would see the knowledge on Fenn's face as plain as nightfall. He forced himself to remain calm. Think, think, you fool! Lord Caecus must be told!

'Yes,' he said aloud. There were transports in the flight bay atop the tower far above, lighters and shuttles that travelled across Baal on regular sorties. All he needed to do was find one destined for the fortress-monastery, and–

'Fenn?' The shock of the voice made his gut twist. 'Don't be shy, serf, I know you're in here.'

He pressed himself into the pew, not daring to breathe. He made out the shape of the figure drifting in from the shadowed doorway; a broad man the size of an Astartes.

'I think we should talk, you and I,' said the impostor mildly. 'I think we got off on the wrong foot. After all, we both share a passion for the same thing, don't we?' The voice became silky. 'The dazzling infinity of the human machine, yes? The quest for perfection of the flesh?'

Fenn watched the figure move slowly toward the altar. With the biolumes at such low levels, it was possible that he would never see the cowering serf. He bent lower, his rational mind warring with the animal need to run. He just had to wait, just a little more. Let him get to the altar, and then he won't be able to catch me before I reach the chapel doors.

'Not talking? That's a pity.' There was a sigh. 'You are a poor sample, Fenn. An intelligent man, oh yes, but a poor sample. It is no wonder that the Blood Angels rejected you as too weak to embrace the power of an Adeptus Astartes. You lack something.' The footsteps stopped.

The sudden silence was too much to bear. With a frantic burst of motion, Fenn exploded from his hiding place and hurtled across the darkened chapel as fast as he could go. He pounded towards the doors, dimly alarmed by the fact that the ersatz tech-lord had not even moved to follow him.

Too late, Fenn realised something was amiss. The thought was still forming in his mind as he collided with a tall, slab-sided shape hidden in the shadows and crashed back on to his haunches, into a heap on the floor. The box-like servitor loomed out of the darkness on its iron claws, stalking toward him.

'Your associate among the communicant,' came the voice. The warmth, the silk of Haran Serpens faded away, replaced by something calculating and impossibly old. 'Such a terrible accident. A freak gust of wind. He fell from the top of the citadel.'

Fenn was shaking, the fear engulfing him in suffocating waves. 'Who?' He pushed the sounds from his mouth. 'Why?'

'You will never know, little man.'

Before him, the sides of the box began to slide open, like some complex puzzle. Fenn saw movement inside, rods and pincers shifting and turning.

'It's better this way,' said the impostor, all trace of the false voice gone now. 'You would only weep when you learned of how I have tampered with your great work. Better you don't live to see it.'

The serf held up a hand in silent entreaty. Inside the open box, a huge arachnid shape of brass legs and glugging pipes coiled and then leapt toward him, metal talons whipping through the air.

RAFEN NODDED TO Ajir as he approached the doors to the Grand Annex. 'Report,' he commanded.

The other Blood Angel inclined his head. 'Little of import, sir. The conclave has reconvened after a short recess.' He leaned closer, lowering his voice. 'I think Mephiston called the pause for good reason. Angered words have reached us here from within.'

'That is to be expected,' Rafen scanned the wide anteroom. As within the Grand Annex, out here every successor Chapter was represented by one or two armoured line troopers – escorts or honour guards for the ranking officers taking part. His eyes met those of Sergeant Noxx, who stood watching him from across the chamber with steady, blank menace.

'The Flesh Tearer has been doing that all day,' said Ajir, with a grimace. 'If he could cut me with that glare, I would be dead and bleeding upon the ground.'

'Don't allow him to irk you.'

Ajir smiled without humour. 'Of course not. I'm not Kayne. I have a better rein on my impulses.'

Rafen let the comment pass. 'Just stay alert.'

'Always,' came the reply. The other Space Marine's dark face shifted, becoming stiff. 'Although I will confess it sits poorly with me to be on a battle footing in the halls of our own stronghold.'

'We are Astartes,' said Rafen. 'We are *always* on a battle footing.'

A commotion drew the attention of the Blood Angels and as one they turned to witness the arrival of Brother Caecus, a woman and a hooded Space Marine in lockstep with him. 'Stand aside,' the Apothecae was saying, 'I must enter the Grand Annex.'

An Angel Vermillion blocked his path. 'The doors are sealed. Our Chapter Masters have ordered it so.'

'This transcends those orders!' Caecus barked.

Rafen stepped up, waving the other Space Marine aside. 'Majoris? Is something wrong?'

He noted at once that Caecus seemed very agitated, his face flushed with colour, his brow knit. 'Open the doors,' he replied. 'Do it now, brother-sergeant.'

Ajir was at Rafen's side. 'Who is this?' The Astartes indicated the woman. 'A servant of the magos biologis, here? Who granted her admittance?'

'I did,' Caecus retorted. 'Nyniq is here on my request. Now open the door! In Blood's name, must I do it myself?'

The Apothecary reached for the control mechanism that would retract the massive iron locking bar, but Rafen caught his wrist in the fingers of his armoured gauntlet. 'You–'

The Space Marine beneath the nondescript robes broke his silence, emitting a low growl, and with preternatural speed his hand snapped out to mirror Rafen's gesture, grabbing the brother-sergeant's arm before he could push Caecus away.

Rafen shot the hooded figure a look; he saw a dark face with a feral cast to it.

'No,' said Caecus, with the force of command behind the word. 'Release him!'

'Brother?' Rafen studied the other man; he did not know him, could not place his strangely-familiar appearance.

'*Brother.*' The hooded figure repeated the word thickly, as if he were unfamiliar with the process of speaking it. The hand around Rafen's wrist dropped away.

'For the last time,' Caecus said, his voice rising, 'open the doors! I will take all responsibility for any censure that results!'

Noxx had moved closer. 'You had better do as he says,' noted the Flesh Tearer.

Rafen turned to Ajir and nodded once. 'Open it.'

UNSURE OF THE protocol for an interruption of this nature, Rafen followed Caecus's group inside, belatedly noting that Noxx was at his heels. He frowned, and walked on. The air inside the annexe was thick with tension; they had intruded into the midst of a forceful argument, of that he had no doubt.

'What is the meaning of this disturbance?' The amplified vox of the Blood Sword Dreadnought Daggan was harsh and grating. 'This is a closed session!'

Caecus spoke before Rafen could frame an explanation. 'Forgive me, lords, but what I have to impart to you could not be delayed. I must speak now, this very moment.'

Mephiston shot Rafen an irritated glare and intercepted Caecus before he reached the circle of leaders. 'Majoris, whatever you have to say, it must wait until the conclusion of this conclave.'

'What I have to say may well change that conclusion!' he shot back. 'I have an answer to the great dilemma!'

'Caecus,' said Dante, a warning clear in his intonation.

'Hold, cousin,' said Sentikan. 'This is your Apothecae Majoris, is it not? Why not let him speak? What harm can one more voice do?'

Dante bristled at the Angel Sanguine's words. 'My Brother Caecus is a learned man. But I fear his reach may exceed his grasp.'

'Not so!' Caecus retorted. 'Not any more! I have mastered the skill of the replicae... I have a success!'

'What does he say?' Seth cocked his head. 'Cloning? It cannot be done!' He bared his teeth. 'If such a thing were possible, the Flesh Tearers would have used it to bolster the numbers of our own Chapter, centuries ago!'

'You tried to use replicae to recover your losses?' asked Orloc.

'No.' The Lord of the Blood Angels became still. His face became granite-hard. 'Caecus. You were ordered to desist in pursuit of this. Did you defy me?'

The Apothecary's bluster faltered in the face of his master's icy manner. 'I… You said only that I did not have your blessing, lord. You did not order me to stop.'

'You dare to play with semantics like some Ministorum lackey?' snarled Mephiston. 'You knew the intent behind the master's words!'

Dante shook his head. 'I am disappointed, brother. I expected better from you.'

'You should only be disappointed if he failed,' said Seth, coming forward with a sudden, new intensity in his eyes. 'What of it then, Caecus? Where is this success you talk of?'

'Here, lords,' Nyniq dared to speak as she reached up and drew back the hood of the silent figure in the robes. 'See the first of them. The first Bloodchild.' The warrior stood unmoving.

An odd silence fell across the room for a few moments as the assembled Chapter Masters studied the clone, each one of them weighing the grave import of its presence. Their reactions ranged from sneers of derision to cold, measuring stares.

'This is a genetic duplicate?' said Armis, clearly unconvinced. 'He appears… a commonplace Astartes, nothing more.'

'This is the first Sapiens Sanguina!' Caecus snapped. 'A fully mature Blood Angel Space Marine force-grown from a nascent zygote sample, made manifest by my will!'

Seth turned toward Dante. 'Why did you keep this from us, cousin?'

'I saw no merit in this work,' came the reply. 'By his own admission, Caecus had nothing to show for his research.'

'That was before,' said the Apothecae Majoris. 'I have…' He glanced at Nyniq. 'Made a breakthrough.'

'Every clone you have created thus far has been unstable,' Mephiston growled. 'All your attempts to duplicate the work of Corax have come to nought. Yet now you enter this chamber uninvited to parade one chance success and call it an achievement?'

'I ask only for what I spoke of before!' Caecus retorted. 'To be allowed to do my part to draw my Chapter back from the brink of dissolution!'

Daggan's torso turned to present his steel face to the assembled masters. 'If this can be done… If this "Bloodchild" is no fluke, then it will mean much for all our Chapters, not just for the Blood Angels.'

'The ability to recoup losses in months instead of years,' mused Orloc. 'It would be a tactical advantage worth having.'

Dante's eyes narrowed. 'Cousins, in this matter I would counsel restraint.'

'That is of no surprise,' said Seth. 'But this is not a time for conservative thought, Lord Dante. If Caecus is as skilled as he appears, then this Bloodchild will solve all your problems, without the need of a tithe.'

'And it will be to the interest of the Flesh Tearers as well,' added Armis.

'Of course,' Seth agreed. 'I make no secret of that.' He walked over to the clone-Marine, studying its face intently. 'The verification of this will be found only in one place.'

'In battle,' said Daggan.

'Aye.' Seth nodded. He snapped his fingers. 'Brother-Sergeant Rafen?' He glanced at the Blood Angel. 'Since you showed such prowess before in single combat, I would ask that you test this Bloodchild for us, in the arena.'

Dante gave Rafen the smallest of nods and Rafen bowed slightly. 'Very well, Lord Seth.'

'Brother-Sergeant Noxx will join him,' said Dante.

Seth turned back to study the Blood Angel master. 'Two against one? That's hardly sporting.'

Dante's reply was cold. 'No confrontation between our kind ever is.'

RAFEN PULLED THE leather strap tight around his arm and secured it. He looked up and saw his face reflected in the triangular eye-slits of his helmet; the Blood Angel's wargear rested upon an arming rack, a hollow man-shape like a red statue. The training tunic was tight around his chest, and the straps pressed into the places where the bruises and contusions from the last combat had still not fully healed.

He sensed a presence behind him but did not turn.

'I admit, I expected to meet you again in the arena,' said Noxx dryly, 'but not so quickly. Or under such circumstances.'

'I'll try not to win so easily this time,' Rafen offered. 'I would hate to shame you twice before all our kinsmen.'

Noxx's insouciant manner cracked. 'You were lucky before.'

'I'm certain you believe that.'

The veteran sergeant grabbed him and spun him about, so that they were face to face. 'I misjudged you, peacock, that's all. It won't happen again.'

Rafen shrugged off his arm and walked to the weapons racks; sickle-sharp glaives and hook-ended short swords hung on belt straps. He drew the sword and tapped a thumb over the keen edge. 'No training blades this time,' he said quietly.

Noxx donned his weapons. 'Of course not. It goes without saying; this will be a fight to the death.'

'How so?' Rafen demanded.

'It's a clone,' Noxx snorted and walked away. 'When it is dead your Brother Caecus can simply hatch out another.'

THE ARENA'S CONFIGURATION had been changed from the previous bout. The mechanisms operating the moveable blocks had been retarded, allowing the combatant the opportunity to fight in an open area, with only the steep inclines of the walls to act as barriers. Rafen reached the edge of the stone bowl and saw the Bloodchild already waiting for them in the centre of the arena. As he watched, a servitor approached and deposited an identical hook sword to the one he carried upon the ground before the clone-Marine. For a long second, the duplicate studied the weapon, staring at it without apparent recognition.

Rafen's lip curled. *Is it even aware of where it is, or what it is?* The idea of replicae, of the test-tube growth of a man from a knot of cells to a full adult, conflicted him. It was a radical concept, and Caecus did not lie when he said the arcane process had the power to heal the Chapter's losses; but Rafen could not help but wonder what kind of men it would create. *What is a warrior if he does not have a past to draw from? A soul to pledge in the Emperor's service? Little more than an organic machine?*

Then, with a quick flash of insight, the Bloodchild flicked the sword off the floor with a jerk of its foot, and caught the weapon by the hilt. It raced through a rapid series of practice moves with seamless ease, as if the clone had been fighting with the blade for decades. But still, in those strangely vacant eyes, there was nothing. Not the dead cold of a warrior hardened by death and killing, not the insane emptiness of a madman; a different kind of nothingness, a void like the absence of something within.

The arming servitor climbed out and clattered to a halt. 'This will be a trial combat. Fight to the shedding of blood, show courage and honour.' The machine-helot bowed its head. 'In the name of Sanguinius and the Emperor.'

'In the name of Sanguinius and the Emperor,' repeated Rafen and Noxx. The words had barely left the Flesh Tearer's throat before he dropped into the fighting pit. Rafen gripped his hook sword and followed suit.

THERE WAS NO hesitation on the Bloodchild's face; the clone-Marine understood what was to transpire in the arena. It pivoted off the back foot and turned into Noxx's approach, the sword coming up to a guard position. The Flesh Tearer's downward blow, augmented by the force of his dive into the pit, hit hard with a resonant clash of steel on steel. The clone dodged backward, drawing sparks off his opponent's blade as he whipped his own sword away.

Rafen ventured closer, out of fighting range for the moment, gauging the Bloodchild, watching him carefully for signs of hesitation, of unwariness.

It was peculiar; by turns the clone-Marine behaved as if it were new to the business of fighting, and then in the next breath it moved like a seasoned veteran. He became aware that the clone's lips were moving, talking to itself in low, hushed tones.

Noxx attacked again, shouting a furious war cry. The clone bellowed back, imitating the other Astartes in pitch and tone with uncanny clarity. Noxx threw out a strike that was a clear feint and the Bloodchild fell for it, overextending. The Flesh Tearer reversed his blow and scored a hit, ripping through the clone's robes and making a shallow cut across his chest. Without losing momentum, Noxx duplicated a mirror of the move, but this time the Bloodchild parried and slammed him away with a glancing blow from his fist.

Noxx's sandals scraped across the stone floor. 'He catches on quickly,' said the other Astartes.

The Bloodchild came about, suddenly coming for Rafen with the weapon in his hand held high; he was copying what he had seen Noxx do, but with twice the speed and ferocity behind it. The Blood Angel ducked low to avoid the feint; it was an easy move, now he saw what it was.

Or so Rafen thought. At the apex of the attack, the clone abruptly reversed and drew down in a falling strike, bright silver lashing at the Blood Angel's neck. Rafen barely managed to turn his hook sword to deflect a blow that surely would have been mortal.

Fool! He chided himself. *Don't underestimate this thing. Noxx is not wrong; he is quick, and he's learning, adapting.*

Rafen flicked the sword and the hooks on each blade came together. With a clash of metal, the curved ends locked, Space Marine and clone thrown into a tug-of-war for control. Noxx saw the opportunity and came in to attack again. The Bloodchild pivoted, sacrificing his hold over Rafen to make a spinning kick at the advancing Flesh Tearer. Noxx was caught off-balance as a heavy foot slammed into his chest and knocked him to the ground.

The clone extended his spin back toward Rafen, slashing the air with his hooked blade. The Blood Angel met the strike with equal force, parrying up as he brought a hard fist into his opponent's sternum. Rafen felt something fracture where he landed the blow, but the Bloodchild did nothing but grunt.

He forced forward, the blades going across one another in a screeching cross of razor on razor. For a moment, his face was a hand's span from the clone's, his gaze locked on those dead, dead eyes.

'Brother,' repeated the duplicate, the word strange and alien upon his lips.

The blades moved and Rafen took the pommel on the chin, but he shook it off. In return, the Blood Angel bucked forward, bending at the waist to drop a headbutt on the bridge of the clone's nose. This time he was rewarded by a cry of pain.

The Bloodchild snarled in anger and punched him back, in time to meet a fresh assault by Noxx. The Flesh Tearer's blade cut again, this time across the clone's seamless abdomen. It fought back, swinging its own sword in a fast arc that tore cuts through both its opponents.

Rafen fell away, a hiss escaping his teeth. There was blood oozing from a wound on Noxx's brow as he shot the other Astartes a look. 'He fights one at a time well enough. Let's see how he does with two at once.'

'IMPRESSIVE,' ALLOWED DAGGAN. 'For something less than a day old, I've barely seen the like outside the ranks of the tyranids.' The Chapter Masters stood in a line, watching the duel from the viewing balconies. 'But can it do more than just fight with blank instinct?'

'He is far more than a xenos insect driven by impulse, lord,' said Caecus, 'the Bloodchild is a pure expression of the genetic ideal of the Astartes. More than a hundred Blood Angels, alive and dead, have their DNA expressed within his physiology. I believe that with the correct stimuli, the clone will be able to assimilate the muscle-recall and genetic memory of each one of them!'

'And what of the implanted organs we share?' demanded Armis. 'Without them, this creation is nothing more than a servitor of better design and breeding.'

'The replicae process duplicates many of the implants within the first budding of the modified zygote,' insisted the Apothecae. 'Oolitic kidney, occulobe, multi-lung, bicopea, the secondary heart organ, all of these are naturally occurring structures within the body of the Bloodchild.' He nodded to himself. 'In that fashion, the clone is superior to a human-source Astartes. He need not undertake the full and lengthy process of adaptation that a normal man must endure.' Caecus dared to throw a sideways glance at his master. Dante did not meet his gaze, his attention fully concentrated on the fight unfolding below them.

'There is a question that no one here has yet asked,' said Sentikan, his eyes glittering deep beneath his cowl. 'If this patchwork being is indeed a distillation of all the potential of the Sons of Sanguinius, then what of the Rage and the Thirst?' The hooded warrior turned slightly towards the Blood Angel Apothecary. 'Have you spliced that out of his genetic code, majoris? Or will your creation still be subject to the curse that touches every one of us?'

Caecus swallowed hard, lost for an answer.

BLOOD ANGEL AND Flesh Tearer came at the clone-Marine from the right and the left, hook swords held chest high, fast and deadly.

The Bloodchild did not waver; something in its eyes, perhaps some hunter's intuition saw that Noxx moved a fraction slower than Rafen, an artefact of the earlier duel in this arena. It employed the feint move again, but this time the clone shifted and left Rafen slashing at open air as it met Noxx's upward-swinging cut. Once again, the curved tips of the swords met, but the Flesh Tearer was unready for it. The Bloodchild executed a perfect disarming move, twisting and dragging the Space Marine's weapon out of his grip before the veteran sergeant could stop him. The force of the motion made the Flesh Tearer's sword describe a loop about the hook of the clone's weapon and down toward the Bloodchild's other hand. The grip slapped into the clone's palm and it snarled, looping both blades about in a lethal arc.

The reticence Rafen had shown toward the Bloodchild evaporated with that masterful display; the clone was indeed every bit the warrior that Caecus claimed it was. Even as he advanced on it, he found himself wondering what kind of heights such a Blood Angel might reach if properly trained and disciplined.

One moment it was forcing Noxx into the wall; the next it turned to attack Rafen with the twin streaks of silver swords. The ferocity of the assault was staggering, and he caught the rush of anger darkening the Bloodchild's face as it came at him. With a colossal impact, the blades scissored across his hook sword and broke it along the length with a screech of rendered metal. The torsion of the blow twisted through Rafen's arm and shocked him backward; for a moment he almost lost his footing.

As fast as it came at him, the clone was roaring into Noxx's face again. The swords fell flat upon the Flesh Tearer's shoulders in a V and closed, shifting to sever his head at the neck with a single motion. Noxx's hands, bloodied and raw, came up to fight against the killing strike. He cried out in pain, his shout warring with the Bloodchild's snarls and growls.

Rafen reacted without thinking, and hurled the broken sword like a throwing knife. His aim was true; the bifurcated blade impacted and set deep into the flesh of the Bloodchild's back, a couple of centimetres beneath his shoulder blade.

The reaction was instant. The clone brayed and spun about, Noxx suddenly knocked aside, the two hook swords falling from its nerveless fingers as it scrambled to reach for the broken weapon, desperate to pull it free.

Bloodchild and Blood Angel locked eyes, clone and Astartes linked by a chain of raging battle-hate. Rafen felt the ebb and flow of the combat rage inside him, metering it by the second as he had been trained to his entire life; but the clone had no such preparation. He saw the shadow of the fury erupt in those lifeless eyes, saw the turn-key of the Red Thirst rising.

With a screech, the clone gripped the broken blade and ripped it from its own flesh, bright vitae cascading off the edge. As Noxx struggled to his feet, the Bloodchild opened its mouth and ran Rafen's makeshift weapon over its tongue, sucking the fluid from its surface. Red stained the white fangs behind its lips.

The clone pivoted and mirrored Rafen's earlier attack, throwing the blade at Noxx. The Flesh Tearer went down again, the broken sword burying itself in the veteran sergeant's thigh.

Rafen gasped as the Bloodchild's torso rippled, the muscles moving and shifting beneath the russet surface of his flesh in abhuman coils. The clone threw itself at Noxx, colliding with him as he tried to rise once again.

Noxx screamed as the clone's mouth opened wide and an arc of teeth clamped into the meat of his shoulder, new blood spitting in rich gushes across the stone floor. A grotesque sucking sounded as the clone-Marine drank deep.

The Blood Angel ran, in a rolling motion ducking low to snatch up one of the discarded hook swords. He leapt into the air and came down sharply; leading with the weapon's curved point. It found purchase in the clone's torso, in the same oozing wound where he had struck moments before.

The clone's back arched and it hooted with agony. Noxx was left to bleed upon the floor of the pit as it swept up clawed hands and gurgled through a mouthful of Astartes vitae. A hammer blow from an off-hand strike knocked Rafen off his feet and sent him sliding backward, his skull resonating with the impact. The strike was made with twice the power of every previous attack; it seemed as if the Bloodchild was energised by the power of the Black Rage, the boiling energy barely contained inside the clone's body.

He was dimly aware of shouting coming from the balconies above, but Rafen could not look away as the Bloodchild came stalking toward him in swift, loping steps. With each footfall, the clone's tanned skin seemed to bunch and tighten. Fingers curved into claws, growing extra knuckles and longer nails. The clone's mouth opened... *and it opened and opened*. The jaw distended, new rows of fangs emerging from the gums. It was mutating before his eyes, twisted by the force of the gene-curse forged into its very flesh.

It bellowed a word, forcing a single sound through a throat choked with thick liquid. *'Blood!'*

'Rafen!' A cry reached him from the galleries overhead and he spied Ajir up there, gesturing wildly. The Space Marine threw something toward him, a slab-sided shape spiralling down toward the pit. Rafen sprang to his feet and leapt, snatching the bolter out of the air. He landed, his finger tight on the trigger.

Without hesitation, Rafen marched the contents of the gun's sickle magazine up the Bloodchild's body, ripping it into pieces in a welter of crimson. The remains of the clone sagged to the stones, twitching and dying.

He could hear his heart pounding in his ears. 'Terra protect us,' he breathed, releasing the weapon to make the sign of the aquila with his blooded hands.

CHAPTER NINE

CAECUS STOOD RIGID as Dante turned away from the edge of the balcony to look directly at him. His legs were leaden, rooted to the spot. The elation he had tasted only moments ago was now ashes in his mouth, the perfect ideal of his Bloodchild warped and destroyed. *Failure. Another failure.*

'I was so close!' he whispered. 'I...'

When Dante spoke, it was a blade twisting in Caecus's heart. 'Apothecae Majoris, I have indulged this fantasy of yours beyond the point of rationality. You have shamed yourself, and shamed your Chapter with this monstrosity.' He pointed at the remains down in the fighting pit.

'I only wished to...' He gulped down air, finding it hard to speak. 'I was so certain...' Caecus cast around, looking for support and saw only measuring stares from the other Chapter Masters. He groped for an explanation, for any vague thread of justification. 'Perhaps I was too hasty. The woman Nyniq was correct, we should have run more trials before–'

'*Enough,*' said Dante. The Lord of the Blood Angels was furious, but it was a cold, cold fury tainted with disappointment and weariness. As he spoke, the full and complete scope of Caecus's error became clear to the Apothecae. 'You will remove yourself from this place and return to the Vitalis Citadel. The method of your censure will be decided on another day, but for now you will *do as I say.*' Dante's face darkened. 'Make no mistake, Caecus, for this is not open to interpretation. This is my command to you. End your pursuit of the replicae project and terminate all works connected to it with immediate effect.'

'I have several nascent Bloodchild clones still in situ,' he breathed, the admission forced from him by his master's steady, hard gaze.

'Destroy them all. No trace of these abominations are to remain.'

Caecus fell to one knee, desperate to find some words he could say to show contrition, to make Dante understand of the pure motives behind his vision. 'Lord, please...'

'No trace,' repeated the Chapter Master, with finality.

Bowing his head, Caecus found the energy to nod but do little else. His mind churned as he caught sight of the mess of flesh and bone that was all that remained of the first Bloodchild. It hardly seemed human now, just a smear of crimson and offal; the traces of a hideous, malformed freak. Dante was correct; he *had* shamed himself, with his hubris and his folly, and worse still he had tainted the sacred ground of the fortress-monastery by daring to bring the flawed clone into its hallowed halls. All this he was guilty of, made worse by the fact that the successor Chapter Masters had been there to witness it. *I have not only made myself a fool, but my master as well.*

Sentikan was speaking. 'Lord Dante. I think we understand now why you chose not to disclose this line of research. None of us wish to follow the path of the Raven Guard or the Space Wolves toward taking beasts into our ranks.'

'Perhaps more research is needed,' suggested Daggan.

'Perhaps,' continued Sentikan, 'but not here. And not today.' The Master of the Angels Sanguine turned his hooded face toward Dante. 'I submit that this matter must be, as you ordered, brought to a close.'

'Someone should be sent, to verify the conclusion of the experiments,' said Orloc.

Sentikan nodded toward his escort. 'I offer First Captain Rydae for this task.'

'Agreed,' said Dante. 'We have much to think on, cousins. I bid you return to your chambers and consider what you have seen and heard today. Tomorrow we will reconvene in the Grand Annex and bring the matter of this conclave to an end.'

'One way or another,' intoned Daggan, pivoting to study the Apothecae.

Caecus kept his eyes upon the marble floor, not daring to utter another word.

IN HIS CHAMBERS, Dante poured a measure of nightwine into a crystal goblet. Normally, the subtle aroma of the fine vintage would grant him a moment of focus, as his enhanced Astartes senses drew measures and depths from the liquor that ranged far beyond those of mortals; but today it was heavy and cloying. His ill mood robbed him of the manner to appreciate the drink; anger tainted it like oil.

There was a rap at the door and he snapped out a terse command. 'Enter.'

Mephiston hove into the room; even without the flayed-muscle pattern of his armour and the crystalline psyker hood about his neck, the Lord of Death still cut an impressive figure. He had come without being summoned; Mephiston knew his master's manner so well the words had not needed to be spoken. 'We have had better days than this one, my lord.'

'Indeed.' Dante's annoyance flared for an instant and the goblet let out a hiss of glass on glass as it cracked in his tightening grip. He slammed it down and grimaced. 'Tell me, my brother, is there any way in which we could have tainted the conclave more than we have?' Mephiston wisely elected not to answer, and his master went on. 'Curse Caecus for his thoughtlessness!'

'He will be punished for his disobedience.'

'Too late,' Dante growled. 'I should have seen it coming. The majoris has always been a stubborn one, and I, a fool to indulge him!' He shook his head. 'His imprudent display of that creature has done nothing but weaken us still further in the eyes of our successors!'

'Word will not spread of this,' said Mephiston. 'Brother Rydae knows what is expected. The magos woman, she will be silenced.'

'I am not concerned with the magos biologis.' Dante's brow furrowed. 'I am concerned with the disposition of our cousins.'

'Lord Seth,' said Mephiston, with ill-concealed scorn.

'And others,' noted his commander. He sighed. 'Perhaps I should not judge Caecus too harshly. I too am guilty of folly, for believing that our kindred would accede to the tithe.'

'What you ask is not unreasonable.'

Dante gave a hollow chuckle. 'Seth would certainly take issue with that statement, brother.' He became solemn again. 'I spent so much time in rumination, careful to hide our state from the galaxy at large, it never occurred to me that the blood of our blood would seek to turn it to their advantage.'

Mephiston took a moment before he answered. 'The Flesh Tearers are insubordinate, it is ever their way. It has been since the time of their first master, Amit. They will push to the very limit of censure and beyond if they believe they can do so. But my lord, do you truly believe that they will defy you when the moment of choice comes?'

Dante's answer was forestalled by another knock upon the door. He called out and Brother-Sergeant Rafen stood in the entranceway.

'Master,' he said with a bow, 'Lord Seth wishes to speak with you. Alone.'

Dante glanced at Mephiston and nodded. 'Perhaps I will have the answer to that question sooner than expected.'

MEPHISTON DID NOT meet Seth's eyes as they crossed paths. The psyker Librarian stepped past him and closed the doors to the chamber. The Flesh Tearer stood for a moment, taking in the scope of the room.

Dante was at the slatted window. The Baal sunset was rich with umber and orange tones. 'How is your sergeant, Noxx?' he asked, without preamble.

'It will take more that that to kill one of my men.'

Dante accepted this without comment. 'Would you care for something, cousin?' The Blood Angel indicated a tall flask of murky wine.

'Only a moment of your time, Dante,' he replied. 'And the opportunity to address you as an equal.'

'You have always been so, Seth,' said the other master.

'That is not true, and you know it.' He crossed the room, examining the elaborate rug beneath his feet; it was a rendition of the Ultima Segmentum, woven in millions of coloured threads. 'First Founding. My kinsmen cannot compare to that.'

'That has meaning, yes. But it does not diminish you.' Dante studied him. 'But I think you have never believed that, no matter how many times I have said it.'

Seth waved the comment away as if it meant nothing, but inwardly he was quietly seething. 'The subject of diminishment is a sensitive one for both of us, yes? Only I have lived with it for far longer than you. I've come to understand it, like one might come to know a constant enemy.'

Dante let out a slow breath. 'I am tiring of this circumlocution. You think I do not respect you. You are wrong.'

Beneath the silver implant, a nerve jerked in the Flesh Tearer's face. 'What I respect is the will of Terra. All the Flesh Tearers are is in the name of the spirit of Sanguinius and the Emperor of Mankind, for their glory. Can the Blood Angels say the same?'

'Of course,' Dante snapped. 'I would strike down a lesser man for daring to suggest otherwise!'

'And yet circumstances might be seen in certain lights to suggest exactly that. The glorification of a false Sanguinius by your men? A schism that nearly destroyed your Chapter? And now, this pitiful exhibition by your senior Apothecae? How are any of these things in service to the will of Terra, cousin?'

'I have given my explanations,' Dante folded his arms, growing colder in tone as he spoke. 'I have explained my reasoning.' His eyes narrowed. 'Do the same, Seth. Why are you here? What do you want of me?'

'I came at your summons, Lord of the Blood Angels.'

'*After* you first refused it. I say again; what do you want?'

Seth allowed a thin smile to emerge on his lips. 'I am here because I see a chance to serve the Golden Throne, by stemming the rot that threatens to eat out the heart of the Blood Angels. I wish to offer you an honourable solution, Dante.' He shook his head. 'Look at yourself, cousin. Look at where your hubris has led your Chapter. You are the great and mighty Blood Angels, First Founding, feared by many, revered by more... But you have allowed yourselves to grow lax upon that reputation. This business with the whelp Arkio and the Ruinous Powers... You should never have let it go so far! But you were too fixated on your own glory or on some other matter to see it until it was too late.' He saw a momentary flash of something like doubt on Dante's face and seized upon it. 'I know you. I know these are all questions you have already asked yourself.' Seth nodded. 'We are Adeptus Astartes. And our greatest fear is not death, but to be found wanting.'

Dante shot him a razored glare. 'You have questioned my leadership once today,' he replied. 'Do it again at your peril.'

Seth stiffened. 'I only give a voice to that which is obvious to all. And I say this to you now, master to master, one Son of the Great Angel to another... Do the honourable thing, Dante. Accept responsibility for what has happened and step down from the stewardship of Baal. Allow another Chapter to take the place of yours.'

A bark of humourless laughter broke from Dante's lips. 'You dare talk to me of hubris and then this is what you demand?'

'There are many who feel as I do,' Seth retorted. 'And more who will be swayed to that same thinking at the conclave tomorrow.'

Dante turned away, toward the window, and Seth sensed the anger rekindling in him. 'Despite what you may think of me, my age does not make me a senile, coddled old fool, and I will meet in the arena any warrior and ten of his brothers who argues that! Leave now, Flesh Tearer, and I will overlook this brazen attempt to wrest control from me as over-eagerness on your part!'

'Do you think I do this for myself?' Seth grated. 'This is not personal, Dante! I want only what is best for the Imperium!'

'Aye,' came the reply. 'I believe that you do. And for that reason alone, I will not have you and your delegation put aboard a ship and thrown back toward Cretacia.' The Master of the Blood Angels faced him once more; Dante's eyes were daggers. 'But if you remain in my chambers a moment longer, I fear you will test my patience beyond the limit.'

Seth hesitated, and then bowed low. 'We will speak tomorrow, then.'

Dante gave a slow nod. 'I do not doubt it.'

CAECUS WALKED AS a man would toward the gallows, lost inside himself, his thoughts in a ceaseless turmoil. Ahead of him, Brother-Captain Rydae strode with ready purpose, the Angel Sanguine with a bolt pistol holstered at his hip and a communicant helot trailing along behind. The Apothecary was aware of the woman Nyniq walking at his side; on his exit from the arena, a single look from him had been enough to silence her. He had no need to explain what had taken place in the fighting pit. His ashen expression spoke volumes.

The wide corridor rose slowly toward the upper tiers of the monastery, toward the southward-facing protected dome where the fortress's compliment of shuttles and atmosphere craft were garrisoned. Caecus imagined those walls closing in around him, the pressure in his thoughts betrayed by his morose mien and the clenching and unclenching of his long surgeon's fingers into tight fists.

Everything was slipping away from him. He admitted a truth to himself. For all the great efforts he had put into the exploration of the gene-flaw, nothing he had ever done toward eradicating the Black Rage and the Red

Thirst had so filled him with the sense of achievement he had in the work of the replicae. The researches of the sanguinary priesthood had been going on for millennia and achieved only little. For a questing mind like Caecus's, to be engaged in a work of that dimension ate at his resolve, knowing full well that he would never live to see a cure for the flaw even if he mirrored the age of Dante himself.

But the cloning... The quest to learn the art of replicae had been different, something that fired his imagination. The discoveries he made had grown and changed by the day, energising him with their tantalising potential. *He was so close!* Caecus could taste it on his lips like cool water. If he could only follow the process through to its logical conclusion, the fate of the Blood Angels would be secure. They would be able to recover from the grave losses incurred at Sabien, and every other battle to come. The replicae was something he could bring about, if only he had the time, the facilities, and the *trust* of his brethren.

A flash of resentment burned hard in him for a brief moment, the force of it directed at Dante; but then just as swiftly it ebbed, overwhelmed by the bleak certainty of his failure. *I was too hasty, and now I have paid for it with my reputation, my work, my future...*

The great burden of his fault weighed him down. He wondered what Fenn would say when he heard of the Chapter Master's orders; Caecus had no doubt his loyal serf would be distraught.

'Wait here,' said Rydae, leaving them at the edge of the hangar bay. He crossed quickly toward a rank of parked shuttlecraft, each of them in the varicoloured reds of the successor Chapters. A pilot-servitor bowed low and began a conversation with the First Captain, discussing the flight plan that would take them back to the Vitalis Citadel. Close by, an Arvus-class ship ran its engines at idle, hot exhaust gasses rippling the air.

Caecus railed at himself. I cannot go back in failure! Had it all been for nought? Every hour of work, every distant place scoured for scraps of information on the process of replicae?

'Wasted,' he whispered. 'All of it, wasted.'

'Not so,' said Nyniq, placing a gentle hand upon his forearm. 'Lord Caecus, you have done incredible things. You have come so far in so short a time! You should be proud of what you have achieved.'

He rounded on her. 'How can I have pride in the birth of abominations? I have done nothing but create monsters, horrible things forsaken by the light of the Emperor!'

'The Emperor... Emperor...' Nerves in Nyniq's face twitched in strange ways and her mouth moved in breathy gasps. She seemed to be having some peculiar form of seizure. 'For... Sake...' Her voice deepened, becoming basso and husky.

'What is this?' Caecus asked, frowning. He pulled her hand away from his arm, and the thin, pale wrist throbbed in his grip. The Apothecae tasted a strange, greasy tang in the air, mingling with the spent-fuel scent of the hangar bay.

Nyniq's eyes rolled up, showing whites, a light flecking of foam collecting at the corners of the woman's lips. Trembling, her face moved towards his. The blank orbs shimmered and moved, turning again to reveal new silver-black pupils lined with threads of gold.

Her lips pulled up in a parody of a smile, an odd mimicry of an expression Caecus had seen upon the face of her master, the tech-lord. 'My... friend,' she gurgled in a low whisper. 'Listen... to me.'

'Serpens?' Caecus could not have explained how he knew that the mind animating the woman was no longer her own, just that he was certain of it. Something about the change of the motion of the flesh upon the bones of her face, as if it were a thin mask of skin stretched over her master's features.

'Forgive me if you find this method of communication alarming, but it is the only way open to us at the moment.' It was Nyniq's tortured vocal chords forming the words, but the manner, the pace and meter of them, they were all those of Haran Serpens. 'The girl has been altered by me. She can function in this manner for a short time, although it is harmful to her.'

Caecus nodded, grotesquely fascinated. Blood was trickling from Nyniq's eyes in pink tears. The analytical part of his thought process wondered after how such a thing was possible. A vox device implanted in her brain-stem, perhaps? Or some form of psyker conditioning?

'I know what has transpired…' continued the breathy echo-voice. 'I am truly sorry, Lord Caecus. I see now that your blood, while potent and strong indeed, was not enough to stabilise the genetic structure of the Blood-child. The amalgam compound degrades before it can bind with the clone's cellular matrix.' Nyniq shook her head in exaggerated, puppeted motions.

'Then… we will never be able to overcome the replication errors.' Caecus said mournfully. 'My blood is pure, it is…' He broke off, suddenly silenced by a thought so shocking it struck the breath from him.

'Yes?' prompted the puppet-voice.

'If we could craft a solution of the amalgam based upon a sample of blood utterly untainted by genetic drift… It would be strong enough to resist the impression of any mutagenic factors…' He felt his heart pounding in a thunderous rhythm.

The reply was disordered and hissy. 'Such a thing does not exist.'

Dare I say it? Caecus looked down at his hands and saw they were trembling. 'It does,' he countered. 'Here, in this very fortress. The purest of blood, free of contamination, protected and unsullied. The preserved essence of Sanguinius himself, drawn from his body and guarded by Corbulo and the ranks of the sanguinary high priests...'

'They would not allow you to take it,'

The Apothecae's flesh chilled. 'I would only need the smallest amount... Only a drop...' He shook his head wildly. 'Impossible! I cannot! It would be a crime, a desecration!' Caecus shot a look toward Rydae; the Angel Sanguine officer was still in conversation with the pilot.

'A crime, a greater crime than allowing the Blood Angels to die out?' Nyniq's twisted voice came out in quiet sobs. 'Do you have a choice? This is your last chance, Caecus! You must, you must you must you must...' The woman stumbled away and broke into a sudden run. 'You must!' she bellowed, and ran screaming from him, toward the resting lighter.

He watched with horror as Nyniq beat her hands against herself as if she were trying to resist the sudden impulses that controlled her body. The girl stumbled into the wake of the lighter's rumbling exhaust nozzles and her flesh blackened; in a moment, she was a shrieking torch, staggering back and forth across the landing platform.

The attention of Rydae, the servitor and every other helot in the bay was instantly on the flaming figure.

The opportunity upon him, Caecus moved to the shadows, slipped away, back into the corridors of the fortress-monastery. He knew where he was heading, even as he tried to pretend he was as much a puppet of fate as the girl had been.

RAFEN BOWED HIS head slightly as Mephiston approached him in the hallway beyond the Silent Cloister. 'Lord,' he said.

The psyker's taut, hawkish face studied him; and as before, *as always*, the Librarian's penetrating gaze swept through him, searching him, measuring him. 'Where is your charge, lad?'

'Lord Seth and his delegation have retired the chambers granted to the Flesh Tearers in the northern tower,' he explained. 'Brother Puluo and Brother Corvus are attending them.'

'Acting as watchmen would be a more accurate description.' Mephiston's lip twisted and he was silent. Rafen found it hard to articulate, but ever since that moment in the Grand Annex, the psyker had seemed…distracted. 'Brother-sergeant, you will be honest with me.'

'My lord, such is your insight I doubt I could be otherwise.'

That drew the smallest of smiles, but then it faded again. 'Tell me the disposition of the brethren. You walk among them while I have been forced to remain with the other Chapter Masters. How does the business of this conclave sit with the men of the line?'

Rafen paused, formulating an answer. 'Each Blood Angel understands the seriousness of the situation.' And none more than I, he added silently. 'We will place ourselves wholly at our master's command, to follow whatever orders he deems fit.'

'What do you think of this… replicae?'

He suppressed a grimace. 'I do not know what that thing was in the fighting pit, lord. I know only that it was not an Astartes.'

'It was hard to kill?' Mephiston asked.

'I have faced worse.' He hesitated, a troubling fragment of recall rising to the surface. 'It…spoke to me, lord.'

The Lord of Death was listening intently. 'Indeed? What did it say?'

Rafen shook his head, dismissing the moment. 'Nothing of consequence. It matters little.'

Mephiston's gaze was steady. 'You would not have mentioned it if you believed that. Tell me, what words did the beast utter?'

'It called me *brother*. I felt for a moment as if… as if it knew me.'

'That is not possible. It was a *tabula rasa*, Rafen. An empty vessel awaiting commands, not like you or I.'

The Space Marine hesitated. 'I wish I could be certain of that, lord.' Rafen's mood grew dark. The shadows playing at the edges of his thoughts threatened to encroach once again. 'After what I witnessed today, after the fight and the conduct of our cousins, a foreboding fills me.' The words spilled out; he had kept the bleak musings to himself since Eritaen, but now he felt a compulsion to voice them, to confess in some fashion to Mephiston. 'After Arkio's death and the repatriation of the Spear of Telesto, I had hoped the wounds of the Chapter would heal.'

'And yours as well,' added the psyker, reading the thought in his eyes.

He nodded. 'The traitor Stele tried to sunder us, and almost succeeded. Now the unity of our bloodline is under threat from within as well as without, and we approach the abyss once again. The brink of conflict, of open dissent. What will be next, lord? Civil war?'

Mephiston shook his head. 'On the grail, I swear to you that will not come to pass, brother-sergeant. Master Dante will not allow it.'

'But if that is the destiny that the Emperor has for us…'

The Lord of Death turned away, gazing out through one of the windows. 'Only He knows the answer to that question, lad. And He will make Himself clear with the turning of the worlds.'

AMONG THE CRENULATED battlements of the fortress-monastery, a single cylindrical minaret stood out among the sharp faces of the towers of rusty stone that reached toward the night sky. Shorter than the rest, the upper tiers were no less impressive. Inlaid with mosaics of ruby and white gold, the decoration was protected from the abrasive storms of Baal by a molecule-thin layer of synthetic diamond. At dawn, the detail would catch the light of the rising red sun, but in the darkness, all that could be seen of them were glitters, fractions of reflection from the lamp-glow of the other towers that clustered about it like a cohort of bodyguards.

The minaret lacked the knife-like tip of its neighbours; instead, it ended in a sphere made of gently curved hex-cut blocks. Around the equator of the vast orb, a ring of oval stained-glass windows looked out in every direction. The dim haze of photonic candles flickered behind them.

The Chapel of the Red Grail was silent within, the brothers who attended it at the evening prayer in the chambers far below. Only the guardians remained, the two machine helots-at-arms in the alcoves at the northern and southern ends of the chamber. Each of them rested down upon one knee, bowing toward the centre of the open space. They were fabricated from metal and ceramite, a thickset approximation of a man-shape cut to resemble an angel at rest. Steel wings of razored feathers were eternally folded at their backs. Their heads were the hollowed-out stone faces of old statues, within them remnants of brain meat and delicate mechanics programmed to ceaselessly watch over the chapel environs. Where men would have had arms, these cyborg slaves had drum-fed bolters, with ornate muzzles and flash guards fashioned in the shape of hands. They were at rest, palms together, as if in prayer.

The mid-level of the chapel was without walls, only a forest of mica-laced granite pillars arranged in arrows to support the upper levels of the spherical construction.

Both guardians inclined their heads toward the shallow dais that was the room's only other feature. Cut from a huge slab of cultured ruby the size of a Rhino troop transporter, the disc-shaped podium glittered with the light spill from the candle rigs. A pillar of faint, blue-white radiance reached down from a concealed null-field emitter hidden in the ceiling; and resting in the grip of that envelope of energy, floating without apparent means of support, was the Red Grail.

In the western alcove, the place of arrival, part of the tessellated floor retreated into itself to allow a rising wave of steps to emerge. Brother Caecus climbed to the top and tasted the blood in the air immediately. He halted and savoured it.

The texture, the invisible aurora of the vitae was rich and heady. A deep, burned copper, it filled his Astartes-strong senses and threatened to make his head swim. His eyes went to the gleaming chalice; there was the cup that had held the blood of his primarch, the contents kept potent by a process of constant exsanguination and exchange. Upon the death of their liege-lord, the san-guinary high priests of the Blood Angels had taken on the holy duty of ensuring that his vitae would never be allowed to perish along with him. His blood kept safe in their very flesh, for ten thousand years the priests had ritually injected and returned the blood of Sanguinius in an endless cycle, bolstering it, never letting it fade.

The Red Grail was the very chalice that had captured the first drops of the primarch's spilled blood, and it was said that it still retained some untouched elements of that first spilling by some arcane manner of technology lost to the ages. It was no lie to say that a measure of Sanguinius would remain captured in that sacred cup for all eternity.

His hands were trembling as Caecus walked across the chapel. The guardians rose smoothly upon their mechanical legs and turned to face him, opening their hands in a gesture that seemed to offer him greeting; but the black maws in their palms betrayed the truth. Inset about the edge of the chamber were a line of glassy tiles. Anyone who crossed that border without due sanction forfeited their life. The machine-helots would kill him where he stood if he was a transgressor.

But he was Caecus, brother of the priesthood, the great and respected Apothecae Majoris, and in the dim recesses of their conditioned organic brains the guardians recognised him as one whose presence here was not prohibited…. only *uncommon*. A mechanical analogue of mild confusion was shared by the twin angels and they hesitated, exchanging clock cycles to co-process this information, unsure of how to proceed. By the letter of Chapter law, in this place Caecus held rank only second to Brother Corbulo; and yet in decades he had not set foot here, not engaged in any of the blood-transfer rituals. In addition, no such rites were scheduled to take place at this time. The helots chattered at each other in machine code, unable to decide what action to take.

Caecus reached the ruby dais and drew the sampler vial from a pocket in the cuff of his robes. He took a wary step up on to the flat stage and found himself staring into the Red Grail, into the crimson fluid there trembling in rippling rings. This close to the ancient artefact, the dampening effect of the null-field was negligible. The radiant power of the chalice crept over Caecus and made his muscles tighten. In combat, when the Red Grail was brought in Corbulo's hands to the warriors upon the battlefield, the mere presence of the cup caused men to redouble their efforts. The sheer force of history within this great object touched the threads of the primarch's legacy in every Blood Angel who gazed upon it. It strengthened them, reminded them of who and what they were.

This enrapture came upon Caecus now, as he gingerly reached out with the vial and siphoned a tiny measure from the contents of the cup. His hands were shaking so much he feared he might drop the glass capsule; but at the same moment he was seized by a powerful will to finish the deed. In a rush, the certainty he had felt at the beginning of his odyssey returned to him, banishing his black and damning mood. I am doing the right thing, he told himself, his teeth baring. Dante will see that. I will show him, I will show them all.

He rocked back and stepped down, basking in the glow of the Red Grail, letting it wash over him. Caecus gripped the vial in his hands, his doubts and fears held at bay. He felt as if he could fight a thousand foes, defeat any challenge–

'Majoris!'

The voice was strident and harsh. Caecus blinked in the lamplight and saw a figure in half-crimson, half-ebon power armour. *Rydae.*

The Angel Sanguine took a step from the entrance alcove, drawing the attention of the guardians. 'I followed you,' he explained. 'Your attempt to slip away unseen failed, Caecus.' Rydae shook his head. 'Your behaviour is inexcusable. Lord Dante will hear of this.'

Caecus advanced toward the other Space Marine, driven by a sudden anger. 'You dare to judge me, whelp? You know nothing of my struggles or the calling the primarch granted me!'

'Nevertheless, you have your orders…' Rydae broke off, noticing the vial for the first time. 'What is that?' Shock entered his voice. 'In the Angel's name, what have you taken?' The Sanguine came forward and grabbed at Caecus's arm. 'You cannot–'

The anger churning inside him found sudden release and Caecus backhanded Rydae, slamming his fist into the Space Marine's helmet. Caught off-guard, the

Astartes shifted with the blow toward the ruby dais. 'You have no right to judge me!' Caecus bellowed. 'None of you have the right!' He struck out again and again, scarring his knuckles on the other warrior's armour, his blows ringing against the ceramite. Each impact felt stronger, better, more satisfying than the last.

'Majoris, do not force me to injure you!' The Angel Sanguine weathered the impacts without fighting back. 'Stop this at once.'

'Stop? *Stop?*' Caecus's voice climbed in pitch. He drew strength from the presence of the grail and spat out a laugh. 'I have come too far to stop now, don't you understand? I am beyond the point of no return! Nothing must halt me!'

Rydae made an inelegant motion, a broad blow that would have knocked the Apothecary to the floor, but Caecus pivoted and gave the Space Marine a vicious shove, taking the other man's balance. The captain's boot scraped backward across the line of glass tiles, bringing the watchful machine-helots to face him. Before he could cry out, the guardians performed their programmed duty. As one, they opened their hands and struck down Rydae with a ripping cascade of bolt fire.

Caecus stumbled away from the discharge, reeling with the stink of new, hot blood amid the chamber's air of ancient vitae.

CHAPTER TEN

THE TOLLING OF the warning bell drew Rafen to the valetudinarium on the atrium tier. He was close, intent on
returning to the barracks for the day's late meal when
the sound reached him. It was no battle drill, no surprise
practice. No one would dare to do such a thing while the
conclave was in residence at the fortress.

He entered and found Brother Corbulo, his white duty
robes flecked with a different kind of red than the crimson bands about his shoulders. The fresh stink of
Astartes blood set off a tumble of sense-memory, of
battles and brethren lost. Rafen dismissed the thoughts
and strode forward. 'Are you injured, lord?'

Corbulo turned his severe countenance toward him.
'Not this day, Rafen.' He gave a nod toward a windowed medicae cell. Inside, Apothecaries and serfs
worked carefully to remove planes of red and black
armour from a torso that lay twisted upon a support
frame.

Rafen recognised the armour and the combat honours affixed to it from the first assemblage of the gathering. 'Rydae?' The Astartes had been mortally wounded; the cratered impact locations of multiple point-blank bolt shots marred every surface of the wargear. Corbulo gave a grave nod.

The question of *how* and *why* was caught in his throat for long seconds, before the tramp of boots announced the arrival of more men drawn by the lowing bell. At their head, the hooded Lord Sentikan came silently into the room and halted with a jerk. Rafen could not see his face, but he heard the thin intake of breath through the Chapter Master's lips.

'Explain this to me,' said the Angel Sanguine. The cold control of his utterance gave Rafen pause.

Corbulo exhaled. 'An alarm from the Chapel of the Red Grail drew me to investigate, lord. When I arrived, I found Brother-Captain Rydae upon the floor. He had apparently crossed the line of censure and walked directly into the weapons of the gun-servitors protecting the sacred relic.'

'He would do no such thing,' Sentikan replied icily. 'We respect the prohibitions of the Blood Angels! He would not enter the chapel without permission!'

'To do such a thing without the company of a sanctioned priest is death,' said Rafen. 'He would have known that.'

Sentikan shot a look at one of his escorts as the other Space Marine approached. 'Master, Lord Dante and his Librarian are here. Others are on their way.' He gestured at the ceiling and the vox-relays in the walls. 'The bell, sir. They have all heard the bell.'

Belatedly, Corbulo spoke a command phrase into a vox device about his wrist and the tolling ceased. Sentikan pushed past him to glare through the windowed wall of the medicae cell. 'What are they doing?' he demanded. For the first time, Rafen heard open anger from the Sanguine Lord.

'Sentikan,' Dante entered, his face set in a scowl. 'I–'

The Angel Sanguine turned about and glared at his fellow master. 'You will have your Apothecaries cease their work immediately, cousin, or I will tear them limb from limb!'

Dante did not hesitate, and nodded to Corbulo. 'Do as he says.'

'Aye, lord.' The Blood Angel slipped through the iris door and into the chamber.

'He might still be alive, perhaps in a healing trance,' began Rafen. 'They could save his life.'

'No,' Mephiston shook his head, his gaze distant. 'Brother Rydae is gone. His spirit has left his body to join the Great Angel.'

Sentikan took a warning step toward the psyker. 'If I suspect you are using your witchsight to peer into the flesh of my kinsman, your eyes will be cut from your head, Librarian!'

The snarling rebuke gave Mephiston a moment's pause. 'I thought only to see the mirror of his final thoughts. Perhaps, to learn what befell him.'

Dante shook his head and placed a hand on his comrade's arm. 'It is not our place to disturb the Sanguine's dead.'

'No one touches the flesh of our fallen,' growled Sentikan. 'Unless he wishes to join them.'

Rafen glanced back at the body. *The hooded faces, the helmets they never removed.* For a brief moment, he wondered again what it was that the Angels Sanguine did not want the rest of the galaxy to see of them.

Sentikan spoke once more. 'I will retire to the battle cruiser *Unseen* with Rydae's body. When I return tomorrow, you will have an explanation for my loss, Dante.'

The Master of the Blood Angels nodded. 'Of course. Cousin, know that I am as shocked by this incident as you are.'

The Angel Sanguine watched him for a moment. 'But now you will ask me not to speak of this, yes? For fear that it will widen the cracks of dissent among the successors?'

'Too late for that.' Dante's answer never came; another voice offered a scowl in reply instead, as more Astartes forced their way into the atrium tier. The Flesh Tearers had arrived, and any chance of silence on this matter fled before them.

CAECUS SENSED IT the moment the drop-ramp opened, the very instant the frosted air drifted into the cabin of the flyer. The keening engines echoed inside the bartizan, but there was no other sound. No voices, no footsteps.

No Fenn, waiting as he always did, at the foot of the landing pad. Caecus drew his robes in tightly around him and ventured out into the hangar, one hand a tight fist around the precious, precious vial. The Apothecae sniffed at the cold, his breath steaming into a haze of vapour. He paused, rocking on his heels. A mixture of scents sent warning signals through his brain; Caecus detected faint traces of chemical preservatives, of fractionating fluid and battery acids. There were other smells as well. Perhaps cordite. Spent cordite and fresh blood. It was difficult to sift though the jumble of them all.

He walked on, into the corridors of the Vitalis Citadel, wary of every shadowed corner, of the silence that fell each time he stopped and held his breath. The complex had a beat of life to it, the motion and sound of the works taking place within its walls familiar – and in its own way, oddly comforting. There was none of that now, though. The strange, ominous quiet was invasive. Caecus listened to his own shallow breathing to be sure that he hadn't simply been struck deaf.

At a lectern in the main atrium he tried the machine-call vox, paging Fenn, then the laboratorium, then the general control chambers on the levels above. He waited a quarter hour there, but no one answered him.

A hundred different scenarios for what could have happened reeled through his thoughts. Had Dante activated some sort of failsafe plan after the business in the fighting pit, eradicating everything inside the building in a fit of fury? Was there a containment breach in one of the other laboratoria, something that had caused an immediate lockdown?

The flyer was still out on the pad; he had the opportunity, if he wished to take it. He could leave, return to the fortress-monastery. Admit to what had happened. Take responsibility for it. Caecus glanced at the vial in his hand. 'But that would be to accept failure.' He thought of the woman Nyniq. She had said those words to him, and he had reacted with ferocity. *Where was that zeal now?* He could feel the twin draws upon his will, one toward the dark and melancholy path, the other toward shrill and angry certainty. He knew without doubt that to turn back now would mean death. He had not lied to Rydae when he told him he had gone beyond the point of no return. Caecus held up the capsule and the light of the biolumes shimmered through the fluid within. *There. There is my zeal, made manifest.*

He threw a last glance over his shoulder. Dante would send men after him, if he had not already. His only hope of redemption lay below his feet, in the heart of the replicae laboratorium.

The bank of brass elevators in the atrium ignored his summons. With care, Caecus took to the spiralling double staircase that ran down the length of the tower, twisting over itself in mimicry of a human genetic helix.

He had only descended a dozen tiers when he heard the noise filter up from below; the clatter of a bolter on full automatic fire, suddenly cut short by a piercing scream.

LORD SETH BARGED past Mephiston, but the psyker blocked the passage of Brother-Captain Gorn. The lord of the Flesh Tearers walked to the medicae cell and gave it a long look.

Rafen saw Puluo at the entrance and moved to his side. 'You were supposed to keep him in his quarters.'

The Space Marine hung his head. 'He is a Chapter Master, lord. Short of putting a gun to him, how could I stop him from exercising his will?'

The sergeant gave a weary nod; Puluo was not to blame, but Seth's intervention here and now would only make this situation worse.

'You would have kept this from us?' Seth demanded of Dante. 'A Space Marine murdered in this very fortress?'

'No one has spoken of murder,' retorted Mephiston. 'This may be a tragic accident, and no more.'

Seth ignored the interruption and concentrated on the Chapter Master. 'You would have concealed it, just as you tried to hide the replicae?' He shook his head. 'I am disappointed in you more and more, Blood Angel.'

'I hide nothing,' Dante retorted. 'I only seek calm in the face of this terrible incident, so that we can learn the full scope of it.' He glared at Seth. 'There are others who will try to turn it to their own ends.'

'You accuse me?' said the Flesh Tearer. 'I see no need to cast blame about! This atrocity took place on your world, Dante. You hold responsibility for it!'

'You tell me nothing I do not already know,' came the reply. 'This will be resolved, have no doubt of it.' The

Chapter Master's eyes narrowed. 'But I say that any who seize upon this misfortune to aggrandize themselves cheapen the honour of every Astartes here!' Sentikan said nothing, watching the two men face off against one another.

Rafen felt a presence at his shoulder and turned to face Mephiston. The psyker spoke in low tones. 'The magos woman, Nyniq. She killed herself on the hangar deck. The serfs there report that Caecus and Rydae both disappeared in the confusion.'

He frowned. 'Then Caecus never left for the citadel?'

Mephiston shook his head. 'A flyer departed the tertiary hanger port in eastern shield wall. Caecus's signet was given as authority for the launch.'

He killed Rydae and fled? The conclusion leapt to the front of his mind, hard and damning. But to do such a thing would be madness!

The psyker nodded, and Rafen wondered if he was tracing the pattern of his surface thoughts. 'It is imperative the Apothecae Majoris follows the orders of Commander Dante to the letter, brother-sergeant, and imperative we learn if he had a part in this… Take your squad and go to the Vitalis Citadel. See to it.'

'As you command,'

'Wait,' snapped Seth, stepping closer, catching the end of their conversation. 'Don't think you can cloud this, Mephiston! If there is investigation to be done, then it must be known to all of us! It must be transparent.'

'This is our world, as you pointed out, lord,' Mephiston noted. 'As such, it is the responsibility of the Blood Angels to keep watch over it.'

'That will not be enough,' Seth insisted, glancing at Sentikan. 'Don't you agree?' The Angel Sanguine did not speak, only nodded once.

'My men will deal with this,' insisted Dante.

'Of course,' Seth snapped, 'but they will do it alongside *mine*.' He smiled coldly, and threw a gesture toward Captain Gorn. 'Consider it an offer to share the load.'

HE HAD NO weapon but himself. He was a scientist, a combatant in battles of different scope than the brutal cut and thrust of fighting; but Caecus had once been a battle-brother as well. He had fought and shed blood in the name of Sanguinius and the Emperor, on warzone worlds in ork space and a dozen Chaos-blighted hells all across the Ultima Segmentum. He could summon the will to do killing, if it was required of him, but in truth he had not walked a battlefield in many decades.

Still; he was Adeptus Astartes. It was in his meat and marrow to be a warrior, no matter how dulled by inaction the blade of his skills might be.

The sounds drew him in, curiosity taking the lead. Caecus had yet to see a single other inhabitant of the citadel. He had come across strange debris on the stairs and the landings of some of the tiers. A scattering of pict slates, fallen as if dropped in haste; torn pieces of a Chapter serf's robes; and here, on this level, strewn casings from bolter rounds, the tarnished electrum glittering dully.

He bent and chose one of them at random, sniffing at it. The cordite stink was still strong. This shot had been discharged recently. He rolled it between his fingers. It was a pistol-gauge round, not the kind of shell a gun-servitor would have carried in its ammunition hoppers. Caecus searched a while for bullet impacts or marks from ricochets upon the stone walls, but found none.

He moved gingerly into the tier, edging around the first open door he found. The room was a minor research chamber, dedicated to the classification and fractionation of blood samples. It was one of many set to such a task in the citadel, one more small cog in the turning labour of the Chapter's study of the gene-flaw. Shattered cubes of armourglass, tiny as pebbles, were gathered at the feet of broken centrifuges. Storage jars and spinner tubes lay open and empty, some with streaks of red within, but most of them drained of their contents.

The blood; all the blood was gone.

Caecus then saw a shape in an untidy heap before a smashed cogitator console. A body. The first sign of life – *of death* – he had encountered since he returned. Stepping over the tiled flooring, taking care not to place his footing in among the broken glass fragments, the Apothecary sank low, to his haunches. Closer now, and he could see that the corpse was in the robes of a mid-ranking Chapter serf.

Old proficiency came back to him with automatic action. He studied the body, checking for anything that could be a booby trap, perhaps an explosive device with a contact trigger beneath the corpse, or a tripwire. In the course of this he got a good look at the dead man. The epidermis of his face was gone, ripped clean away, and the flesh beneath was pallid like meat boiled too long in the pot. More details became clear. There were what had to be claw marks upon the arms and torso, rents in the cloth of the robes that could only have come from slashing wounds.

But little blood. Very little blood at all, and then only in the lines of drag marks where the corpse had been pulled from the doorway to here, into the centre of the room.

Caecus froze. *The centre of the room.* What point was there to make a kill, be done with it, and then move it to here, in plain sight?

Trap.

From the deep shadows behind the fractionator columns came a thin thread of red, the targeting laser dancing as it settled upon a point between Caecus's eyes.

'Righteousness is our shield,' intoned a voice. 'Faith our armour...' He heard the snap of a safety catch as it released. 'And what else? Say the words.'

The Apothecae was very careful not to move. 'Hatred. Hatred is our weapon,' he said, completing the fragment of the Alchonis Axiom.

At once the targeting beam dropped away. 'Terra's bane. I thought you were one of them.' A figure emerged from the darkness clutching a gun, and Caecus recognised the man, one of the lower-ranked Apothecae Minoris.

'Brother Leonon?'

The Blood Angel hesitated. 'Majoris? Majoris, is that you? Forgive me, I did not recognise you...' He trailed off and gestured to a roughly-applied bandage across his face. 'My sight was impaired. The glass...' He indicated the floor. 'I have not been able to remove all of the fragments from my eyes.'

'Leonon, what has happened here?' Caecus straightened, slipping into the mode of seniority he habitually wore in the halls of the citadel. 'What was that business with the axiom?'

'They don't seem to have the intelligence for anything more than a few words,' he husked. 'They can look like us from a distance. I had to be certain.' Leonon shook his head. 'I saw men kill one another because they were unsure.'

A horrifying awareness was forming in Caecus's mind, his gut tightening with a sense of revulsion, of self-loathing; and perhaps, of fear. 'Where are the staff?'

'All dead, or if not they are isolated and waiting for rescue as I was.' Leonon blinked owlishly at him with his one good eye. 'How many men did you bring with you? How did you get past them?'

Caecus ignored the questions and nodded at the dead serf. 'Who did this?'

The next word from the Blood Angel's lips made his heart tighten in his chest. 'Mutants.' Leonon shook his head. 'I saw only the one, but there must be several of them. How else could the citadel be silenced so quickly?'

In his mind's eye, Caecus relived that horrific moment in the arena, when the Bloodchild's perfectly sculpted form went into flux. He remembered the festoons of teeth, the warped limbs and other aberrations in the failed clones that he had terminated throughout the length of his work. This was far worse than one freak gunned down in front of the Chapter Master. If the iterations in the embryo chambers had suffered some kind of spontaneous mass metamorphosis, there might be dozens of deviant creatures running loose in the complex.

He thought of Fenn and Serpens. Were they already dead, torn apart by maddened clones with no control over their baser natures? He struggled to keep himself in check, fighting the urge to curse in front of the Space Marine. 'I must continue onward,' he told Leonon. 'To the secure tiers. The source of this… concern is there.'

The other Apothecary's face set grimly. 'It is a charnel house down there, majoris. Those things are feasting. I heard them.'

'This is an order!' he snapped, his temper rising. 'You will come with me!' From the corner of his eye, Caecus saw a shadow move slightly, against the glow of the chamber's biolumes.

Leonon had seen it too, and was turning, bringing up the bolt pistol. The shadow disconnected from the rest of the dimness and crossed the chamber in one quick, loping surge. It moved so fast that Caecus was left with only impressions of it, a sheet of talons and a mouth like a lamprey, eyes red as ruby. Leonon's gun was cut from him and Caecus saw only the red beam of the laser streaking around and about as it spun away, out into the darkened corridor. The attacker ignored him and ripped across the room, dragging the Apothecae Minoris with it, spinning Leonon about and savagely ripping into the Blood Angel's flesh. The creature struck in the manner of a sand shark, biting down with its distended jaw and shaking furiously, tearing the flesh to ribbons.

Caecus stumbled after the lost pistol, sickened by the gargling scream of the Space Marine as the mutant crushed his throat and choked him on his own blood. Falling to his knees, he found the weapon on the stone floor. A length of Leonon's forearm and hand were still connected to the grip, the severed end a stream of red rags. He ripped the detached limb away and took the bolt pistol, taking aim back through the open door. The mutant looked up from the twitching body of the Minoris, face painted crimson with viscera.

Caecus fired, the first round sparking off the tiles, the next shots impacting hard in the torso and abdomen. The creature howled, and it sounded almost like a man.

The pistol made a hollow snapping sound and the mechanism stalled in his grip. The Blood Angel cursed and grabbed the slide with his other hand, working at the breech; the gun was fouled, a bolt cartridge caught upright in the ejector port like a stove pipe.

The blood-rimed fiend did not come for him. It watched, cocking its head. Then, with a sickening lurch, it began to retch, shoulders twitching and rocking. After a moment the creature spat a thick bolus of oily vomit on to the tiles and gave a wheeze.

Caecus heard the jammed shell ring as it flew free and the gun snapped back to the ready. The mutant did not wait. With one hand of grotesquely misshapen talon-fingers, it pierced the chest of Brother Leonon and grabbed him by the cage of his ribs. On coiled, rippling muscles it leapt at the ceiling, clawing open a ventilation duct set into the stone roof. It flowed into the space, compacting itself to fit into the narrow space, dragging Leonon as it went. Caecus heard the Space Marine's bones fracture and snap, as it pulled the Apothecae Minoris into the vent with such force that his robes were torn away.

Rattling echoes grew fainter and fainter as the thing fled from the room along the shaft, finally becoming silence once again. In the pool of liquid ejecta, objects glittered and Caecus ventured closer, daring to take a look. Amid the glutinous blood-laced bile there were two distorted discs of metal, resembling the caps of fungal growths. The Apothecae nudged one with his finger. It steamed slightly, still warm with the heat of passage through the mutant's flesh. Caecus had a flash of memory from his service as a battlefield medicae. He had seen the same thing many times when called upon to extract spent rounds from his injured brethren, the distended heads of bullets flattened by impact with dense flesh.

He got back to his feet, checked the pistol once again, and then resumed his passage along the downward spiral.

THE THRUSTERS FLARING at maximum output, the Thunderhawk plunged toward the ice fields at near-hypersonic velocity, speed bleeding off in a cherry glow about the wings as the transport aircraft entered the terminal phase of its suborbital flight from the fortress-monastery. Through the viewing slits in the hull, the polar zone was a ghost-grey in the washed-out light reflected from Baal Prime. The first moon was high in the sky, its larger sister still low to the horizon, hidden behind the thick bands of dust clouds.

Rafen looked away. He felt more at ease now he was back in his wargear. After everything that had transpired since the return from Eritaen, some part of him had longed for the cool familiarity of his battle armour about his body. Now so sheathed, he felt his confidence strengthen. All the politicking and talk of the conclave was anathema to him; he longed for the simple equations of battle. His armour was an old friend, a comrade. Encased within it, Rafen once more became the red blade of the Emperor, ready to do His bidding.

The vox-bead in his ear chimed and he inclined his head. 'Speak.'

'Corvus, lord,' said the other Space Marine, transmitting from the Thunderhawk's flight deck. 'No reply to the cogitator's interrogation signal. The citadel's communicants do not answer. Something is amiss.'

Rafen accepted this, musing. When they were closer, they might be able to pick up signals from hand-held short-range vox-units; but then again the Vitalis Citadel was built into a cairn of dense rock, which meant that anyone attempting to communicate from the lower tiers would not be heard at all. 'Place the summons on auto-repeat, brother. Then return to the drop bay and be ready for deployment.'

'Should we inform the fortress?'

'Not yet. Not until we have something definite to report. Lord Dante has enough to occupy him.'

'Aye, brother-sergeant.' Corvus's voice faded away and Rafen became aware of someone standing in the gangway down the middle of the transport's troop compartment. He shifted in his acceleration couch.

'Rafen,' began Captain Gorn, 'a moment of your time before we arrive at the target.' The officer had his helmet in the crook of his arm and showed the Blood Angel a mirthless smile. 'Deploy your men in a staggered twin-tear formation after touchdown, and I will move with Brother-Sergeant Noxx–'

He held up an armoured hand to halt the Flesh Tearer's speech. 'Your pardon, lord, but there appears to have been some miscommunication. This sortie is under my command. Lord Dante himself authorised it.'

Gorn bristled. 'Does a captain's rank mean nothing to you?'

'Your rank has no bearing upon this, *sir*.' He put a hard emphasis on the honorific. 'This is Baal. And no mission progresses upon her surface that is not led by a Blood Angel.' He made a show of glancing around. 'I appear to be the ranking Astartes of that Chapter here present.'

Irritation tugged at the corner of the captain's lip, but then he smothered it with another false smile. 'As you wish. We are your guests, after all. However, perhaps you will accept my tactical counsel, should the situation require it?'

'Perhaps,' allowed Rafen. 'But this is not Eritaen. This is not a combat zone.' The Thunderhawk shuddered through a thermal and the deck tilted. Gorn was about to offer some rejoinder, but Rafen beat him to the punch. 'We have entered the landing phase, brother-captain. You should return to your acceleration couch. The air over the pole can be quite changeable.' As if to underline his point for him, the transport dropped sharply through a pocket of turbulence.

Gorn walked away, back to where Sergeant Noxx and his squad were already strapped in. He leaned close to his men to exchange sullen words with them.

Rafen's vox chimed once more, this time with a rune on his helmet display indicating a signal on discreet channel. 'He does not look happy,' said Turcio. 'I wouldn't be surprised if Gorn's men cut from us the moment our boots touch rock.'

'Respect the rank, if not the warrior, brother,' he replied. 'As for the good captain's happiness, that is an issue I don't consider to be important.'

Turcio was two racks behind him, likewise sealed into his armour so that no other man would hear their conversation. 'Why did the master even agree to let them accompany us? They have no business in the citadel.'

Rafen frowned behind his breather grille. 'Lord Dante has his own troubles to address. We are merely his instruments.'

'*Ave Imperator*, then,' said Turcio.

'Indeed,' nodded the sergeant, drawing into his own thoughts as the Thunderhawk drew nearer to their destination.

THE CLOSER CAECUS came to the replicae laboratorium, the worse it became. At first he found the odd body part, or severed limb whitened through blood loss; pieces of people discarded by their killers, lying on the broad bands of the stone staircase. The debris left behind by a pack of predators.

Then there were the levels he passed without daring to investigate them further. Through the doors that led into their depths there were the occasional sounds of motion, and once a faint, peculiar mewling. At the forty-seventh tier he was forced to constrict nerves in his nostrils because of the death-stink that wafted over him. He paused to listen and heard a lapping sound, removed some distance down a radial corridor. There were no lights down there, but the floor glistened in the spill from the stairwell as if it were slick with wetness.

The bolt pistol only had three more rounds remaining in the magazine. He moved, spiralling, descending.

THE HEAVY PRESSURE doors were open, and beyond the actinic blue lights of the purification antechamber were flickering and buzzing. The guard cages on the walls were open pits in the carved rock, the bands of metal across them twisted away. Pieces of iron and stained brass littered the floor; of the gun-servitors there was nothing else. The floor was sticky and it dragged at Caecus's sandals as he walked slowly from the stairwell, the bolt pistol in a two-handed grip. The crimson thread of the targeting beam reached out in front of him, fingering the walls.

He hesitated on the threshold, kneading the gun. There could be no turning back now.

Inside, the laboratorium was red. Blood covered every surface. It dripped in places from the ceiling and collected in shallow pools. Caecus felt the odour of it penetrating his flesh, tasted the metallic flavour on his tongue with every breath he took. He was at once sickened by the sight; but there was a fraction of him, a piece of the primal Blood Angel soul that savoured the sinister fragrance that lay thick in the air. The Apothecae recalled the sensation that the Red Grail had briefly instilled in him; this was a sense of the same thing, but less marshalled, more feral.

He blinked, forcing away the dark thoughts, and took stock of the devastation. Everything was wrecked. Every device, every storage cylinder, every servitor and cogitator, all of them torn to pieces as if a hurricane had been contained within the chamber and allowed to expend its fury upon them. Across the length of the laboratorium, he saw that the door to the replicae chamber was hanging open at an angle, the upper hinge torn off by some incredible force. He approached, stepping into the compartment. It was gloomy with inky shadows and Caecus forced his occulobe implant to adjust his vision spectrum. His eyes prickled and a shape became clear: a man of his size and stature.

The tech-lord stood at a console examining a piece of torn meat with casual indifference. He discarded it and turned as Caecus approached, with no more concern than a host welcoming a visitor into his parlour. He inclined his head. 'Ah, majoris. I'm pleased you came. I confess, I suspected you would falter before this point.' A smile drew across those misshapen lips. 'It pleases me I was mistaken.' His gait seemed different, hunched somehow, as if a great weight were upon his back.

Caecus saw the gestation capsules for the clones, every one of them shattered from the inside, every one of them empty. 'You did this,' he husked, the words that had been pressing at his lips emerging in a dry rush.

'I merely helped the process down a road it was already upon.' The smile grew a little more. 'I am sorry to tell you that for all your hard work, you were doomed to fail just as Corax did.' He chuckled, as if at a private joke. 'But then Corax was always a fool.'

'Serpens!' Caecus snarled his name in accusation, as the other man shrugged off the coat over his shoulders, letting it drop into a heap. 'I trusted you! What purpose was there to this?' He blinked. 'My staff... Leonon... Fenn?'

'I would be surprised if they were not all dead by now. The Bloodfiends are such brutal and efficient killers, don't you agree?' Something moved at his back, clicking and unfolding.

'Bloodfiend?'

He got an indulgent nod in return. 'I like that name better.'

Caecus twitched, his self-control cracking beneath the strain. He glanced at the gun, still gripped in his hand, as if he had forgotten it was there. The Apothecae took aim. 'I will kill you for this!'

'Don't you want to know why?' The man reached his long, bony fingers up to his face and played with the skin there, pulling at it, pinching at the cheekbones and the line of the jaw. 'You are a scientist, Caecus. Cause and effect, reason and process, these are all things at the cornerstone of your self. Can you really kill me without understanding why this happened?' There came a tearing noise and parts of the magos's face peeled away in fatty strips, dropping to the floor where they began to deliquesce. Caecus saw other flesh beneath, tight upon a hard-lined and ancient skull.

'Speak, then, Serpens!' he shouted. 'Confess if you must!'

Another laugh escaped him, the register shifting to a deep, bone-crack dry tonality. 'I have been Haran Serpens for a time. But he is ill-fitting, tight about my breeches. I tire of him.' The ripping went on, and the skin flayed itself. A white gale of stringy hair emerged and fell about the man's shoulders. He took a step closer, so that the flickering lights of the chamber could better illuminate him. 'Do you know me, Brother Caecus? Think now. I imagine you recall my name.' Brass splines sighed and extended from behind him, and with a start the Apothecae Majoris realised that what he had thought to be the play of shadows was actually a spidery contraption upon the impostor's shoulders. 'I know you and all your kin,' he continued. 'I walked the same earth as your primarch. I once looked him in the face.' He laughed openly. 'What a poor distillate of his grandeur you are these days. He would be ashamed.'

'Do not speak of Sanguinius, pretender!' Caecus gasped. 'Do not utter his... his name...' The heat in his blood instantly flashed to ice as recognition crept upon his thoughts. '*You!*' He felt his gut twist. 'It cannot be!'

'Your primarch was always an arrogant one, Blood Angel. You are no different, ten thousand years after Great Horus struck him down like the fool he was.' The impostor opened his arms wide and a festoon of brass limbs exploded from the monstrous thing upon his back. 'Do you still not know me?'

The Apothecae fired blind, but the rounds screeched as the spider-legs spun out to deflect the shots. A black, cold pall filled the chamber.

'Then, please allow me to introduce myself.' The impostor bowed low, revealing the chattering machine upon him in all its grotesque glory. 'I am the primogenitor of Chaos Undivided, Master of Pain, Lord of the New Men.' His voice was thick with mockery and venom. 'I am Fabius Bile. And you have something that I want.'

CHAPTER ELEVEN

THE ASTARTES DISEMBARKED from the troop bay of the Thunderhawk even as the transport was lowering itself to the deck on its landing gear. Blood Angels and Flesh Tearers streamed out of the craft and formed a perimeter. The men with search lamps on their shoulders shone the bright sodium-white beams about the interior of the bartizan, picking out the hard-edged shadows of parked fuel bowsers, cargo crates and resting flyers.

At Rafen's side, Puluo inclined his head slightly and gave his commander a meaningful look, flaring his nostrils. Behind his helmet, the sergeant caught the scent as well; spilled blood, underscoring everything.

'I have something here,' Roan, Sergeant Noxx's second, called out from the starboard side of the Thunderhawk. Rafen ducked under the wing of the transport, ignoring the ticking and clicking of the cooling fuselage, coming to the Flesh Tearer's side.

Noxx was already there. 'What is it?'

Roan turned his shoulder lamp upon the prow of a parked Arvus lighter. The slope-faced cockpit of the craft was wide open, the angular metal frame peeled back where it had been torn open. Jagged pieces of green armourglass lay about it on the decking. In the dimness, the craft's running lights were soft yellow dots, blinking every few seconds. The glow of the cockpit instruments was also visible.

Rafen led with his bolter, peering down the length of the gun into the ragged hole where the windscreen had been. Inside, there was a mess of shorn mechadendrites lying like slaughtered snakes across the active control console. Oily residue and processor fluids speckled the cockpit walls. Where another craft might have had a command couch, there was nothing but a stubby metal podium ending in pipes that gave off the smell of ozone and human effluent.

'There should be a pilot-servitor in there,' said Roan.

'Yes,' noted Noxx. 'There *should* be.'

Rafen studied the twisted metal frame and ran his gauntlet along it. He found a set of curious indentations that seemed to have no pattern, until he realised they matched the spread of fingers on a human hand. 'Someone removed the pilot and killed it.'

'Caecus, perhaps,' offered Captain Gorn as he approached them. 'He wanted to ensure no one left after he landed.'

Puluo indicated the ranks of other shuttles. 'This is not the only aircraft in the hangar.'

'I imagine we will find them similarly gutted, then.'

Rafen was half-listening, peering hard into the dark corners of the landing bay. His helmet's optical array set to preysight mode, he searched and found no heat sources save for the thermal exchanger pipes across the walls and ceiling. He returned his vision to normal, noticing from the corner of his eye that Sergeant Noxx had been doing the same.

'Why would the majoris do such a thing?' said Puluo. 'Would he even have the strength?'

Gorn shrugged. 'He killed an Angel Sanguine. He fled like a coward. He is one of your kindred. Tell me, in your opinion, are those the actions of a brother still rational in mind?'

Across the hangar, in a pool of dull biolume light, a hatch ground open and a figure in hooded Apothecary's robes entered the chamber. The new arrival approached with steady, careful steps, apparently undeterred by the array of guns that were immediately trained upon him.

The captain of the Flesh Tearers did not wait for Rafen to speak. He rocked off his stance and strode forward, through the line of his men around the Thunderhawk. 'You,' he demanded. 'Halt and be recognised.' Gorn placed one hand on the hilt of the falchion at his waist, drawing a length of the barbed short sword in order to indicate his willingness to use it.

The figure slowed to a halt and then bowed low.

'Speak up,' Gorn demanded. 'That's an order.'

'Brother-Captain!' warned Rafen.

The Flesh Tearer glared at him across the glossy black ceramite of his shoulder plates. 'Sergeant–'

In the instant his eyes left the hooded figure, the attack came. It was a blur of action, almost too swift for the Astartes to catch the full motion of it. The robes burst open and a taloned hand of deep red-purple flesh shot forth. Palm flat and fingers in a blade, it extended beyond normal reach and caressed the skin of Gorn's neck where the Flesh Tearer's throat was bare.

A gout of crimson fluid arced into the air, steaming in the cold. The captain's hand's swept up to clutch at the wound, a strangled cry escaping him; but only for a moment. On the back-stroke the talons twisted and tore into the cut they had just made and opened it wider.

Gorn stumbled toward the hooded figure and it leapt upon him, the two of them crashing to the deck.

A ripple of hesitation shot through the men, none of them willing to fire the first shot for fear of hitting Captain Gorn. Noxx bounded forward, his flaying knife hissing from its scabbard.

There was a grinding, crunching noise and Gorn's head separated from his body, rolling away across the blast plating. Blood spat in pulsing fountains as the hooded killer nuzzled into the stump of the captain's neck.

Puluo's heavy bolter sang, the cruciform muzzle flare backlighting the Space Marine. Gorn's slaughterer was blown backward, the dense rounds ripping cloth and ruddy flesh alike. Incredibly, it skidded about and tried to stand up once more. Skin, talons and bony arches flexed beneath the shredding robes.

'Movement!' called Ajir, shouting to be heard over the roar of the support weapon. 'Above!'

Rafen looked up, to the spaces overhead he had scrutinised only moments ago. Pieces of the roof detached and fell toward them, air snapping through cloaks as they dropped. But there was nothing up there... The preysight showed no heat sources...

He pushed the thought away and bellowed a command. 'Weapons free!'

Lightning-flash discharges of yellow cordite exhaust flared all about him as a dozen bolters released their force all at once. He heard Corvus and Kayne shouting the Emperor's reproach at their enemies, adding to the cacophony of the clash.

AJIR FIRED A three-round burst into something fast and howling. He couldn't be certain if the bolts found purchase; his attacker did not seem to slow. The mutant ploughed into him with a bone-shaking impact that threw them both against one of the Thunderhawk's support legs. It pressed into him, shoving Ajir back so he could not bring his bolter to bear, scraping and clawing at his armour as if it wanted to climb inside with him. Eyes red as madness glared from a knotted and deformed head, and a hot slaughterhouse stink of foul breath washed over Ajir, disgusting him. He punched and butted the creature, but it was like striking a piece of leathery meat. No blow he landed seemed to make any difference to the hooting, spitting freak. Ajir tried to twist away as its neck extended grotesquely, jaws running wide to display the barbs of curved canine teeth. It went for the jugular vein on his neck, but Ajir struggled and instead the lamprey mouth bit a twist of skin and meat off his cheek.

Holding him locked in its obscene embrace, the mutant probed into the wound it had just made, sucking at the rush of blood. The Space Marine kicked out and felt a bone break beneath the heel of his armoured boot. The creature spat and drew him tighter, the sinuous limbs distending into forms closer to tentacles than arms.

The rattling snarl of a chainsword came closer and Ajir saw another armoured figure at the edge of his vision. The unmistakable sound of spinning blades meeting bare flesh reached his ears and the mutant howled, suddenly releasing him.

Ajir's rescuer pressed the weapon into his attacker's spine and let the weight of his blow do the rest. The matrix of adamantium teeth churned the ruddy flesh into ragged gobbets and pierced the beast's abdomen, opening it to the air. It fell away with a gargling screech, only hanks of sinew and bared white bone keeping the two halves of the torso together. It shuddered and bled out in surges, still clinging to life.

Swearing, Ajir fumbled for his helmet where it hung upon his belt, cursing himself for being foolish enough to go without it. His comrade came closer, offering him a hand to steady himself. 'That'll scar well,' said Turcio.

Ajir ignored the hand and got up, burning with annoyance.

'Not even a thank you?' said the other Blood Angel. 'Or is it beneath you to show gratitude to a penitent?'

He said nothing and took a step toward the gasping mutant as it tried to drag itself away. Ajir touched his gun barrel to its head and pulled the trigger.

THEIR ATTACKERS MOVED with a speed that seemed impossible for things of such density and bulk, propelling themselves with the sheer force of oversized bunches of muscles, or clawing from point to point, scrambling over gantries and across the fuselage of parked ships.

Rafen heard a deep wail and spun in place as Noxx came closer, irritably reloading his weapon. The death-cry was from another of the Flesh Tearers; three mutants fell upon him and tore his limbs from his body, retreating into the shadows with their grisly prizes as bolt rounds snapped after them.

'Warp-cursed things,' spat the veteran sergeant, 'they soak up shots like they were rainfall!'

Rafen fired into the dark at a hazy shape, and heard the thud of impacts. The creatures were retreating now, and silence descended, broken only by the moan of injured men and the rattle of spent shells rolling at their feet. With Noxx a step behind, he crossed the deck to where a mess of meat lay strewn over a metre's length of flooring. The creatures had left little of Captain Gorn behind in their frenzied assault.

He hesitated, a piece of clawed, fractured armour plate at his feet, the saw-tooth sigil of the Flesh Tearers staring up at him. 'This is no way for an Astartes to perish,' he said quietly.

'The Emperor knows his name,' Noxx offered. 'I always believed Captain Gorn's overconfidence would be the death of him.'

The two sergeants exchanged glances, in a rare moment of shared understanding. 'The beast in the pit. The clone,' said Rafen. 'These are the same.'

Noxx shook his head. 'Not the same. *Stronger.*'

'Aye.' He paused, thinking. 'They shirked the preysight. They were of a larger mass, but faster with it. How is that possible?'

'The one we fought, it only mutated at the very end. Perhaps these...' He gestured at the wet streaks across the decking. 'Perhaps they have evolved.'

'It's the blood,' Rafen grated, remembering the desperate hunger in the eyes of the creature in the arena. He saw Noxx's hand drift to his shoulder, where the beast had bitten into him. 'The more they ingest, the stronger they become.' He shook his head. 'The one that killed Gorn... Nothing should be able to withstand the barrage from a heavy bolter.'

'Like the old legends,' Noxx's voice dropped to a whisper. 'The blood-letters, the man-predators. The *vampire.*'

The ancient curse-word drew a sharp look from the sergeant. 'These things are malforms. Twisted mutations bred in some vial.' He looked up as the rest of the men approached, Blood Angel and Flesh Tearer alike. 'Our mission remains the same. Execute them all.'

'What about Brother Caecus?' asked Kayne, absently nursing his bandaged hand. 'And the rest of the brethren in this place?'

'The majoris is beyond our reach now.' Rafen's face set in a grim mask. 'Survivors are of a secondary consideration. We all saw what those things can do.' He cast around. 'How many of us were there? And how many of them did we kill?'

'We barely marked them,' said Turcio.

Puluo nodded. 'They cannot be allowed to leave the citadel.'

Ajir was fuming. 'Aye. Those creatures are an offence against our bloodline!'

'This facility is as broad as it is deep,' said Roan, turning to Noxx. 'It will take us days to sweep every tier.'

'And we have no idea how many of those beasts await us down there, or how quickly they are changing. They fight with tooth and claw now, but how long until they take up guns and flamers?' Noxx watched Rafen steadily. 'I believe a more immediate solution is required.'

'We agree on something at last, then.' Rafen nodded and beckoned Corvus to him. 'Brother. You studied the design of this place during the flight here. Where is the citadel's terminatus chamber?'

'You intend to obliterate the entire complex?' asked Turcio. 'Lord, is that wise?'

'The Vitalis Citadel is built upon a geothermal vent,' explained Corvus. 'A mineral aquifer heated by a magma chamber kilometres below the surface.' He pointed at the exchanger pipes across the walls. 'Channelled by the works of the Mechanicus, it provides warmth and power for the whole facility. The terminatus chamber contains a governance system that will disengage the vent's regulator.'

'Anything the Mechanicus create, an Astartes can destroy,' said Rafen. 'And we are beyond the point of a surgical strike now.' He looked up. 'We kill this place, and we kill those monstrous freaks with it.'

None of the assembled men questioned the severe logic of the statement.

Corvus produced his auspex and held it up. On the screen, a wire-frame map showed a skeletal model of the complex's layout. 'The terminatus chamber is below us, Lord. Ten tiers down.'

Rafen nodded. 'Kayne, Turcio. Remain here and guard the Thunderhawk. If you are overrun, get into the sky and stand off. Wait for my recall signal.'

The two Blood Angels saluted. Noxx nodded at a pair of his men. 'You and you, assist them.'

There was a flurry of activity as the Space Marines took a moment to prepare themselves, reloading their weapons and checking the integrity of their armour. Rafen allowed a long, slow breath to escape his lips.

'Into the arena once again,' said Noxx. 'But a different one this time.'

'Aye,' agreed the Blood Angel. 'There'll be no reprieves here.'

CAECUS HAD LOST sensation in his right arm after he had fended off the fourth – or perhaps it was the fifth? – of the attacks. The useless limb dangled at his side, all purpled meat and white bone protruding from torn and sodden remains of his sleeve. A steady drip of blood fell from his nerveless fingers, dotting the floor as a measure of his passing. He was drawing a line across the heart of the madness, up along the spiralling stairs, down the corridors. He wondered what he would find at the end of it.

Pain made it hard for him to think clearly. Claw wounds covered his body, the cuts both shallow and deep, singing with new jolts of agony each time he took a step. He could feel the fevered work of his Larraman implant as it struggled against the blood loss; it was a battle the Space Marine's body would eventually lose.

At first, Caecus could not understand why the bastard Fabius had not simply murdered him as he had Fenn, the other Apothecaries, even his servant Nyniq. It came to him in fits and starts as the mutant clone-Marines attacked, drove him out of the laboratorium and back through the reeking halls of the citadel. The Chaos renegade was amused by it. He was watching in some fashion, perhaps through the scrying monitors in the corridors, perhaps through the eyes of the mutants themselves. The creatures did not come at him all at once, and if they had he would have been dead in moments. No, they had chosen to end him slowly, through attrition. At intervals, the Bloodfiends dropped from the dark or thundered into him, cutting and beating, then fleeing into the shadows once again. Without a weapon, he was reduced to fighting barehanded, but they were so very fast and he was slowing with each step, bleeding out, struggling to place one foot in front of the other.

He was dying by inches, and he had nothing to show for it.

'No!' The shout escaped him with sudden vehemence. Caecus spat bloody spittle from his bruised lips. 'I am not done, not as long as I have… I have it…' His good hand fumbled at the pockets of the matted, sodden robes, looking for the vial that he had carried back from the Chapel of the Red Grail. Dread rising in his gullet, Caecus pulled at the pocket and his hand emerged through a claw-rent torn in the material. 'Empty…?' He felt as hollow as the word he spoke. 'No…'

The glass tube was gone. He turned in place, stumbling backward, searching the floor for it. The pain of the numberless cuts made him list on his thickset feet. *The blood.* The mingled blood of a hundred centuries of priests and the primarch himself, the raw vitae of his Chapter, lost. Caecus let out a moan, voicing an agony deeper than any other. 'What have I done?'

He thought he could hear mocking laughter in the distance, faint and scornful. Not lost, then. Taken. Taken by Fabius. Caecus's good hand reached up to his face and he felt hot tears streaking his bruised cheeks. He stumbled and collapsed.

* * *

HE AWOKE WITH a start, an icy-cold sensation at his throat. Caecus blinked and found himself surrounded by towering shapes in red and black ceramite. There was the hiss of a narthecium injector. The cold rushed into him and some clarity returned to his thoughts. The pain seemed distant and trivial.

'It's him,' said a low voice, close to his ear. 'The majoris.'

One of the giants bent low. Caecus saw a blurry face. Anger radiated from the dark-haired warrior like heat. 'Is he alive?'

'Barely.' The low voice came again, with hesitation. 'If we get him back to the Thunderhawk, there's a chance he might survive. The medicae-servitor on board can induce a sleep of stasis.'

'Caecus,' said the angry one. 'It's Brother-Sergeant Rafen.'

'Lord, did you–'

Rafen looked in a direction where Caecus's head could not turn. 'I heard what you said. Now step away, Corvus.'

He tried to speak. The first attempt was a thin wheeze. 'It is much worse than you think,' he managed, at last. 'They are loose. The Bloodfiends... The hand of Chaos is behind it.' Caecus's breath caught in the words and he coughed up black blood. Something inside him was broken, he could feel it with every laboured breath he took. 'Fabius Bile. He is here.'

The Blood Angel snatched at his robes and pulled him up. '*Here*?' he snarled. 'On the home world?' Some of the other Space Marines spat reflexively at the mention of the renegade's name. Rafen's face darkened as he struggled to control his anger. 'This is your mistake, you self-absorbed fool! You opened the door to this.'

'I gave him what he wanted...' He managed a nod. 'I will be damned for my hubris. I will be damned...'

Rafen released his grip and the Apothecae fell back against the wall. 'So you will,' came the reply. The black maw of a bolter rose to fill his vision. 'Caecus. In the Chapter's name, I judge you and find you wanting. You will find no forgiveness in the Emperor's light.'

'So be it.' He managed another breath, a strange kind of calm coming over him as at last he embraced the truth of his failings. 'I deserve nothing less.'

THE GUNSHOT ECHOED down the corridor, and each battle-brother there turned his face away from the act of justice.

Rafen stood to find Puluo watching him. The Space Marine tapped his chest, over the spot where his progenoid glands were implanted. The tiny knots of flesh contained the complex DNA required for each generation of Blood Angels, and their recovery from the bodies of the fallen ensured new life in the shadow of death.

'No,' said Rafen. 'No harvest for him. Caecus's crime has tainted him beyond the point of exculpation. No trace shall remain.' The sergeant gestured to Roan, pointing at the Flesh Tearer's hand flamer. 'You. Burn him.'

The gush of ignited promethium billowed and engulfed the corpse. None of them spoke as the majoris's body was turned into ashes.

Noxx's dead eyes were hooded, and finally he broke the silence. 'If an agent of the Ruinous Powers is within these walls, how did our psykers not detect him?'

'Does that matter now?' asked Ajir. 'Every Astartes knows the traitor Fabius Bile. He is ten millennia old. To survive that long, he must have tricks we can only guess at.'

Rafen gave a slow nod of agreement. Once an Adeptus Astartes himself, the warrior who had been Brother Fabius of the Emperor's Children Legion gave himself to the Chaos Gods during Horus's insurrection against Terra in the 31st millennium; he turned, along with his primarch Fulgrim and the rest of the III Legion, and embraced the way of the traitor. There were many tales of the man who renamed himself Fabius Bile, self-styled 'primogenitor' of the Chaos hordes, all of them sickening and hateful. No longer allied to his former band of corrupted turncoats, he was known to act as a free agent among the arch-enemy, a mercenary offering his knowledge of twisted science to any he chose. Fabius Bile had crossed paths with the Blood Angels on many occasions, but never before had he dared to venture this close to the heart of their Chapter. 'Nothing has changed,' said the sergeant. 'If anything, we now have greater cause to obliterate this place if Bile's corruption has touched it.'

'Excise it like a cancer, and kill him into the bargain,' said Corvus. 'He must be the cause of the mutants.' The Space Marine dared to glance at the smouldering corpse. 'He used Caecus to strike at the Chapter.'

Noxx snorted. 'And you believe this blackguard will simply stand still and allow us to drown him in boiling floodwaters? If he has not already escaped?'

Kayne shook his head. 'No ships have left the citadel in days, none save the flyer used by the majoris. There are no other ways out of the complex.'

Corvus held up the auspex. 'That is not true, brother.' He showed the display to Rafen, and the sergeant's eyes widened. 'A teleportarium?'

'On this very tier, lord, used for the transit of delicate genetic samples,' said the Space Marine. He frowned. 'There are dozens of starships in orbit–'

'If that traitor whoreson reaches any one of them, his escape is virtually certain!' Roan shook his head.

'We need to split the unit,' said Noxx, his thoughts following the same pattern as those of his Blood Angel counterpart.

'Agreed,' Rafen nodded. 'Corvus, you will join Sergeant Noxx and the Flesh Tearer squad. Guide them to the terminatus chamber and enact the rites of obliteration. The rest of us will locate the teleportarium and render it inoperable.'

Noxx gestured at Roan. 'Take him with you. I won't have Mephiston say I left my cousins a man down.'

'For Sanguinius, then.'

Noxx nodded. 'In the primarch's name, aye.'

THE MUTANTS WALKED in a wary train behind him, heads turning in jerks of motion like birds of prey seeking food animals. Some of them lowed and snapped at each other with angry ill-temper. They had fed so much and yet they were still hungry. The primogenitor wondered what it would take to sate that unending appetite. How much blood? How many kills? Part of him was sorrowful he would not be able to stay behind and observe. It was of interest to him, but truth be told, only in a tangential way. He had much more important things to do. Much more important experiments to enact.

Fabius's long fingers tapped out a rhythm upon the flesh-pouch on his belt, the draw-string bag made from the flayed head-skin of a small girl he had caught, on some hive-world whose name escaped him. Behind the sewn-shut eyes and mouth slit, resting there was the vial that foolish Caecus had delivered to him. The largest of the Bloodfiends, the one that walked at the front of the line, had brought it to him. That one was the farthest along, the most developed. Bile could see the glint of emerging intelligence in its eyes. It was carrying a stolen bolter and bundles of ammunition plundered from the citadel's weapons store. The clone cradled the weapon in a way that was both unfamiliar and commonplace.

He allowed himself a smile. They were exceptional things, these replicae, almost the equal of the New Men of the primogenitor's own creation. Such a shame, such a pity that genetic material of rich potential would be wasted. But then, it was in the service of a better cause. The precious vial made all sacrifices worthwhile. The geneforms locked within that undying fluid would advance *his* great work by decades.

The renegade left the teleportarium's doors wide open and moved to the command console, pausing only to snap the neck of the servitor waiting there. As an after-thought, he tossed the corpse toward the clones and let them harry it for a while. He worked quickly at the rune-dotted panel, his hands and the brass limbs sprouting from his back at a blur; during this he became aware that the large Bloodfiend, the pack's 'alpha', was sniffing the air and shooting him wary glances. The mutants had shown Fabius an almost instinctual deference, as if they understood on a cellular level that he was in some way their creator. But now they were becoming agitated.

He pressed on; other matters were more crucial, and the time was drawing near. He could sense the slow build of pressure in the back of his skull. The Gate would open soon, and then he would flee this place. The last of his pretence at being Haran Serpens would be removed, and he would truly be himself once more. He longed for the feel of his trusty tools in his hands, his rod and the needler. They were his orb and sceptre, the implements that crowned him Gene-master of the Eye of Terror.

But before he could return, he had to ensure he would not be followed. The first step in that had already been set in motion. He could feel it in the slow chilling of the air. The second step... He was almost done.

Fabius eschewed the rituals of activation and the tiresome litanies of thanks to the Machine-God that the teleporter's drone-mind demanded. Instead, the chirurgeon upon his back extended a needle-arm and injected a euphoric poison into the mechanism's braincase, letting it drown in pleasure. So released, he was free to impose a new set of target coordinates and set the matter-energy conversion process to begin accumulating power for a transit.

The humming chains of energy were nearing their peak when the howls of the Bloodfiends turned clamorous and shrill. Through the open doors came a squad of Space Marines, and the renegade laughed at them. 'What kept you?' he snorted.

NOXX'S MEN MOVED with a swift and predatory competence that was at odds with the manners they had displayed on Eritaen. Corvus kept pace with them, the auspex in his hand, his bolter at the ready.

The Flesh Tearer sergeant disarmed a laser trip-mine array hastily erected about the door to the terminatus chamber and opened the thick hatch.

'Shouldn't that doorway have been locked?' said one of the Flesh Tearers.

Corvus didn't register the man's words, his thoughts on the task ahead. He had already drawn the deactivation scripts for the geothermal regulator device, and he strode in beside Noxx, ready to offer them to the citadel's machine-spirit.

What he saw made him stop dead. The glyphs on the control consoles were shining a hard, uniform crimson. Corvus had barely registered the fact when he sensed a faint tremor through the soles of his boots.

Noxx swore. 'This is bad.'

Corvus shook his head, his mouth going dry. 'No, sergeant. This is worse.'

'FABIUS BILE, I name you traitor!' Rafen spat out the malediction and opened fire, shooting from the hip. Bolt-fire cascaded into the command pulpit and the renegade dived away, through the mass of cables strung from the power vanes that circled the teleport pad like a giant's coronet.

The Bloodchild clones – no, the *Bloodfiends* – went wild and attacked, but this time the Astartes were ready for them. With pinpoint barrages of fire, they corralled them, forced them across the humming hex-grid of the chamber floor. Energy crackled all about them.

'Back!' shouted Puluo to the men. 'Stay back!'

Roan was at the front of the group and faltered. Rafen's eyes widened with shock as he saw a clone, this one larger than the rest, bring up a bolter and return fire. The Flesh Tearer dodged away, skidding across the grid as emerald motes of light began to form in the air. Noxx had been correct; the creatures *were* evolving. He remembered the Bloodchild they had fought in the arena, the way it had drawn from their fighting styles and learned in seconds. These things were doing the same, quicker and quicker with each confrontation.

'Where is that traitorous snake?' demanded Ajir.

Rafen spotted movement across the far side of the teleportarium. He had expected the renegade to be standing among the clones but the opposite was true. Bile was making for another doorway, the claws of his spinal mechanism flailing, ducking low to avoid the rounds that snapped at his heels.

The clones howled and battered at the decking, a lanky and stringy one striking out and snaring Roan about the ankle. Rafen burst from cover, meaning to dive headlong after him, but Puluo swung his heavy bolter and batted the Space Marine back on his haunches. 'Sir, no!'

The Blood Angel sergeant realised too late what was about to happen. With a crackling, buzzing hum that reached into his marrow, Rafen let out a gasp as viridian light blazed through the chamber. There came a sharp thunderclap of displaced air and suddenly the teleport platform was empty; only wisps of ozone drifted where moments before a host of screeching clones and one Flesh Tearer had stood.

Rafen snarled and bolted across the still-sizzling transport stage. He was halfway across when the renegade threw a cluster of metal eggs toward the workings of the teleporter's power train. 'Consider them a gift!' shouted Fabius, pulling the far hatch shut behind him.

The krak grenades detonated on impact and a flat disc of force flashed out across the chamber. Rafen felt the deck leave him as he was picked up and tossed into the air. The Blood Angel was hurled into a crystalline regulator column that shattered into jagged fragments around him.

THE TREMORS WERE coming every few seconds now, and at the edge of his hearing Corvus caught the rolling rumble of the boiling floodwaters churning their way through the levels beneath them. At a run, the Astartes vaulted the broad stone steps three at a time, spiralling upwards. The Blood Angel's world narrowed to the back of Noxx in front of him, the sergeant's fusion-pack bobbing as they ran to reach the upper levels.

'Brother-Sergeant Rafen, the destruct process has already begun!' he called into his vox, his breath coming in chugs of air. 'Bile got there before us! You must retreat to the Thunderhawk!'

He heard only static over the open channel.

IGNORING THE DARTS of agony that rippled down his body, Rafen dragged himself from the wreckage of the burning teleporter stage and dove through the growing flames. He shouldered open the hatch and pushed inside. Beyond, there was an access gantry that ranged over a forest of power conduits. The companionway travelled for several metres and ended in a sheer ferrocrete wall.

His senses sifted the sensations in the air about him. There was a thickness to the atmosphere here, a sickly tang that felt greasy upon his tongue even through the filters of his helmet. A slime pattern lay about the sheer wall. Rafen pressed his palm to the hard sheet of artificial rock, searching for a hidden door, some sort of concealed exit, but there was nothing, no means of physical escape from the dead-end chamber. He frowned, for the first time sensing the shallow trembling in the walls around him.

In quick succession he ran through the different modes of vision open to an Astartes in power armour – electro-chemical, ultraviolet, and infrared. Only when he turned to preysight mode did he catch it, and by reflex the Blood Angel batted at the shape that suddenly appeared in the air. It began to disperse, moving like slow smoke.

Rafen bit back a surge of disgust in his throat. The shape of the ghostly vapour was falling apart, but for a single moment he had seen it intact. It was an image, a crude sketch hovering in the air.

A howling skull-shaped gateway as big as a Space Marine, and between the teeth of its open mouth, a star with eight points.

MEPHISTON STOPPED ABRUPTLY in the light of the tall window and hissed as a line of pain crossed his face.

'Kinsman?' said Dante. 'What is it?'

The psyker shook his head. 'Something… I felt it before, but I could not be certain. This time, though… The touch of darkness…' He swallowed, tasting metal in his mouth.

And then the green flash erupted in the sky high above the central courtyard of the fortress-monastery.

CHAPTER TWELVE

THE AIR WAS damp, acrid with the smell of metallic salts and sulphur. Ahead of the churning floodwater, gusts of furious steam were being pushed down the corridors of the Vitalis Citadel. The searing, superheated vapour reverted back to droplets where it touched the chilled outer walls of the tower, turning into rains that sluiced over brick and steel. The rumble of the deluge was constant now, the tremors rippling through the decks.

On the Thunderhawk's drop-ramp, Turcio threw a quick glance down the length of the ship's troop bay. At the far end, he saw Kayne in stern discussion with the pilot-serf. The transport's engines were revving, the winglets shuddering as if the craft was desperate to take air and leave the citadel to destroy itself. 'How much longer can we wait?' demanded the Astartes.

Kayne looked his way and spoke over the vox. 'The pilot tells me we may have already tarried too long.'

Turcio grinned wolfishly. 'I'd prefer a more optimistic estimate.' He went to say more, but movement at the doors to the landing bay brought him to a ready stance with his bolter at his shoulder. He relaxed an iota when he recognised the figures of Space Marines streaming across the deck. 'Brother-sergeant?' he called.

Rafen was at the rear of the pack of men, urging them on. He threw a look over his shoulder and cursed. Turcio spied the first shallow drools of yellowed water sloshing over the threshold and knew that their time was up.

'Get the men aboard!' Rafen roared. 'Forget the ramp, get them in and lift the ship!' Turcio stood back as a mass of mingled Blood Angel and Flesh Tearer warriors scrambled into the Thunderhawk's open troop bay. Some of them bore injuries, but not a one of them allowed such trivialities to slow them. The Flesh Tearer sergeant, the veteran Noxx, propelled Brother Corvus ahead of him, and then turned on the lip of the ramp to extend a hand to Rafen. The Blood Angel accepted, and no sooner had Rafen's boot touched the aircraft than the Thunderhawk's engines shrieked with the application of new thrust. The floor of the landing bay fell away as the gunship lifted vertically through the bartizan and out into the polar air. Boiling floodstreams laden with debris came up after them, churning in coiled waves at the rising craft's wings.

Turcio saw it happen through the open hatch. As the pilot-serf pulled them away, the deluge exploded out of the citadel's flanks and for one brief instant the red tower became a fountainhead; then the frothing, streaming geyser overwhelmed the building's structure. Beneath a plume of dirty, magma-fuelled water, the Vitalis Citadel was crushed back into the ice-covered mountainside. Hot and cold met in a scream of reaction, sending up a wall of steam and billowing snow.

The concussion rocked the Thunderhawk and sent it tottering toward the spikes of the ice ridges, the pilot-serf making frantic corrections to keep them airborne. The Astartes who had not secured themselves were tossed about the cabin like toys. Turcio hung on grimly, and saw Rafen lend his strength to Noxx to keep him upright. A marked change from their behaviour in the fighting pit, he mused, keeping the observation to himself.

The turbulence eased and the flight became more stable as they accelerated away. The Blood Angel caught a few words from Noxx. 'We're short a body. Where is Roan?'

As the hatch finally closed, Rafen detached his helmet and ran a hand through his unkempt hair. 'He was upon the teleportarium's stage when it activated. The traitor Fabius used the device to spirit the mutants away before he fled the tower, and Roan was caught among the Bloodfiends.' He frowned. 'I regret his loss.'

'Where did Bile send them?' demanded Noxx.

'I have an inkling,' Rafen returned, his expression grim. He looked at Turcio. 'Brother. Tell the pilot to push this ship to the very limits, to fly it apart if he has to. No time can be spared. We must get back to the fortress-monastery.'

THE TELEPORTATION FLUX tore the air from his lungs in the shattering moment of transition. The Flesh Tearer felt every atom of his body become fluid and ghostly, for one horrible millisecond existing as nothing but a mass of free particles in a sea of seething non-matter; and then suddenly Brother Roan was whole once again, the equilibrium of being restored as quickly as it had been taken.

The shocking transition was not new to him. Roan had taken part in teleport assaults on more than one occasion, but it was not something that he relished. He had seen brothers twisted inside by perturbations in the flux, and worse still the warpings of flesh and ceramite that resulted from an incorrect reintegration, that had to be put down like diseased animals.

His was not to share that fate, however. Fabius Bile was too accomplished a scientist to make an error of that stripe. No, the twisted genetor had led the Astartes to a wholly different manner of perishing.

Roan was barely aware of himself before he realised he was *falling*. Dark sky and black earth tumbled around him, exchanging places as he fell into the grip of gravity. The citadel's teleport had sent them to the fortress-monastery, clear across the hemisphere, but not to a point within its walls. Roan, along with the snarling, roaring Bloodfiends, had rematerialised a half-kilometre above the central courtyard. The ground rushed up toward him and the Space Marine picked out the towers of the central block, the dome of the Grand Annex growing closer by the second. Death was spreading its arms wide to welcome him.

About him the mutant clones shuddered and wailed; for a moment Roan grinned, believing that perhaps Bile *had* made an error, positioning the re-mat point in the wrong place, condemning the Bloodfiends to share his demise. I will die, but so will they.

But that too was snatched away from him when the flesh across the backs of the freaks rippled and split, issuing out great sails of veined skin that caught the air and buoyed them like raptors.

Roan shouted out a curse in the old tribal tongue of his clan, damning the renegade Fabius to suffer death at the teeth of the terrasaurs that roamed the jungles of Cretacia.

He hit the ground and punched a shallow crater into the flagstones with his passing. The clone-beasts, unsteady but swift on their new mutations, dropped down around his corpse, some bending to lap at the puddle of blood and meat Roan had made.

THE SHUTTLE BEARING Master Sentikan and the body of Brother Rydae back to the *Unseen* had barely become a glitter in the sky before Lord Seth rounded on Mephiston's commander once again and reiterated his demands.

'This conclave of yours is fast becoming a disaster, Dante. You should have come to me first, alone. We could have discussed these matters, found a solution that we could impose together.'

'I will *impose* nothing,' Dante replied firmly. 'I will ask my kindred to aid me, and trust in them that they will do as the Emperor wills.'

'And if the Emperor wills that you do not prosper, what then?'

Mephiston fought back the urge to speak; this conversation was not for men of his rank, but only between the masters.

And then came the pain. *The touch of darkness.* The silent knife of psychic shock being drawn across the surface of his soul. He faltered and heard his lord speak out to him. The Librarian hissed through clenched teeth. Before, in the annex, there had been the smallest of moments when he thought he sensed something, but it had vanished so swiftly that he could not capture it. This time was different. He tasted the brief musk of psi-spoor, sensed the impression of a roaring skull opening its mouth to swallow a man draped in an aura of death, then slamming shut.

Mephiston gathered himself to sift the moment for meaning, just as an emerald glow burst in the sky high overhead. *A teleport discharge?* He sensed the sudden emergence of new minds, feral and rage-driven.

'An attack!' he shouted, with abrupt force. 'They're here!'

FIRST CAPTAIN LOTHAN died when the mutants came up from the service ducts beneath his boots.

Argastes looked up to see Mephiston and Dante racing along the corridor toward them, with Seth at their side. Lothan had thrust a bolt pistol into his hand and bid the Chaplain to follow him, to find the Chapter Master and ensure his security. One of Lothan's men, the honour guard Garyth, told Argastes of the energy-seers that had screamed as they detected the formation of a teleport bubble above the monastery. The elaborate sense-servitors were the fortress's early warning system, but even their panicked reactions were not fast enough. There were creatures, the battle-brother told him. Creatures like the one from the arena, but dozens of them, and faster with it. Guard posts and serf barracks across the gothic complex had gone silent or reported glimpses of things that moved like Astartes but stank of mad blood-hunger.

But it didn't seem possible. These things, like the one that Rafen had terminated in the pit, they were mindless flesh-proxies, little more than organic automata. Lethal, aye, but surely without true intellect…

Why then, could they not be caught? Where were they hiding? Argastes could see that Lothan had already asked himself the same questions and drawn the same answers. The beasts moved in hit-and-fade attacks, in battle-rote straight from the Chapter's indoctrination tapes and the pages of the Codex Astartes. Striking and fleeing, taking kills and, if Garyth was to be believed, *feeding* upon them. Moments ago, Argastes had spied an eviscerated scroll-servitor heaped in an alcove off the sunward prayer halls. The stark, bloodless pallor of the dead drone's flesh was not lost on him, and beneath his breath he spoke a verse of warding from the Litany Vermillion.

Ahead of him, Lothan was reaching out to beckon Dante toward him when it happened. The steel gutters over the ducts exploded and beasts that massed too much to fit inside so small a space extruded out and tore into him. The first captain spun about in a welter of blood, and he came apart.

MEPHISTON FELT BROTHER-CAPTAIN Lothan's mind die along with his body, the impact of it a discordant string amid a chorus of thought. The mutants spilled into the corridor, assaulting the men in Lothan's squad, clawing and biting and slashing. Gunfire barked loudly inside the echoing companionway as the Lord of Death released a snarl and fell into the melee. He cursed himself for not having his force sword to hand – the Mindblade Vitarus was in his chambers, left behind at Dante's behest for the duration of the conclave – but still the psyker had weapons in his employ no mere freak of nature could hope to resist. Mephiston released the psionic reservoir of his inner quickening, tasting the might of heroes as it lashed though him. He became fluid, faster than light, striking and tearing at the beasts.

He gathered up Lothan's fallen chainblade and cut at a mutant with barbed fangs sprouting from all over its flesh. He slashed it down and ended it with cruel, unyielding blows, then went on to another, ripping a sinewy thing with rope-like arms off the Space Marine it was attempting to strangle, killing by cutting it in two.

Mephiston had flashes of the other men in the fight; there, his lord Dante with a rescued bolter in either hand, coldly blasting mutants into wet slurry; Argastes, beating an eyeless, entaloned man-beast with the crest of his crozius arcanum; Seth, choking another clone in the crook of his arm; and others, fighting and dying.

* * *

IT WAS OVER swiftly. The mutants scored their kills and then fled, spattering blood from their wounds and their kills, fleeing in every direction, dragging torn meat behind them. Each moved like it had a purpose – as if, Throne take it, they *knew* the fortress. Knew it as well as Argastes and his brothers did, where every alcove and place of retreat might be among the kilometres of stone and steel and glass.

More than a hundred Blood Angels, alive and dead, have their DNA expressed within his physiology. Caecus's pronouncement upon the first replicae returned to him. The clone will be able to assimilate the muscle-recall and genetic memory of each one of them. Argastes shared a look with Mephiston and knew the Lord of Death thought the same thing. The Apothecae Majoris had not lied. These things are more than animals. It is as with the forsaken of the Raven Guard, but now within our Chapter.

He took a moment to moderate his breathing. The attack had been so quick, with such unbridled savagery that it left them reeling.

Dante was speaking into a vox-unit about his wrist. 'This is the commander, to all posts and barricades. Sound the cloister bell and seal the fortress,' he ordered. 'All gates barred, all barriers lowered. Nothing is to be allowed to exit the structure without my mandate.'

Seth had made a kill of his own, and paused in the business of clearing blood and particles of flesh from his tunic. 'We should be driving those things out, not bottling them up.'

'I disagree,' came the growled reply. 'These creatures cannot be allowed to roam unchecked. They will be corralled and then exterminated.' Dante's eyes flashed. 'I will see to it.'

The Flesh Tearer dropped into a crouch, staring at the corpse of one of the mutants with open fascination. 'Curious. Such a blood-thirst and precision of brutality.

These things are quite the monsters, aren't they? I would not have thought someone like Brother Caecus capable of creating something like this.'

'Nor I,' agreed Dante.

Against his better judgement, Argastes too was drawn to one of the dead beast-men. 'Only in the hosts of the Death Company have I witnessed such lust for blood, and even then only for the spilling.'

Mephiston nodded slowly. 'They are driven by the Rage and the Thirst to a degree absolute, Chaplain,' he said. 'It is to them what air to breathe is for you and I. These vat-grown freaks are *us*, stripped bare to the animal beneath the man.' The psyker spoke with the bleak candour of one who had seen such darkness in himself. 'We have no choice. We must kill every last one of them.'

'If blood is what the seek,' said Seth, 'then they may strike again to find it. Perhaps in the medicae complex, or elsewhere.'

A cold disquiet crossed Dante's face. 'Where is Brother Corbulo?'

There came a lowing toll at that moment, as the great cloister bell began a mournful peal through the halls and corridors of the fortress-monastery.

FOR THE SECOND time in the span of a single day, the sanguinary high priest followed a summons to the Chapel of the Red Grail. Corbulo's stewardship of the holy artefact demanded that he dedicate his full attention to ensuring its safety; as such, when the cries of the servitors called warning of an imminent attack upon the fortress, the chapel was his first destination. He did not waste time upon thoughts of who or what the attackers could be; Corbulo did not allow himself to dwell on the fact that, in thousands of years, Baal had never been victim to such an invasion. He only turned himself to the defence of the Red Grail.

Gripping his chainsword in his hand, Corbulo took the steps to the chapel. Laser sensors hidden in the eyes of death masks upon the walls fanned him with red light and took his measure, opening the tiled floor above so he might enter.

He emerged and took stock; as always, his eyes were drawn at once to the copper chalice above the ruby dais, hovering in silence. A spark of irrational fear, that he might arrive and find it gone, faded – but only for a moment. Corbulo passed through the stone pillars toward the altar, and it was then he realised that the darkness outside the windows about him was wrong; not the depths of a Baalite night, but black as ink, and shifting. He heard the scrape of claws and drew the chainblade to him, his thumb resting against the activator rune.

There were forms outside, clinging to the marble and stone of the minaret, massing against the glass. With sudden violence, great cracks lanced from floor to ceiling and the ornate panes shattered with a thunderous report. Corbulo's weapon came up to battle-ready as the mutants, all of them the duplicate of the Bloodchild in its last monstrous moments of life, forced their way inside, yowling and sniffing at the air.

The sanguinary priest felt his gut tighten; all at once, he knew exactly what it was the beasts wanted, and he bellowed out a denial, breaking into a run.

There were only a handful of them; one mutant, the largest of the group, grunted out something – *a command, perhaps?* – and made for the ruby dais. The others swarmed toward Corbulo, fangs out and talons wide. He met them with the chattering teeth of the chainsword, carving into them, but they were hard to hit, harder to kill.

Ahead, he saw the guardians rising from their rest and opening their hands to the large beast-clone. It was easily the mass of a Space Marine in Terminator armour, perhaps more so. He saw light from the photonic candles blink off a looted ceramite shoulder plate about the monster's body, a black curve of wargear spattered with colour. The brute threw itself over the line of glass tiles and the guardian fired. Bolt shells thudded home into the dense flesh, but to no apparent effect. The creature reached the gun-servitor and uprooted it from the tiled floor. Metal wings tearing, rounds still discharging, the mutant Bloodchild used the machine-helot like a massive club to knock down its twin.

Corbulo shook off his attackers and raced to the dais, anger fuelling his speed. The mutant's crooked face showed red-stained teeth and it mounted the platform ahead of him, clawed fingers reaching into the glow of the suspensor field to grab at the relic.

'No!' he shouted. 'Damn you, no!' The priest lashed out just as the creature's hand caught the chalice, his hand swiping through empty air.

The mutant swung the Red Grail at Corbulo and struck him across the face with it. Hot blood splashed from the cup across his eyes and nostrils, searing his skin, and the priest was thrown backwards, off the ruby podium, landing hard to skid back across the polished tiles.

Corbulo's hand crossed his face and came away stained with the potent vitae, the mingled lifeblood of his fellow priests, of *him* even, in blend with the still-living essence of Sanguinius. The fluid was fiery upon his skin, and the power of it made his head swim.

But the warrior's reaction became revulsion when the mutant tipped the contents of the cup into its open mouth and drained it to the dregs. Corbulo felt his gut rebel and he retched at the sight of such barbaric desecration.

The creature howled and *laughed*, laughed just as a man would. With a sudden shock of motion, the figure thickened and grew, muscles bunching and expanding, that ragged slit of a mouth widening to show new buds of teeth. The mutant's mass increased by half again just from the draught it had taken. It threw back its head and roared, the cry a very definite, very clear word. *'More!'*

With a savage jerk of the wrist, the beast threw the grail away and Corbulo dived after it, scrambling to snatch the empty cup from the air. The Blood Angel caught the holy chalice before it could strike the ground. His hands trembled with fury at bearing witness to such an act in so holy a place as this.

Corbulo whirled about, his chainsword ripping at the air, ready to kill every mutant he could lay his hands upon in answer for their sacrilege; but they were already retreating, fleeing back through the broken window and dropping into the night winds.

DANTE STRODE INTO the hall and Mephiston walked at his master's side, entering a room filled with warriors in disagreement and ill humour. Seth came with them, and the Lord of Death noted that for once, the commander of the Flesh Tearers had left some of his usual swagger behind. The lowing of the cloister bell underscored everything; it seemed like only days since Mephiston had been in this chamber, listening to Dante eschew Caecus's experiments and charging his men to seek out the successors for the conclave. *Matters are not unfolding as my lord had wished, that much is certain.*

Armis of the Blood Legion was the first to speak. 'At last! What is the meaning of this? We are roused from the guest chambers and brought here under armed guard... Do you mean to compel us to your side at gunpoint, Dante?'

'Don't be so melodramatic, cousin,' Seth grunted, before the other Chapter Master could answer.

'Kindred,' Dante said firmly, 'the fortress-monastery is under assault by malforms of as-yet unknown number and disposition. You have been brought here for your own protection.'

'The teleport flash,' said Orloc. 'I saw it from the residence tower.'

Daggan's metal fists rose. 'What is the nature of the enemy?'

'It shames me to say, but they are of our creation.' Dante bit out the words. 'The clone-Marine that Brother Caecus brought to us… These are more of the same.'

'They are better,' Seth broke in. 'Faster and more lethal than the one culled by Noxx and Rafen.'

'How did this happen?' Armis demanded.

'It appears that Caecus was more industrious than he admitted,' Seth replied. 'The Apothecae has broken with his brethren, quite possibly turned from the face of the Emperor into the bargain–'

'There is no evidence of that!' Mephiston said hotly, although with less conviction than he would have liked.

Seth went on. 'These freaks are skulking in ever chamber of this building. They are feeding, cousins. Nourishing themselves on the very blood in our veins.'

'This is Baal. This is a matter for the Blood Angels to deal with.' Dante's cold anger churned behind his flinty eyes, so strong that Mephiston could almost see it spilling into the psychic realm in a hazy red cloud. 'You will be taken under escort to the flight bay and thence to your shuttles. I will ask all of you to return to your starships in orbit and allow my men to deal with this…infestation.'

Daggan gave a metallic grunt. 'Is this an insult? You ask us, a gathering of the heroes of Sanguinius, to flee in the face of some *mutants*?'

'This is my fault,' Dante admitted. 'It is not upon any of you to shoulder that burden, nor shed blood for it.'

'Agreed,' said Orloc. 'But we shall stay and do so anyway, yes?' He glanced around at the other Masters and gathered nods of the head in return. 'Baal is yours, Blood Angel, that is without question. But it is the home of our shared liege-lord, and that makes it our heritage as well. As the Venerable Lord Daggan says, to be kept from this might be thought a slur toward us on your part.'

'We stay,' repeated Armis.

Mephiston watched the hint of a smile touch his master's lips. 'Then you do my Chapter an honour. We will fight side by side, as our primarch would wish.' Dante turned to his trusted lieutenant. 'Have a detail of battle-brothers bring armaments for every warrior here, and loads for the Lord Daggan's cannons.'

'As you command,' said the psyker, bowing.

The next words came with casual menace. 'And summon my armourer. I want my wargear and my weapons.' Dante's smile went away. 'This folly has gone on long enough. We will make an end to it, before the dawn rises.'

THE THUNDERHAWK WAS on fire as it fell from the sky. The thrusters, pushed to a point beyond their safe limits, began to consume themselves. Sun-hot fusion flame distorted and buckled the engine manifolds, and great black trains of smoke marked the gunship's downward passage. White sparks of broken metal fell in their wake, like spent tracer.

Within, a hell-light bathed everything. Crimson warning strobes blinked incessantly, although Rafen had swiftly silenced the braying of the alert klaxon in the troop bay. 'How much longer?' he shouted.

'We are on final approach,' replied Kayne. In order to convince the pilot-serf to take the Thunderhawk on a suicidal suborbital dive, the sergeant had dispatched the youth to the cockpit to provide some encouragement with his bolter. The plan had worked, and their return flight had taken a fraction of the time of their outward sortie; the only problem was the cost. This ship would never fly again; at best, the Techmarines would use it for scrap.

And that is if we can make it the last few kilometres without coming apart in mid-air, Rafen thought grimly. But the Emperor had taken them this far without calling them to His side, and He would not take His favour from them now, not with Mount Seraph and the fortress-monastery in sight.

Noxx had his head bowed and his lips were moving. He was leading his battle-brothers in a prayer, amid the juddering, plummeting flight. Rafen saw the words he spoke and echoed them. 'We are the Emperor's Chosen. Hear His great anger in the roar of the bolt pistol. See His almighty fury in the blades of the chainsword. Feel His undying strength in the protection of your armour.'

The simple litany brought him focus. Each word seemed right and true. Back there, in the citadel, Rafen had felt a small sting of doubt in the moments before he passed judgement upon Caecus. The poor fool; the Apothecae's intent had been pure, even if his methods had not. He shook his head. There could be no forgiveness, now. Caecus had opened the door to corruption though his arrogance and brought disgrace to his Chapter.

Rafen's gaze went to Noxx once more and he wondered: *do all the successors see us as men of that stripe? Superior and wilful, convinced of our rightness even to the point of irresponsibility?*

'Stand by for egress!' Kayne's shout was loud.

Rafen bowed his head once more and whispered a final invocation. 'Lord of Terra, Lord of Baal. Grant me safe landing. Let me take my fury to those who should know it.'

The words had barely left his lips when the Thunderhawk shuddered as if it had been hit by a gigantic hammer, and crashed into the monastery's great courtyard.

THE SHIP BOUNCED off the flagstones, snapping a trio of pennant masts before landing again, this time so hard that the undercarriage crumpled, the metal skis snapping from the wing roots. Churning out coils of heavy smoke, the craft skidded and lost first one wing, then the other. Reaction fuel gushed out in spurts as the armoured fuselage was punctured. The Thunderhawk shed pieces of itself and flipped on to its port side, slowing as it carved a black streak toward the great statue on the central podium in the middle of the quad. Velocity bled away and it creaked to a halt, sparking, aerofoils twitching in machine-death.

The drop-ramp blew out on explosive bolts and the Space Marines disembarked in a flood of armour. Rafen and Kayne were the last to exit, dropping to the stones. 'The pilot?' said the sergeant.

'Expired,' said the youth. 'The strain of the flight was too much for his heart. He died as the aircraft did.'

'His duty was done. That's all that matters.' Rafen looked up at the statue of the primarch Sanguinius towering over their heads, and he gave it a silent nod of thanks.

On the thin, cold desert winds came the mournful sound of a hollow tolling and every warrior stiffened. 'Cloister bell,' hissed Corvus. 'We were right to hasten back.'

'Those creatures are here,' said Ajir. 'I can smell them.'

Rafen looked and found Noxx a short distance away, crouching at the edge of an impact crater. As he watched, he saw the Flesh Tearer spit and then made the sign of the aquila, his men following suit.

'Roan,' said Puluo, his face unreadable.

'Aye,' nodded Rafen.

Beside him, Kayne's attention was still on the statue. 'Lord, do you see that? Something up there… But nothing visible on preysight…'

Rafen spun around, bringing up his bolter, in time to see a flurry of muscled shapes throw themselves from the shoulders of the great stone angel, webs of skin flapping open beneath their arms to slow their fall.

GUNFIRE ERUPTED AROUND the wreck of the Thunderhawk as a pack of the Bloodfiends attacked. The largest of them, still drunk upon the rich cocktail of vitae it had swallowed in the chapel, hung back and let its smaller brethren take first cut.

Within the collection of animal drives and base impulses that were its mind, the mutant clone was torn by a kind of madness. Chattering meme-voices, fragments of self and old, dead personalities warred with each other. They could only be stopped by the drowning of them in the deluge of stolen lifeblood.

The creature was, like every one of its kind, a shattered mirror reformed in the image of a Blood Angel, but lacking in any of the qualities that could be thought of as human. If it had a soul, a spirit, then that too was a broken and distorted thing. Given hundreds of years of test and study, of careful experimentation and practice, the replicae might have become something akin to a man; instead, the mutations that cursed them had been accelerated by the machinations of Fabius Bile, and with each drop of bright blood they consumed, the thirst that dominated the Bloodfiends grew stronger. The pack alpha perched upon a piece of wreckage and sniffed at the air. It could smell the coppery scent on the wind. Not the commonplace blood that spilled now about its feet, torn from the veins of the Space Marines, but something more, like the fluid from the grail but much, much more potent.

It would seek it out. Consume it; and perhaps, in the taking, finally silence the madness.

'THEY WILL SEEK it out...' Mephiston froze, his armour suddenly tight around him, his crystalline sword in his hands.

'Lord?' At his side, the honour guard shot him a questioning look.

The psyker hesitated in the corridor beyond the great hall, the faint light of the burning Thunderhawk catching his dark eyes through the arched windows. The strength of the feral animal-thought was so sudden, so strong that it caught him unawares. It was there and then gone, a flash of lightning on a stygian night. He blinked and refocused, seeing Corbulo racing toward him. The sanguinary priest had a drawstring bag of heavy leather clutched to him and his chainsword in the other hand. Blood stained the edge of the blade and Corbulo's robes. Mephiston's battle-brother was marked with contusions across his face, but he didn't seem aware of them. Instead, he bore an expression of mingled distaste and horror.

'Librarian!' Corbulo gasped, shaking his head in disbelief. 'I have... What I have just seen sickens me! Those beasts, they invaded the chapel!'

'Yes,' Mephiston tried to hold on to the fleeting though-pattern of the Bloodfiend, but it was like mercury, breaking apart, slipping away. He saw images; the chapel, the Red Grail. He sensed the echo of sensation; the deep taste of old, old blood, blunt iron upon torn flesh. 'It took the draught. All of it...'

Corbulo nodded, shamefaced. 'I could not stop them.'

'It won't be enough,' said the psyker, as the brief spark of contact finally guttered out and died. 'They want more. By the Throne, brother, they want it all.'

'They can't bleed every one of us!' snarled the priest.

Mephiston's face became stony as an understanding came upon him. He whirled about, his crimson cloak flaring open, and raced back into the chamber.

LORD DANTE TURNED at the sound of his name. His eyes narrowed. He had seen the Lord of Death in many aspects, from warrior to scholar, but never with the face he saw now. *Revulsion*, pure and unadulterated, was etched upon him. 'Brother, what is it?' He halted in mid-dress, the golden vambrace on his armour still hanging open.

'Infamy!' shouted the psyker. 'Atrocity and desecration, master! They must be stopped!'

'It is the witchsight,' said Orloc, nodding grimly. 'What have you seen?'

Mephiston halted, all eyes upon him, and made a visible effort to control himself. 'The creatures… The Bloodfiends… They penetrated the Chapel of the Red Grail, took the vitae of the chalice!'

A surge of shock went through everyone in the room. Dante heard Daggan crackle out a curse.

'The blood,' said Seth, the colour draining from his face. 'Throne and damnation… They went for the blood of the grail!'

'And they want *more*,' husked Corbulo. 'They are feeding off it, enhancing themselves with every mouthful. I saw it with my own eyes.'

The psyker nodded. 'The Red Grail won't be enough. Now they have the taste of it.'

Seth's eyes searched Mephiston's, then turned to meet Dante's gaze. 'If this is so… Then there can be only one place to which they will be drawn.'

'The Sarcophagus,' Dante's voice was a whisper in the sudden stillness of the hall. 'The flesh of the primarch himself. If they absorb that, they will be unstoppable.'

To consider such a thing was a horror, an offence of such dimension that not one of the Astartes spoke; it fell to the Master of the Blood Angels to break the silence.

He turned to Corbulo. 'Brother,' he began, 'contact Lord Sentikan aboard the battle cruiser *Unseen*. Disclose to him the scope of this… outrage. Relay this request.' Dante sighed. 'Tell Sentikan that he has authority to stand as acting commander of all warships in Baal orbit.' None of the other Chapter Masters showed any signs of disagreement, all of them certain of the seriousness of this moment, and of what Dante was about to say next. 'Tell him to have lance cannons trained upon the planet, to this location. If we fail to stop these creatures, Mount Seraph is to be destroyed. We will not suffer abominations to live.'

CHAPTER THIRTEEN

LIGHT CAME UPON the silent cadre of warriors in a slow wave as they entered the ossuary antechamber, biolume floaterglobes rising from their cradles to cast colour and shadow about the hall. A pathway made of iron crossed from one side to another, narrowing as it did to the width of two battle-brothers shoulder to shoulder. Every other surface was dull white with bone. Hundreds of skulls stared sightlessly out from the walls and the ceiling, some of them unadorned, others whorled with etchings of devotional script or illuminated pictographs. The bones of the chosen few were of men whose deeds were of such magnitude they were allowed to be interred so close to the body of their primarch. These dead had not just been heroes, for all Astartes were heroes; they were men of singular courage, soldier-saints of vision and utmost purity.

Dante, the light glittering off the polished gold of his wargear, was at the head of the group, and for an instant his gaze dropped to one single skull, low down among the others. He knew where it lay, because it was his hands that had put it there. Kadeus, the Chapter Master who had ruled before Dante, a mentor and a friend, long dead now but still watching over him. He wondered what advice the old warrior would have had to offer him if he were alive at this moment. Every Master was here in this room, from the brothers who had been granted the fortune of walking in Sanguinius's shadow, to the men who had led his Legion through ten millennia of ceaseless galactic war. Dante hoped that he too might one day be laid to rest among them, but for the first time he wondered if that fate might not be open to him.

If we fail, Sentikan will follow his orders to the letter. He looked around. *All of this… It will become vapour and ashes.*

Dante stiffened as he approached the massive circular door at the far end of the antechamber, dismissing the thought with action. He twisted the wrist of his golden gauntlet and removed the glove. In the middle of the door was a fist-sized hole, and the Blood Angel thrust his hand into it. With a sharp clank, metal pins stabbed out from the door's inner mechanism and clamped his forearm tightly in place.

'I am Dante,' he said to the air. 'In Sanguinius's name, know me.'

A cowl of thick needles coiled around his bared flesh and sank to the hilt, penetrating his veins and deep to the marrow in his bones. Arcane gene-sense technologies tasted him and considered for long moments, before snapping away, releasing the master's arm. He wiped away a stray droplet of blood and replaced his gauntlet. 'Open the doors,' he commanded, and so they did.

* * *

MEPHISTON FOLLOWED HIS master into the sepulchre with a reticence he had thought himself incapable of. At the edges of his thoughts, the psyker felt a distant pressure upon his telepathic sense, like a faraway storm. As the antechamber's cogwheel gate rolled away into the walls, so did two others at equidistant points around the circular shrine, the priest's door and the penitent's door. Overhead, the walls vanished toward a curved roof covered with elaborate frescoes that showed spacescapes and the arc of the galactic arm. Picked out in clusters of gemstones and precious metals were the locations of Terra, Ophelia, Sabien, Signus and dozens other significant systems from the Chapter's history, arranged as if glimpsed from the surface of Baal on a clear night. But there had not been a clear night on Baal since the War of the Burning that scourged the planet with nuclear fire; and the surface was high above them, through layers of rock and countless tiers of the fortress-monastery.

Free-standing ramparts taller than a Dreadnought ringed the centre of the space, set out at regular distances. The middle of the chamber was an open pit, in cross-section an inverted cone. From where he stood. Mephiston could see the ramp that dropped away, following the walls downward in a spiral walkway leading to the very bottom, and to the great and holy resting place.

The other Astartes filed in around him, sharing his silence, his reverence for this place. All of them looked to the dark pool of shadow that was the vast opening, all of them knowing what lay down there, untouched and forever preserved. As one, without command or gesture, each warrior bowed their heads and sank to one knee, making the sign of the aquila across their chests.

When they rose again, Mephiston found Dante looking at him. 'Speak, my friend,' said the Chapter Master. His words were quiet, in respect for the place in which they stood. 'Say what is on your mind.'

Mephiston glanced down at the force sword sheathed at his belt, his hand suspended over the weapon's hilt. 'This is a place of veneration, lord. Yet we cheapen it by bringing blades and guns into its environs. What does that say of us?'

Dante placed a hand on his comrade's shoulder. 'Battle is our church as much as any stone-built cathedral, kinsman. Our faith is dust unless we are willing to kill for it. And die for it.' The Chapter Master nodded toward the pit. 'He knew that. And he will forgive us this trespass.'

BROTHER CORBULO LED them down through the corridors, along the great tunnels and passageways with the screams and hoots of the Bloodfiends as their constant companions. The beasts were following them, of that Rafen was certain.

The sanguinary high priest had gathered them from the courtyard as the mutants fell back to regroup, explaining on the way what had transpired in the fortress. Rafen listened, aghast, as Corbulo told him of the confrontation in the Chapel of the Red Grail, of Lord Dante's orders to Sentikan and the massing of the men inside the holy walls of the great sepulchre.

At that, the muscles in Rafen's legs stiffened and he halted clumsily. 'I... We cannot enter that place, priest.' He cast around at his own men, at Noxx and the squad of Flesh Tearers. 'We are unworthy.'

Corbulo fixed him with a hard glare. 'Don't be a fool, lad. Have you learned nothing in recent days? We face a threat unlike any other, and if to fight it we must bend rules and ancient doctrine, then that *we will do*.' He gave a grim smile. 'Once it is done and all is well once again, we shall ask the Emperor's forgiveness. He will grant it if we do not fail him, I have no doubt.' Corbulo turned to Turcio, looking at his penitent brand. 'Dogma cannot oppose the realities of battle, it can only form a frame-work for the fight.'

'Unusual to hear a blood priest say such a thing,' said Noxx.

Corbulo gave a weary nod. 'We are all of us learning many lessons this day.'

As difficult as it was to put the greater meaning of the place behind him, Rafen and the other line Astartes did so, following Corbulo through the antechamber and, at last, into the sepulchre. They paused to kneel and show deference before stepping forward once more. The sergeant saw the mix of men from every successor at the conclave, all of them handling their guns and swords with care, as if they feared to make too much sound and disturb the worshipful air about them. Noxx gathered the survivors from his squad and marched to his master's side, and for a moment Rafen thought he saw a flash of genuine empathy on Lord Seth's face at the return of his warrior and the absence of Brother-Captain Gorn. Scattered around, the men of the other Chapters were in similarly close-knit groups, speaking quietly of what was to come.

A figure in hard planes of gold emerged and came to them. Rafen bowed his head to his Chapter Master; even in the dim light of the sepulchre, Dante cut an impressive figure in the shining artificer armour. In respect for where they stood, the commander went without his combat helmet; fashioned in the image of the primarch's death mask, to wear it in this place seemed unmannerly. He rested one hand upon the butt of his Inferno pistol, casting a measuring gaze over the Space Marines. 'Was your mission a success, brother-sergeant?' Argastes and Mephiston approached in his wake, watching for Rafen's answer.

Rafen met his master's eyes. 'The Vitalis Citadel is no more, lord. In its destruction, all trace of the replicae laboratorium was obliterated.'

'A high cost. And what of Brother Caecus?'

'Dead by my hand.'

Dante's eyes narrowed. 'Why?'

Rafen frowned, framing his reply. '*Chaos*, lord. The hand of the Ruinous Powers was corrupting his work, although it was only in the end he saw it. He accepted my judgement without question.'

At the Chapter Master's side, Mephiston's lip curled. 'I knew it! The moment in the annex, and again in the halls… I sensed something unhallowed, too fast to be seen in the light of reason.' He showed his teeth. 'These clones, these Bloodfiends. They are tainted by the touch of the warp.'

'Aye,' agreed Rafen. 'Caecus's works were fouled by an agent of the arch-enemy. The renegade Fabius Bile. It disgraces me that I could not kill him before he vanished.'

'Fabius dared to set foot on our soil?' For an instant, Rafen sensed that Dante was on the verge of open fury, the same heartsick anger that he had felt on confronting the twisted primogenitor; then the warlord's expression became icy. 'He sent the Bloodfiends here. To sow anarchy and disorder throughout the fortress. To divide us at the very moment when unity is needed.'

'A gate to the Eye of Terror opened, a warp tunnel forced through our spirit-wards and defences.' hissed Mephiston. 'Yes, it is clear to me now. He fled Baal and left this disorder in his wake.'

Dante nodded once, and again turned his iron-hard gaze on Rafen. 'I will have a full accounting of things from you in due time, brother-sergeant. But for the moment, other issues press us to their resolution.'

'What would you have us do, master?' Rafen said stiffly.

'Fight,' Dante growled. 'Fight until the Emperor claims you. The mutants are coming here, drawn to the scent of the greatest blood as moths to a flame. We know this. We set the line here, and kill them as they come.'

'Lord,' ventured Argastes, musing. 'If we could obliterate these aberrants swiftly... Perhaps, we should employ one of the archeotech weapons in the armourarium–'

'The Spear of Telesto?' The name escaped Rafen's lips and he glanced at Mephiston.

The psyker shook his head. 'The Spear would not end these brutes, brother. Its brilliant fires are gene-locked by some manner of science from the Dark Age of Technology. Any Blood Angel who falls beneath it emerges untouched.'

'And the Bloodfiends are alike to us on a genetic level,' Argastes frowned, understanding. 'The flames would be turned from them.'

Dante nodded again. 'It will be force of arms, the will of the Sons of Sanguinius that turn this battle, not other powers. The fortress is sealed, brothers. There will be no reinforcements, no more men for these creatures to prey upon and bolster themselves. We alone will break them. We must.' He glanced around at the mix of crimson armours. 'This is something only we can do. To prove the truth.'

'What truth?' said Corbulo tersely, forgetting himself for a moment as dejection clouded his face. 'That we are being driven to the brink of extinction?'

The Chapter Master turned on him, his eyes flashing. 'That we are worthy, brother! That is what we must affirm! To ourselves, as well as our successors, even to Sanguinius and the Emperor!' He drew in a breath, raising his chin. 'In this place and this time, this *ordeal*, my brothers, it is the price that we are paying for our arrogance.' He glared at Rafen and the Blood Angel felt a moment of connection to his commander. 'Look at what has befallen us. The machinations of Chaos, first through the ordos traitor Stele and his puppetry of good, loyal men; men whose failing was to be prideful to the point of blindness. The deaths at Sabien and the diminishment of our numbers. And now this, these twisted, freakish mirrors of our baser natures, given flesh and let loose in our most sacred places. What is the root, kinsmen? What sin opened the doorway to these attacks upon the very soul of our Chapter?' Dante's temper was rising, his face darkening. 'Conceit! And we can lay the blame nowhere but at our own feet!' He shook his head. 'My cousin Seth did not lie. We *have* allowed ourselves to become arrogant. To rest upon our laurels as the First Founding, to believe that the name Blood Angel is protection enough!' Dante's voice fell. 'We reflect our liege-lord in so many ways, but we have allowed one of his greatest traits to run thin in us.'

'Humility,' whispered Rafen.

'Just so,' said his commander. 'And perhaps this is the way the Emperor seeks to remind us. By pitting us against the beasts cut from the cloth of our own folly.' He turned and stalked away toward the great pit, drawing his Inferno pistol.

DANTE DREW HIMSELF up to his full height and held his gun in the air, a sullen glow playing around the barrel of the master-crafted weapon. All heads turned to give him their attention.

'Sons of Sanguinius! Heed me. We make our stand here, on the cusp of the sepulchre, in sight of the Emperor of Mankind and in the aura of our primarch.' He pointed down into the open chasm. 'The Great Angel lies below us, sleeping in light, forever preserved. The beasts that come to savage his memory are as nothing we have fought before. Not daemons, not xenos, but a malform that shares our strengths, our will, and more than that, a dark and animal heart. Make no mistake; this will be a hard-fought battle. Some of us will not see daylight again; but know that if you die, it will be at Sanguinius's side, and he will spread his wings to carry you to the Emperor's right hand.' Dante fell silent for a moment, and in the quiet, the sounds of the enemy reached down the stone corridors to the assembled men, growing closer by the moment.

'These past days we have been consumed by words. Dissent and divisiveness have cast long shadows over this conclave, and to my chagrin not one moment of this has gone as I planned it.' He gave a rueful smile. 'But then, as our staid comrades in the Ultramarines always say, no battle plan ever survives first contact.' The smile faded. 'The time for words is over, kindred. Now our deeds must carry the day.'

Daggan's scratchy vox-coder crackled. 'For Sanguinius.'

'For the Emperor,' added Orloc.

Armis nodded. 'For the future.'

Dante gestured towards the three doorways. 'The Bloodfiends are on their way. Our reports on their numbers vary, but I suspect half-company strength, perhaps more. With each door to the sepulchre open, we will force them to divide their approach.' He glanced at the Dreadnought. 'Lord Daggan? I ask you to take command of the men defending the penitent gate.'

'I offer the arms of the Blood Drinkers for the priest gate,' said Orloc.

Armis nodded again. 'If the Lord Orloc will accept, my men will join his.'

'Gladly. And I will offer the Angels Encarmine a place at my side, if they will take it.' Orloc got a silent nod in return from the Master of the other Chapter.

'Lord Seth,' said Dante. 'Will you stand with the Blood Angels at the great gate?'

'Never let it be said that Cretacia's Finest refused a fight,' hissed the Flesh Tearer.

* * *

RAFEN WATCHED THE groups of Astartes form up; the
Blood Swords joined by the Angels Vermillion and the
Flesh Eaters; the Red Wings, Angels Encarmine and the
Blood Legion coming together in a moment of shared
battle-prayer; and other squads from the rest of the successor Chapters forming into combat squads, bolters
and blades at the ready. For each cousin-warrior, there
were Blood Angel battle-brothers to stand with them,
but once again, as he was in the Grand Annex on the first
day of the gathering, Rafen was struck not by the differences in armour and livery, but by the similarity between
the warriors. 'We are all one cadre now,' he said aloud.

Rafen's gaze went to each of his men in turn. 'Brothers,' he began, 'This one will test us hard, make no
mistake about it. We are fighting ghosts in a hall of
priceless mirrors.'

Puluo hefted his bolter cannon. 'Ready,' he said simply.

Corvus forced a smile. 'Of course we are.' He nodded
at the youngest of their group, whose hand was still
swaddled in a bioplastic bandage. 'Look at Kayne, here.
He's fighting with his off-grip just to give the mutants a
fair chance.'

The youth snorted with gallows humour. 'I only need
one hand to make a kill.'

Turcio was looking at the other Space Marines. 'Where
is Lord Sentikan?'

Ajir jerked his thumb toward the ceiling. 'In orbit,
behind the guns of his starship.'

'He has a different task to attend to,' said Rafen, shooting Ajir a warning look. 'Let us pray we do ours well
enough that he need not perform it. We will take to the
line, and hold fast–'

'You will not,' said Mephiston without preamble,
striding into the middle of the group with Brother
Argastes at his side. The Chaplain's black wargear

shimmered in the gloom, in stark contrast to the blood-coloured armour of the psyker. Rafen caught the play of faint electric blue sparks around the Lord of Death's towering psychic hood. 'Our Master Dante has charged me with a singular duty and I need men of courage to assist me.'

'We are yours to command,' Rafen said, without hesitation.

Mephiston beckoned the Blood Angels with an armoured hand. 'Follow me.'

As one, Rafen's unit fell in and made formation to do as they were ordered; but they had only taken a few steps when the brother-sergeant was compelled to speak. 'My Lord?' Mephiston was leading them toward the pit, toward an arch of spun electrum and gold that marked the start of the spiral ramp leading down toward the heart of the sepulchre. 'We cannot venture…'

The psyker halted and scanned the faces of the men. Rafen felt his penetrating gaze weighing each of them as if they were handfuls of sand in his grip. 'Our orders are to stand as bulwark to the Golden Sarcophagus, brother-sergeant. If need be, to places our backs to it and defend it with tooth and nail.' He glared at the Blood Angel. 'You would refuse? Do you think your men unworthy, or incapable of executing that edict?'

Rafen heard the rush of blood sing in his ears. 'It will be our singular pride to give our lives in service to this command.'

Mephiston grunted. 'Let us hope it does not come to that.'

DANTE SIGHTED DOWN the barrel of his pistol. The weight of the ornate weapon felt right and proper in his hands. It seemed too long since he had used it in anger. *The demands of authority have kept me away from the field of battle.*

Seth was watching him, a plasma gun ready at his side. The screeching of the Bloodfiends was loud now. The mutant horde could only be moments away from them. 'Are you prepared for this, cousin?' asked the Flesh Tearer.

'Nothing could prepare for this,' said Dante. 'We can only meet the enemy as they come.'

'I hope you're up to it.'

Annoyance flared in the Blood Angel's eyes. 'And still you test me, Seth. Even now, as battle is about to break upon us, you still seek to goad me. What do you hope to achieve? Answer me that!'

Seth sniffed. 'For all your years and wisdom, you still do not know me or my brethren…'

'I know this! You deliberately challenge me at every turn; you oppose every word that falls from my lips as if it were your sole reason for living!' Dante fumed. 'You foster discord, Seth. You thrive upon it!'

The Flesh Tearer smiled. 'I stand corrected. You *do* understand my kind after all. You've cut to the heart of me.' His head bobbed. 'We are disorder, that is true. But that is what we were made to be. The wild and the random.' Seth's voice was gravelly. 'If each successor embodies traits of the Great Angel, then that is what the Flesh Tearers are, just as the Blood Swords are his martial prowess, the Sanguine his secrecy, the Flesh Eaters his carnivore's fangs!' He laughed in a short, harsh bark. 'But the Blood Angels are the melding of all those things, and that is why I will always envy you, cousin. I challenge you because I *must*. How else can you be sure that you remain upon the primarch's path?'

The Chapter Master felt a feral grin tighten his lips. 'And so you justify yourself? You are my watchman, is that it?'

'We are all our brother's keepers, Dante. The Emperor created us to be so.'

A cry came up from one of the Angels Vermillion; the mutants were in the corridors, boiling toward the sepulchre in a frenzied flood.

The Master of the Blood Angels took aim. 'When we are done here, you and I will speak more of this.'

'I do not doubt it,' Seth allowed, the inductor coils atop his weapon glowing blue-white with power.

THE BLOODFIENDS DESCENDED upon the vast, circular chamber in a storm of talons and fire. The blunt jags of development coursing through them pushed the mutants toward rough cunning and base intellect; for every two that attacked with claws or teeth or club-like fist, there was one with a looted weapon and the innate skill to use it. The clones carried the formation of an omophagea organ in the structure of their flesh. Almost identical to the function of the implant in the bodies of the Space Marines, the complex knots of nerve-sheath and organic bioprocessor keyed to viable elements of genetic memory in any ingested matter. The blood they consumed, still warm and raw from men drained dry, awakened locked muscle-recall and conditioned responses. The more they fed, the more they became.

But it also opened doors to fractured pieces of self, caught by the vagaries of evolution. Fragments of memories from the hundred-fold donors whose DNA formed Caecus's zygote code emerged, conflicting, strident and unstoppable. The thirst of the Bloodfiends drove them to consume; but in that act they only intensified the insanity that churned inside them.

The first wave of them broke through all three gates at once, each torrent of ruddy flesh meeting bolter fire and energy beams. They could smell the great bounty lying just beyond the antechambers, and it maddened them beyond the point of self-preservation.

The beast that Corbulo faced inside the chapel was the oldest of them, if such a concept applied to beings force-grown in synthetic wombs, the furthest along through the tortuous process of its awakening. The pack alpha tried to form words, but they escaped it. Frustration heaped upon the anger that burned within it. The killing rage grew ever stronger, the lust for blood and direction-less hate a wave that carried them forward.

DAGGAN SPUN IN place, his drum-shaped arms slamming into a Bloodfiend's torso, the mutant's chest distending with the impact. The Dreadnought registered the hit, the power of which would have crippled an Astartes. These things were dense, though, as large as Terminators but as fast as a fleet-footed Scout. The Master of the Blood Swords discharged the assault cannon on his right arm and blew the clone off it, the point-blank impact tearing it apart.

His sensor suite registered one of the Flesh Eaters in the heavy, slow armour of a veteran assault warrior. A guttural cry escaped the Astartes as he was torn from his wargear by a cluster of Bloodfiends. His helm in pieces, the Flesh Eater was ripped out in rags through the neck of his black torso armour. Daggan granted him the Emperor's Peace with a sustained burst of fire, laying shells across his attackers as he did. He cursed when only one of them fell dead, the others shrugging off glancing shots.

'Rot these freaks, but they do not perish easily!' Charging his chainfist, the Dreadnought lumbered forward and sliced into the mass of mutants pressing against the penitent gate. A pair of Angels Vermillion in shining Terminator armour kept pace with him; he registered them beating back smaller clones – those close to the size of a line Astartes – with thunder hammer and lightning claws. Daggan aimed his cannon into the cluster and fired again, a spear of muzzle flare roaring through the air. The reverent silence of the sepulchre was a dim memory. This sacred place was now another battlefield, a crucible of death.

One of the Angel Vermillion advanced, and took his hammer to a Bloodfiend larger than the rest of them. Daggan saw the creature emerging from the spitting, growling pack and measured its mass. This new enemy was almost the size of the Dreadnought, horribly inflated to gross proportions in a parody of brawn and strength.

It landed a closed fist upon the skull of the Terminator and Daggan's audial scanners picked up the crunch of bone beneath shattered ceramite. The Angel Vermillion fell to the marble tiles, his life extinguished with a single blow.

A hissing crackle escaped Daggan's vox-coder and he swung his ponderous mass toward the towering Bloodfiend, blocking its path toward the great mausoleum. His palette of sensing devices cast x-ray, preysight and sonic energies over the clone's body, instantly pouring information to the twisted clump of meat and brain tissue that was all that remained of Lord Daggan's flesh. The seasoned warrior's mind interfaced seamlessly with the iron musculature of his machine-body, searching for points of attack. Bolt shells fired artlessly from the beast's gun sparked off his armour-plated facia, and through the veil of the Dreadnought's synthetic senses, Daggan saw a very human smile spread across on the mutant's face.

All other foes forgotten, the Bloodfiend screamed and leapt at him.

THE SPIRAL RAMP fell quickly downward, describing a course around the inside of the conical chasm toward the circular stage at the heart of the great sepulchre. As was right and proper, the Chaplain Argastes led the way, intoning the ritual passages from the Book of the Lords at each arch they passed. The photonic candles flared into red flame upon the delivery of the Chaplain's words; it was his duty to ensure that every spirit-ward and hidden trap was correctly addressed before they could proceed to the next. Rafen was behind Mephiston, who walked at Argastes's back with his hand upon the hilt of his force sword. The pskyer's face was set in an expressionless mask, but his eyes were stark and troubled. The sergeant wondered what ethereal energy might lurk unseen by him in such a place as this, a tomb where a demi-god lay in solemn rest.

Rafen was acutely aware of the thundering noise of his heartbeat rushing in his ears. He clenched his hands into fists to stop them from trembling and tried to keep his focus; but it was difficult to hold on to his warrior's detachment. The Blood Angel looked straight ahead, not daring to let his gaze drop down to the resting place. His eyes found the intricate murals that followed the spiral path, the paintings and carvings in varicoloured stones, metals and gems; a mosaic that chronicled the life of Sanguinius from his creation at the Emperor's hands to his death by the blade of the Arch-traitor Horus. Here, Rafen saw a depiction of the primarch at Signus, engaged in battle with a swarm of Furies, surrounded by battle-brothers under the command of the noble Chapter Master Raldoron.

For a moment, Rafen lost himself in the sapphire eyes of the man in the frieze. It was Brother Raldoron who had built this place beneath the fortress-monastery, and he, it was said, who alone had borne the Golden Sarcophagus down the spiral ramp on the day the primarch's body had returned to Baal. Rafen tried to imagine the incalculable sorrow the man must have endured at that moment. To have lived when Sanguinius

was alive, and then to have seen him struck down…
What horror that must have been.

The Blood Angel found himself drawing strength from
the image. If Raldoron had survived such grief to carry
on the legacy of his Chapter, then in comparison the
challenge laid before Rafen was insignificant. *Fight until
the Emperor claims you,* Dante had ordered. *So we
shall.*

He allowed himself to look down, and there he saw
the honeyed glow of rippling gold light, thrown from
the shifting, liquid heart of the primarch's casket.

THE DREADNOUGHT WAS an obelisk of war, a living, moving monument to the battle prowess of the Blood
Swords and the honour of Sanguinius. A leviathan of the
field, Daggan had served first in flesh and bone and then
encased in steel and ceramite for more than four hundred years. His was to be part of a heritage of great
heroes, Astartes who fought beyond injuries that would
have killed lesser men. Like the noble Furioso, first and
greatest of the Sons of Sanguinius to live again within a
sheath of steel, and his descendants Ignis, Dario and
Moriar, Daggan was a fist of flesh encased in an iron
glove. His coffin was his weapon, his injuries the spur
that turned him to fight anew.

But the pack leader of the Bloodfiends saw only meat;
meat shrouded in metal.

It struck Daggan with clawed hands, landing hard
enough to rock the Chapter Master back on his
hydraulic legs. Too close to employ his assault cannon
without blinding his sensors with the muzzle flash, Daggan pressed his chainfist into the clone and spun the
toothed blade.

The beast howled and tore at the Dreadnought's
ornate faceplate, gouging great scars through the armour
plating, cracking the outer surface with punches that

rang like a tolling bell. It brought down its bony, ridged skull and butted the narrow armourglass slit over Daggan's casket-pod with a heavy blow. The glass webbed and shattered.

The meat-stink of the Blood Sword warrior's corpse flesh body issued out. The monstrous clone caught the smell and it brayed; tormented rage aroused by the scent of ancient tissue kept alive by the engines and biological arcana of the Mechanicum.

Daggan's chainblade scored through layers of skin as hard as plasteel and bony discs of natural armour. Thin fluids oozed from the wound, but the beast-warrior only attacked with greater fury, shredding the Chapter Master's votive chains, his purity seals and the fine inlaying of ruby and white gold across his faceplate.

His battle-brothers attempted to rally to his side, but the defence of the penitent gate was shifting, pushed back by the sheer pressure of Bloodfiend numbers. Clones shot down and thought dead would recover and remount their attack, even with stumps that trailed blood or flesh in tatters; anything short of decapitation seemed to be uncertain of stopping them.

Daggan tried to snatch at his assailant, but the Dreadnought's clumsy mass worked against him. The pack leader scrambled about, shifting out of the Chapter Master's grip, constantly defeating any attempt to pin him.

A hand of talons raked his facia and found purchase in the broken-open eye-slit. With a monumental roar, the Bloodfiend's distended biceps knotted and metal gave way with an agonized screech. The faceplate, decorated with bones and shards of red jade, was torn free and sent spinning back down the corridors. Revealed, the remnants of Daggan's organic body lay in a thick soup of processor unguents, haloed by coils of mechadendrites and neural ducting.

He had taken the Path of the Steel and Eternal in the wake of a battle on a nameless planetoid, after coming a heartbeat's count from dying in the burning acid discharge of a tyranid spore-mine swarm. From that day until this one, no breath of air had ever touched Daggan's flesh. In the midst of all the melee, the sense of warmth across his skin sparked strange recall in the Chapter Master's mind.

But he was granted no time to savour it. With lightning speed, the Bloodfiend alpha opened its jaws wide and bit deep, tearing Daggan into shreds, ripping him from the husk of the Dreadnought to be consumed like the sweet meat of a splintered crustacean.

The iron warrior twitched and collapsed with a crash into a kneeling stance, as if Daggan were mirroring the penitent figures carved into the stonework around the third gateway.

As one, the Blood Sword warriors let out a cry of anguish. The mutants took up the sound and made it a feral howl. The stink of blood heavy in their nostrils, the clones surged forward, shattering the lines of the Space Marines.

CHAPTER FOURTEEN

IT WAS AT once more beautiful and more terrifying than anything Rafen had ever encountered. In silence, for each one of them was struck mute by the sight of it, the Blood Angels stepped off the last length of the spiral ramp and gathered in a cluster at the far edge of the tomb platform.

Argastes, as was his duty, took to his knees, bowed his head and began a prayer. His words were so quiet that Rafen could barely hear him speaking; but none of them needed to. Each warrior knew the invocation as well as their own names, and they took the same stance, mouthing the verse without a sound, eyes averted.

Mephiston glanced over his shoulder and bid them to rise with a slight gesture of his hand. Rafen did so, fighting back a tremor in his legs as ingrained training told him he should still be on his knees in the face of such glory.

'Look,' husked the Lord of Death, pointing toward the far end of the circular stage. 'We do not shy away like virginal pilgrims. Show your liege-lord your faces. Let him see you.'

Each of them removed their helmets and let the amber glow wash over them. It was like standing in sunlight on a perfect, cloudless day. The colour was magnetic, it was transcendent. It was this and a hundred other things, reaching deep and stirring emotions in Rafen that he could not find a voice to describe. From the corner of his eye he saw Puluo wipe a tear of joy from his scarred cheek.

It seemed like an eternity ago when Rafen had laid his hands upon the Spear of Telesto, the ancient weapon that had once been wielded by his primarch; and when his fingers had touched it, there was a moment when the Astartes believed some fragment of the Great Angel made itself known to him. A vision, perhaps. Some manner of connection awakened briefly, and then gone before the power of it could burn out his warrior flesh. The ghost of that sensation now returned to Rafen, and he felt fearful, as if he might be consumed by his proximity, charred to ash by it.

Rafen wanted so much to reach out and touch the aura of his demi-god, but he could not. There was an enchantment upon them all, a binding that held them in place before such magnificence. Awe, veneration, wonderment; each of these words were stripped of colour and made meaningless by the sheer intensity of divine radiance that moved through the Blood Angels.

The heart of the great sepulchre was a monolith at the opposite side of the platform, cut from three tall blocks of red granite. They were polished to a mirror-bright sheen; each mined from the living rock of Baal and its two moons, and crested with a single Terran ruby the size of Rafen's fist. The granites and the gemstone signified the worlds of Sanguinius's birth, his childhood and maturation. Emerging from the monolith were two huge extended angel's wings, curving up and around to form a protective cowl. The individual feathers were made of steel and silver and brass, each one etched with words of remembrance. So the Chapter's chronicles said, many of them were cut from the hull metal of loyalist starships that fought during the time of the Heresy, given in tribute by brother primarchs such as Guilliman, Dorn and Khan, by the Legio Custodes, even the admirals and generals of forces that had fought in the shadow of Sanguinius and counted themselves in his debt.

And between the wings; amid them a single giant hoop of spun copper burnished to the colour of Baal's red giant star, suspended there upon rods of milky crystal that intersected the ring like the points of a compass, in echo of the design upon the floor of the Grand Annex.

Inside the copper halo lay the glowing heart, living and yet dead, forever in motion but always still. The Golden Sarcophagus was not a casket in any conventional sense of the word. It was a sphere of molten gold, rippling and flowing, pendant in an invisible stasis envelope generated by unknowable technologies buried beneath the stonework. In the ebb and flow of the fluid form, one might imagine they could see brief conjunctions of motion that suggested a face, a countenance of most pure and handsome aspect.

Contained within a globe of suspended time, the mantle of liquid metal had never been allowed to cool and solidify, not once in ten thousand years; for beneath it lay the flesh of the Emperor's son, the Great Angel and Lord of the Blood, Master of the IX Legiones Astartes, primarch among primarchs, the most noble Sanguinius.

'My life may end now, and I will be content,' Ajir managed, forcing a faint whisper out of his dry, bloodless lips. 'For I cannot witness a greater glory than this sight.'

'That is not for you to choose,' Mephiston said, making a physical effort to turn away. He pointed toward the sarcophagus once again. 'It is for him to decide.'

'In his name,' intoned Rafen, without hesitating.

'In his name,' repeated the rest of the men, their eyes shining, each of them ready to hold back hell itself to keep this place inviolate.

HIGH ABOVE THEM, a torrent of rage was breaking upon the defenders of the three gates.

Daggan's killing drew away balance from the Space Marines and forced them to regroup, to bulwark the gap cut into the line. At the priest gate, a coalition of warriors from five different Chapters fought in serried rows, red upon red, crimson upon crimson, bolters and plasma guns answering the approach of all foes.

Lord Orloc's gun ran dry and he used the inert firearm to club down a Bloodfiend brandishing a pair of knives; the clone's mutation was more progressed than some of the others of its kind, limbs strangely warped into forms more tentacles than human arms. It growled through a toothed mouth and tried to bite him.

The blade of a power sword burst from its chest and tore upwards along the line of its sternum, cracking bone and spilling innards across the tiled flooring. Fluid spattered across Orloc's face and he turned away as the blade ended its cut. In pieces, the clone fell apart revealing Lord Armis standing behind it, sneering.

'These damnable monsters,' began the Master of the Blood Legion, 'they're tenacious. They seem to know our tactics by rote!'

'I appreciate the assist,' Orloc allowed, quickly reloading his storm bolter. The Astartes licked the spent crimson of the creature off his lips, measuring the essence. 'Curious...' he allowed. 'It has a strange musk to it.'

Armis raised an eyebrow. 'As long as these things bleed, I care nothing else about them.'

The Bloodfiends moved like ocean waves, slamming into the lines of the defenders, retreating, returning and attacking again. They gave little time to react to each frenzied assault.

The Blood Drinker aimed on the move and the storm bolter sang; his fellow Chapter lord followed suit, lending his pistol to the fray. 'They're coming in again!' Orloc shouted, as a horde of red-tanned figures forced themselves through the arch of the priest gate.

Armis spun about, opening the neck of a beast with his sword-point. 'How many this time?' he demanded.

'All of them,' growled Orloc, as the wave of killers struck.

THE GREAT GATE of the sepulchre was the largest of the three, and so it was the largest of the Bloodfiend numbers that burst through it, the clone-Marines hurdling one another in mad abandon, screaming, driven by their desperate thirst.

Seth knew the thronging, wild melee of hand-to-hand battle as well as any Son of Sanguinius. In the depths of such conflict, the fight drew away from issues of tactics and forethought, gradually becoming nothing more than an exercise in steady butchery. A warrior's war diminished to the patch of blood-slicked stone on which he stood, the victory or loss weighed in the spaces within the reach of his hand or the sweep of his sword. The Flesh Tearer gave the right to his name, with the blade in his hand cutting deep into any mutant that came too close, tearing flesh, rending it, slicing it.

He had become separated from Dante; he was dimly aware of the blink of smeared golden armour somewhere to his right, he saw the fall of a terrible swift axe blow and the spin of a head cut clean away. Seth swung his sword in a flashing arc, the plasma gun in his other grip hissing sun-white death into the attacker mob again and again. But still, despite every punishing kill, the defending line was compressed backward under the mass of the assault. Blows that would have broken ranks of ork or eldar did little to deter these bestial parodies of Space Marines. They were simply obsessed to such a degree that pain was not a barrier for them; the lust for the pure blood down in the pit was blocking out everything else. Seth thought of the men he knew who fell into the Black Rage, strong-willed warriors destroyed by the gene-curse and condemned to fight to their ending in the Death Company, under the watchful eye of his Chaplain, Carnarvon. These Blood-fiends shared a similar madness, but without the balance of duty, of ingrained obligation bred into every Adeptus Astartes. The mutants were a force of nature, feral beyond even Seth's definition of the word.

The plasma gun was sizzling in his grip, heat hazing the air around it as overload runes blinked fiercely at him. He turned the weapon away just as a wiry Blood-fiend collided with him. Seth barely had time to react before he was shoved to the rear by the impact, his boots sparking as they skidded over the stones. A sinewy hand with too many joints grappled his wrist and held it rigid, preventing a swiping riposte from the sword. The mutant pushed and pushed, forcing Seth back toward the sharp drop at the edge of the pit. Its neck, an elongated and sinuous thing, wove back and forth like a snake, the head snapping at him.

The plasma gun stalled, the weapon's machine-spirit refusing to release another shot until it cooled for fear of an explosive burnout. Angered, the Flesh Tearer snarled and forced the weapon's white-hot muzzle into the meat of the clone's bare chest and held it there.

Flesh crisped and smoked, drawing a hooting cry from the mutant. In furious agony, it pounded on Seth's armour and threw him to the floor, pushing the Flesh Tearer over the rim, on the cusp of a sheer fall.

For one dizzying moment, Seth saw down into the depths of the chasm, catching sight of the golden sphere shimmering below; then the moment of elation at seeing the sarcophagus with his own eyes was torn away as twisted shapes rushed past him, dropping into the pit on vanes of thick, misshapen skin.

ARGASTES CRIED OUT, pointing upwards with the glowing rod of his crozius. 'To arms, Blood Angels! They've broken the line!'

Rafen glared toward the mouth of the chasm high above them, his lips twisting in fury as dark shadows fell toward them, dropping through the glow of the photonic candles, spinning and turning to dodge the pulse-blasts of laser turrets concealed in the sepulchre's walls. Kayne gave a cry of victory as one of the mutants exploded, the lasers converging to boil it in an explosive burst of concussion; but that was only one kill, and there were so many more of them.

'Wings!' snarled Ajir. 'The damned things can fly!'

'They glide,' Mephiston corrected, drawing his sword. 'The flesh between their limbs only slows their fall.' He aimed the force blade and blue lightning crackled around his psychic hood. The sword twitched and a pulse of ethereal energy leapt from the tip, channelled from the psyker's blazing mind. It swept up and found a mutant, smiting it from the air. 'It makes them better targets,' he concluded.

'Squad!' Rafen shouted. 'Weapons free!' Every gun fired, the storm of shot and shell rumbling like thunder about the walls of the pit.

THE BLOODFIENDS FELL upon them as raptors coming after prey. Puluo's heavy cannon ate up bandoliers of ammunition in shining brass ribbons, the blazing muzzle sending rounds tearing through flesh and bone. At his side, Kayne sighted down the auto-sense targeting scope atop his bolter, carefully pacing bursts of three rounds into each mutant that came within range. He frowned behind the gun at the paucity of immediate kills – the shots were only slowing the attackers – but he did not hesitate, reloading with quick, mechanical motions.

Through the sights, he saw the clone-beasts cleaving to the walls of the chasm, some of them dropping to land on the spiral ramp, others digging their clawed hands into the ornate sculptures to gain purchase. Part of Kayne felt sickened by the idea of these polluted freaks penetrating so far into the heart of the fortress-monastery, and he lamented the damage that each errant shot or mutant talon wreaked on the perfection of the chamber's walls. He felt the warmth of the Golden Sarcophagus upon his back, but did not turn to look at it, as hard as it was to resist the temptation. Instead, he let the glow guide his focus, he allowed it to centre him. He ignored the nagging pain from the knitting bones in his hand and fired again. This time, he marched the rounds up a creature brandishing a pair of short swords and saw it plummet into the steep walls of the ramp. To his disgust, a pair of the mutant's comrades surrounded the fallen Bloodfiend and fed upon it.

'Their hunger has crazed them,' said Puluo. 'The closer they come, the worse they will feel it.'

Kayne took aim again. 'Then it will be a kindness to put them from their misery.'

'RELOADING!' SHOUTED TURCIO, ejecting a spent clip.

'I have you, brother,' Argastes snapped, covering the Space Marine with shots from his bolt pistol.

Turcio nodded, a small part of him marvelling at the esteemed company he found himself in, at the conjunction of events that had brought him to this place. His skeletal bionic forelimb whined as he slammed a fresh magazine into the open breech of his bolter. The Chaplain Argastes was a figure from the Book of Heroes, as were Mephiston and Dante and all the men who were engaged in combat high overhead. These were brothers of note, warriors of iron will and great reach whose deeds were committed to slate and canvas by the Chapter's chroniclers.

And I? I am only Brother Turcio, a penitent and a line Astartes. No songs written about me. No remembrancers crafting poems of my deeds.

Argastes threw him a nod and Turcio returned it, the two of them combining fire on a group of mutants storming the platform from the ramp's edge.

Perhaps on another day, he might have been saddened to think that he would die unsung if he fell at this moment; but he was fighting in the shadow of Sanguinius, the shimmer of molten gold playing around him.

This is my duty; that is enough.

'For the Emperor!' cried Mephiston, his words strong and clear.

Turcio raised his voice to join him. 'And the Great Angel!'

AJIR FOLLOWED A Bloodfiend down as it leapt from the curve of the ramp over his head, describing a swoop toward the floor of the platform. It let out a very human sob of agony as the Blood Angel's rounds hit one after the other, each bolt impact punching a red fist of discharge from the mutant's leathery skin. It landed hard and shuddered, trying to climb back to its feet, groping for a bolt pistol tethered by a lanyard to its thickset forearm. Ajir sneered and reset his weapon to full automatic fire. 'You will not defile this place!' he shouted, and executed the clone with a burst-shot that churned the meat of its torso into blackened slurry.

'Brother!' He heard the alarm in the cry and spun in place, instinct saving him from losing his life to the sweep of a clawed limb bristling with bony spines. The new attacker had come from nowhere; it was some error of replication still walking and breathing. The humanoid's bone structure was grotesque; an overdeveloped thing covered in barbs and skin the texture of tree bark. Ajir fired at it and chips of ossified matter splintered away without apparent affect. Faster than it had any right to be, the creature's drum-shaped fist punched him in the chest and his lungs emptied under the force of it. The Space Marine tasted metallic bile in his mouth, trying to shake off the shock of the blow.

The mutant reeled back for another strike, and the daggers of pain across Ajir's ribcage warned him that a second hit would break bone, likely crush vital organs. He brought up his hands to ward off the blow, but it never came.

The braying of a chainsword cut through the cacophony of the battle and the mutant howled, falling to the floor. Corvus cut the beast down with savage, precise strikes, panting with effort. 'Are you injured?'

'I will live.' Ajir pushed him away, 'I did not need your help!'

Corvus scowled. 'Because of *this*?' He pointed at the penitent brand on his cheek. 'Can you not see beyond it? You should–'

The barbed mutant lurched suddenly, rising again in some last spasm of hate despite the damage done to it. Before he could react, a claw ripped Corvus across the side, opening his arm and tearing his throat into a second, red-lipped mouth.

Ajir's trigger finger jerked reflexively, emptying the rest of his bolter's magazine into the Bloodfiend, blasting it back across the flagstones.

Corvus slumped, gasping, his eyes filled with agony.

Ajir grabbed him. 'Why?' he demanded. 'You repentant fool, why did you do that?'

The other Astartes looked up at him, blood forming a pink froth at his lips, clutching at his throat to hold it together. 'You...' he rasped, confusion at the question there in his dying gaze. 'You are my kinsman...'

Ajir began an angry reply, but it was too late for Corvus to hear it.

THE SWORD WAS gone from his grip and still Seth's pistol refused to obey him, the warp-cursed device spitting and fizzing. The Flesh Tearer made it a club, then, slamming the gun into the Bloodfiend's head over and over. His blows crushed in the orbit of the sinewy clone's skull, but it seemed oblivious to the pain. Talons curved in sickle blade claws raked over his armour with ugly squeals of noise, catching his neck ring and lacerating his face.

The old scar on his cheek reopened and pooled with fresh, bright blood. The mutant chattered and pounded on him as Seth's arm flailed, trying to find something to take hold of before he fell. Beneath his back, the Chapter Master felt the stonework around the lip of the pit fracture and give way.

Seth discarded the plasma weapon and snatched at the Bloodfiend, digging his fingers into the flesh of his attacker; the armoured digits sank into the sallow meat, which parted like the thick rind of a cheese. If he were to fall to his death, than at least he would end his life by taking this monstrous affront with him. Seth had come to this place many times in his life, to the gates of his ending, and he did not fear it; but strangely, there was a new emotion that tightened inside him, so brief and so fleeting. *Regret*. He would not live to see a resolution to the events set in motion by his kindred.

The clone reared back, thick spittle flying from its pallid lips, eyes rolling to show the bloodshot whites. The thing was utterly insane, broken and burned, consumed by its obscene hunger.

Gravity pulled at Seth and he lost his grip; and in that moment the light of a punishing, vengeful sun washed over him, a beam of blazing energy catching the wiry Bloodfiend in the fan of its full power. The creature twisted and became fluid, corrupt flesh sloughing from blackened bones, then the bones themselves turning molten and then to vaporous ash. Seth reached up to bat the cinders away and the rim of the pit collapsed in a snarl of broken rock, throwing him into the empty air.

'*Brother!*' With the shout came a flash of smoke-smeared golden armour, and a hand reached out to grab him. Seth caught hold and his fall was arrested. The Flesh Tearer growled and hauled himself up to safety, blinking away streams of blood from his eyes.

Dante released his grip and Seth spat out a mouthful of ruby spittle. The lord of the Blood Angels gave him a level look, the thickset shape of his Inferno pistol still smoking from the blast that had destroyed the mutant. Seth bent to recover his weapons.

'Gratitude might be in order,' Dante said mildly.

At last, the plasma gun had cooled enough to fire once again. 'You called me brother,' Seth noted. 'Not *cousin.*'

'I suppose I did.'

'Am I worthy of such address?'

Dante smiled as the clones surged into the Space Marines lines again. 'Am I?' he asked, and turned his weapon on the screaming horde.

Seth let out a wolfish laugh and joined him in the battle.

THE PACK ALPHA ignored the screams of its kindred as they died beneath the guns and the swords of the Space

Marines. The Bloodfiend's addled mind barely registered the sounds of murder and destruction. All that mattered was the colour, the red, the fluid ruby tears; the sweet perfect scent of wet copper, the dense perfume of the vitae, rich and succulent. Saliva flooded the beast's misshapen mouth, ropey strings of discharge frothing at its lips. The kill it had recently made, the dead and old flesh from inside the machine-hulk, was weak and tasteless in comparison. It wanted more. It longed to be sated, even if on some level of barely human understanding it knew it could never be.

The incredible, unstoppable need overwhelmed every other consideration, any question of the preservation of self. The mutants poured through the lines of the Astartes, killing as they went, roaring forward in a tide of ruddy flesh that flooded over the lip of the great pit, cascading through the stone funnel toward the prize at the sepulchre's shining heart.

On muscled legs as thick as support pillars, the eldest and most evolved of the twisted clone-Marines threw itself downward, leaping across the chasm from one side of the sloping walls to another, cuffing its smaller, slower cohorts into the paths of the lasers, dodging or shrugging off the glancing sparks of bolt fire that chanced to reach it. The pack alpha would not be denied its feast; ignoring the dead of its own kind and the bleeding bodies of fallen Astartes, it came down toward the sarcophagus, embracing the call of the Blood of Sanguinius.

It would drink and drink until there was nothing left.

RAFEN SAW THE mutant coming, and a gasp caught in his throat. He knew at once that it was the same creature that had led the horde after the Thunderhawk had crashlanded in the courtyard, the one that had fled before the Blood Angels could regroup and execute it.

It was different now. Larger, and if anything more feral in aspect than it had been before. His thoughts returned to the clone he had dispatched in the arena once again; was this thing what it might have become, if allowed to run its course? Rafen shuddered at the thought, that such twisted atrocities as these could be spun from the gene-matter of a noble Space Marine. He fired, bracketing the Bloodfiend with bolter fire, but it was swift and powerful, matching his Astartes-strong senses point for point, always a heartbeat beyond his kill shot.

The monstrous pack leader landed on the floor of the sarcophagus platform with a massive crash of displaced air, knocking the Chaplain Argastes off his feet with the shock of it. Without a second of uncertainty, the Dread-nought-tall Bloodfiend snatched at the black-clad warrior and hauled him up, a rag-doll in the hands of a hulking, brutal child. Rafen cried out as the creature threw Argastes across the span of the dais, the Chaplain pinwheeling through the air to collide with Mephiston, halting the psyker's headlong advance, both men slamming into the walls so hard they made a shallow crater in the mosaic.

The beast bounded forward, each footfall cracking the stones beneath it, taking a direct line toward the shallow ziggurat of steps leading up to the copper halo, and the shimmering gold sphere. Rafen saw its eyes were solid panes of ruby, hazed by the full, unchained force of a red fury.

Only Puluo and he stood between the Bloodfiend and the sarcophagus, the rest of the squad pinned down by hordes of smaller mutants or hobbled by injury and circumstance. The Space Marine showed his fangs and unleashed the whirlwind of his heavy bolter, each blazing shot from the man-portable cannon finding points upon the creature's hide to cut flesh or rip open newly-scabbed wounds.

The mutant roared and bit at itself where the searing shots fell, at one moment stumbling beneath the onslaught but never slowing. Puluo stood his ground, shouting out hate at the beast as it came upon him, still firing.

In return, it swept out a thick arm and punched the taciturn Space Marine, striking the bolter cannon with such force that the weapon broke apart. The blow did not cease there, the power of it slamming Puluo down into the marble floor. Rafen saw one of his battle-brother's legs twist and snap back against the line of the bone and Puluo fell in a nerveless heap.

Rafen retreated, moving back toward the great glowing sphere. Steadying his hands with a grimace, the sergeant aimed down the iron sights of his bolter and began to fire, one shot at a time, directing each round toward the curdled, shifting mass of flesh that was the alpha Bloodfiend's face. He aimed for the soft tissue of the eyes, seeking to blind the beast if his bolter could not kill it outright.

It yowled and batted at its flesh as it came closer, clawing at the bolt rounds as if they were nagging insects. Rafen could see it was covered in hundreds of wounds, sword cuts, plasma burns and bullet impacts, none of which seemed to slow it. If anything, the pain appeared to drive the Bloodfiend on.

The bolter's breech clattered open on an empty magazine and Rafen's ammunition was spent. He threw the gun at the mutant and it knocked it away, closing to the reach of its arms. The Blood Angel tore his combat blade from the sheath on his hip, the length of polished fractal-edge steel catching the amber luminosity dancing in the air around him.

Digging the flattened heads of bolt rounds from its undulating flesh, the creature came on undaunted. The meat of its face was a shifting, twitching mass that seemed incapable of holding a single aspect, as if the bones and musculature beneath were struggling to define what it was; who it was. Its mouth hung open, and for the first time Rafen heard the disorder of its mewling, howling voice, the gurgles and grunts, the fractured and incoherent pieces of speech that might have been words.

In the turmoil of its countenance, for one brief moment he glimpsed the pattern of a face familiar to him from years of comradeship, rising to the surface through the muddle of twisting, distorted skin. An old face, a trusted face, the aspect of a warrior who had been mentor and comrade to him, lost now as so many others had been.

'Koris!' he spat, unable to believe what he had seen; and yet he knew it was no illusion. Caecus had taken the genetic material of dozens of Blood Angels, living and dead, and used that to forge the synthetic pseudozygotes that grew into these distorted malforms. The ideal that some element of his old tutor might be part of the Bloodfiend sickened Rafen to his core.

Even as the twisted face flowed and changed, the creature swung at him – *so fast, so horribly fast* – and he ducked, slashing at the thick, leathery skin. It did little good, eliciting only snarls and pops of spittle as the monstrous freak tried to snare him, bite him, stamp him into the stones. The back stroke of a clubbed fist caught him off-guard and Rafen stumbled, bouncing off a wide curve of razor-edged steel.

The wings. He spun, startled, as the great sculpted pinion creaked and rattled under the force of his collision, the ancient metal feathers scraping against one another in discord. Rafen's shock was so great that for an instant he forgot the enemy at his back; the Bloodfiend had pressed him to the very foot of the Golden Sarcophagus, into the corona of radiance that spilled across the chamber.

Rafen's gaze crossed the glittering sphere of churning liquid colour, and he saw something within the depths of the molten metal; the hazy ghost of a figure, perhaps a man with his head raised to the sky, his arms open and palms raised, the shadow of mighty wings to his back.

Sudden tears streamed from the Blood Angel's eyes and he shook them off, the moment of timelessness snapping like a broken thread. The beast advanced, slowing, savouring the moment. A toothsome grin, a maw crowded with fangs opened to him. Curled hands, fingers distending into needle-mouthed tentacles, reached toward the sphere. A rabid hunger leaked from every pore of the mutant.

And he was all that stood before it, the last line of defence between this abomination and the flesh of his primarch, between the vampire and the last vestiges of his Chapter's purest blood.

Rafen raised the combat knife and grinned back, baring his own teeth. 'This is as far as you go,' he spat.

The Blood Angel threw himself at the mutant, leading with blade point-forward. The creature reacted, the sudden attack unexpected, but too slow to stop Rafen finding his target. He pressed the knife into a ragged chest wound already thick with clotting fluids, felt the tip slice through muscle and scrape over the dense bones of the ribcage. Ignoring the bellow of pain from his target, he turned and pushed the weapon home until it punctured the Bloodfiend's heart, burying the blade to its hilt in the folds of fibrous skin.

The mutant stumbled back from the sarcophagus, tearing and clawing at the Astartes even as thick, oily blood pulsed from the cut. It staggered and snarled, finally knocking Rafen away to the floor.

Liquid streamed over the red flesh, pooling around the beast's feet, and still it did not falter. It took a slow, painful step toward him, back toward the sarcophagus.

A sudden flash of understanding struck the sergeant. The heart... *But this is a replicae, a genetic duplicate of a Space Marine...*

And in the mirror of every Adeptus Astartes, the Bloodfiend had a secondary heart, just as the Blood Angel did.

Rafen.

A guttural voice came to him, not through the chaos of the battle-thick air but hammered directly into his thoughts, bright as diamond. He turned and through the melee saw Mephiston across the chamber, his force sword in his hand. There was a firm understanding in the psyker's eyes.

Finish it.

Mephiston's arm came up in a sweeping motion and the Mindblade Vitarus left his hand, wheeling and spinning about, carving through the air toward Rafen. He reached for it, something preternatural guiding him. The lengthy, barbed blade turned along its own span and fell into his grip, as easily as if it had been made for him.

Without the incredible power of a psyker behind it, the crystalline metal of the weapon could not channel the ethereal forces of the warp, but even robbed of that, it was still a sword of near-matchless quality. And it was more than enough for Rafen to do what was needed.

Turning the weapon about, Rafen shouted and charged the Bloodfiend. 'For Sanguinius!'

The mutant hesitated on the edge of the steps, angered at another interruption. It saw the sword coming and animal panic lit across its expression. It clawed at the blade, desperate to stop it. Rafen denied the creature and pressed Vitarus into the blood-flecked torso, piercing the skin above the knot of pulsing flesh that was its secondary heart. The inert force sword whispered through the dense meat as if it were vapour, slicing the organ in two, pressing onward until it erupted from the Blood-fiend's back in a welter of black fluid. It staggered, pain squeezing the air from the beast's lungs, and collapsed atop the steps beneath the copper ring.

But some things do not die all at once.

Life leaking from it in sluggish pulses, the clone made a last, desperate attempt to claw itself closer to the sar-cophagus, reaching out, raising itself up to feel the warmth of the golden glow upon its trembling skin.

Rafen took the hilts of the sword and the knife in either hand and gave both a savage, final twist.

A last rasp of breath escaped the lips of the Bloodfiend as death finally claimed it. For a man standing close by, for a man who turned the blades that killed the accursed creature, that breath could have been a single word.

'*Brother?*'

EPILOGUE

FROM THE BATTLEMENTS of the fortress-monastery's shield wall, the broad scope of the Oxide Desert could be seen stretching away into the wilderness, toward the Chalice Mountains. In the warm light of the day, the towers of black smoke from the death pyres extended upward into the clear sky, tilting to the west with the motion of the winds that carried them. Rafen could see the red slabs of Rhino transports dallying at the points of each smoke trail, and on the air he tasted the faint tang of burning flesh and spent promethium.

'How can we be certain that we killed them all?' said Kayne, watching the same sight from the sergeant's shoulder.

'The Chapter serfs will sift Caecus's records just to be certain,' he offered, 'but I know there are no more. Their birthplace in the citadel was obliterated. All of the hatched came to the sepulchre. All of them perished there.'

Kayne frowned and looked away. 'I still…' He stopped.

'Speak, boy,' said Rafen. 'If you serve in my squad, you speak your mind when I tell you to.'

'Lord, while I honour and revere Lord Commander Dante as much as any Blood Angel, I am still…*troubled* by what he did.'

Rafen nodded slowly. 'The opening of the sepulchre?' He sniffed. 'The mutants would have found it on their own eventually. He only made it happen sooner.'

'But the Golden Sarcophagus…' Kayne's voice trembled as he said the name. 'It has been sullied.'

'The master let them come because he is a tactician. Because he knew that they would all be drawn to that place, that their blood-hunger would cloud them and rob them of any other focus. Imagine if we had been forced to hunt the mutants down one by one, if they had been allowed to hide in shadowed corners of the fortress. We would have lost many more men, and much more time.' Rafen turned away from the pyres and studied the youth. 'Blood washes away, brother. Broken stone can be mended. But faith… That is eternal. And Lord Dante knows that faith such as ours cannot be crushed.'

'And what of broken men? What of our brothers Puluo or Corvus?'

Rafen looked away again. 'Puluo is strong. He'll live.'

'And Corvus?' Kayne pressed. 'He gave much for his penitence.'

'So he did.' The sergeant nodded once. 'The Emperor knows his name.'

They stood in silence for a time, until the youth ventured to ask another question. 'Brother-sergeant… What is to become of the Blood Angels now?'

Rafen's gaze fell to a pennant turning in the breeze; a banner upon which lay the sigil of a droplet of blood flanked by angel's wings. 'That choice is beyond our reckoning, brother.'

DANTE CAST ABOUT the Grand Annex, his gaze dwelling on each warrior there, on Armis and Sentikan, on Orloc and Seth and all the others. He frowned as he thought of Daggan, blunt and candid, steadfast and strong, now lost to his Chapter and his kindred alike. As with Rydae before him, and Gorn and Corvus and all the other Space Marines lost to this sorrowful business, their remains were aboard their ships and votive scrolls bearing their names hung in the Chapel of the Red Grail to honour their sacrifices. It was the first time in living memory the rites of the heroes had been spoken there for warriors who were not Blood Angels. It was only fitting, though. They had died in the name of the same primarch, and that was enough.

Dante stood in the centre of the stone star and bowed his head. 'Kindred. Cousins.' He looked up and caught Seth's eye. 'There are no words I can voice that will express my gratitude for your aid in Baal's hour of need. We have paid for the sanctity of the Great Angel with our dearest blood. And in the aftermath of this misery I must take accountability for what has happened.' The lord of the Blood Angels let out a slow breath. 'I am to blame. The responsibility for this atrocity falls to me and I accept it without recoil. As my honoured cousin Lord Seth said, the state of my Chapter can only be laid at my feet. It was my hubris that brought us to this place.'

'Fine words,' said Orloc. 'But what of the choice you asked us to make, Dante? What of this tithe that you request from our Chapters? What are we to do upon that matter?'

Several of the assembled warriors glanced toward Seth, expecting the outspoken Flesh Tearer to speak, but he remained silent.

'The appeal remains,' said Dante. 'I can do no more than ask for your help. But I will bear no malice to any Master who decides against me. I make no motion to compel you. The choice is yours to make.'

'And it must be unanimous,' said Sentikan. 'Without unity, it will be meaningless.'

Armis shifted. 'You realise the import of this, Lord Dante? Let us be clear. If the vote is carried against your tithe, it will mean the dissolution of the Blood Angels.'

Dante gave a solemn nod. 'I will abide by whatever choice the conclave makes.'

'Then we shall make the ballot.' Sentikan's hooded head bobbed. His words hung in the air; no one was willing to speak first.

Blood Angel and Flesh Tearer, Angels Vermillion, Sanguine and Encarmine, Blood Legion and Blood Sword, Flesh Eater, Red Wing and Blood Drinker, these warriorlords and each of the other successor Chapters gathered in the chamber, they stood in a silence that seemed to go on forever.

At last, it was Seth who stepped forward. His face was still seared with the colour of his knitting wounds, but the intensity behind his eyes was undimmed. 'In my Chapter, there is a litany that we recite upon the final day of testing, when a warrior completes his induction into our ranks and earns the name of Adeptus Astartes.' He walked slowly toward Dante. 'The Invocation Initiate. Each Chapter has its own variation, but it is at the core of what we are. These words empower our bond, our strength of purpose.' Seth paused, and when he spoke again it was with a brusque honesty that gave every warrior in the room pause. 'For he today that sheds his blood with me shall be my battle-brother eternal.'

The Flesh Tearer produced his flaying knife and drew it across his palm, a line of blood emerging behind it. Seth offered his hand and the blade to Dante. The Blood

Angel copied the gesture and the two masters clasped their palms together, the crimson mingling.

'I will give you the men,' said Seth. 'And so will every successor here. Your future will be secure.'

There was very little that surprised Dante, but he felt that emotion now. 'Why?'

'Because it is the will of the Emperor.' Seth smiled. 'He brought us to this place, to this condition for a reason, for a *lesson*. To test you. To remind us.'

'To remind you of what?'

Seth's grin grew to show his fangs, and Dante found himself returning it. 'That we are not cousins, Blood Angel. We are *brothers*.'

WITH CARE, TURCIO removed the segments of his battle-brother's power armour from the rack in the armoury chamber, taking a moment to speak a few words of the Prayer to Weapons over each piece.

Ajir watched him, aware that the penitent was ignoring him. Finally, he spoke. 'He gave up his life in vain,' said the Astartes. 'You understand that?'

Turcio hesitated, then continued in his work. 'Is that what you believe?' The Space Marine ran a fine cloth over the ruby sigil across the wargear's chest plate.

'Did Corvus think that letting himself die would somehow complete his atonement? Is that why he did it?'

'Corvus did what he thought was right. That is why I was proud to call him my battle-brother.'

Ajir picked up the dead warrior's helm and shook his head. 'He died for nothing.'

Turcio put down the chest plate and turned to present Ajir with a severe stare, the brand upon his cheek livid and red with anger. 'If you truly believe that, then you did not know him. And because of that, I feel sorry for you.'

'I do not understand.'

The other Space Marine shook his head and turned away. 'That is clear. If you knew Corvus, if you saw the man instead of the brand... Then perhaps you would.'

Turcio walked away, leaving Ajir to stare into the eyes of an empty helmet.

RAFEN WATCHED HIS battle-brother go. The wounds of the past days were still fresh, and it would take time for them to heal. The sergeant returned to his own duty, working at his bolter with the cleaning rods, the simplicity of the task helping him to maintain a focus.

A shadow fell across him and he looked up. 'Brother-Sergeant Noxx.'

The Flesh Tearer's head bobbed. 'Brother-Sergeant Rafen. I have news from the conclave. I thought you would wish to know. The tithe has been approved by all the Chapter Masters.'

A sense of relief washed over the Blood Angel. 'Thank you.'

'My master and our delegation are to return to Eritaen to conclude the campaign there,' he continued, 'but before we do, there is another matter of which I would speak to you.'

'Go on.'

Noxx's hooded eyes bored into him. 'We do not see eye to eye, the two of us.'

Rafen gave a humourless smile. 'That much is certain.'

'But I wish you to know this. In the sepulchre... I was reminded of something. Of commonality between us.'

'I, too.' Rafen admitted.

Noxx gave a nod. 'And perhaps, I dislike you a little less now.'

'I feel the same way.' Rafen offered the Flesh Tearer his hand. 'Until our paths cross again, then?'

Noxx shook his hand. 'I have a feeling that will be sooner than either of us expect–'

At the chamber door, a Space Marine in the gold-trimmed robe of an honour guard entered, interrupting them. 'Brother-Sergeant Rafen?'

'Who asks for me?'

'The Chapter Master,' came the reply. 'You are summoned to his presence.'

DANTE LOOKED UP from the stained glass window as Rafen entered and bowed. The commander beckoned him forward, and the Astartes crossed the chamber.

Rafen saw Mephiston standing in the lee of the window, in the shadow cast by the red sunlight. The psyker nodded to him; he bore no outward signs of the injuries he had suffered in the previous night's battle. Rafen's hand twitched with a fleeting ghost-memory of the force sword in his grip. On the other side of the room, Brother Corbulo waited, watching.

'Master, my lords. What do you wish of me?'

Dante faced him, and there was grave concern etched upon his expression. He held a data-slate in his hand. 'This is an initial report from the Techmarine squads sent to sift the ruins of the Vitalis Citadel. Pict spools recovered from Caecus's laboratorium have provided some very troubling information.'

'Fabius?' Rafen asked, his throat tightening at the renegade's name.

Dante nodded as Corbulo spoke. 'Before Caecus fled to the citadel, he stole a measure of the sacred vitae from the Red Grail.' Rafen's blood turned icy at the thought of such a thing. 'It… appears that the vial was appropriated.'

'The traitor has it,' Mephiston rumbled. 'It was doubtless upon his person when he fled through the warp-gate.'

Rafen's heart pounded in his ears. 'And I let him escape…'

'The blame does not fall upon you,' Dante replied. 'All of us were remiss in this. We share it equally.'

'But what does he want with the blood of the primarch?' Rafen blurted out the question. 'In Terra's name, what sorcery could he do with it?'

Dante exchanged glances with his lieutenants. 'We cannot know. All that is certain is that such a heinous transgression will not stand unchallenged. For too long, Fabius Bile has been a blight upon the galaxy. And now, he has awakened the full wrath of the Sons of Sanguinius.'

Rafen nodded, a sense of purpose coming over him. 'I am at your command. What would you have me do?'

'Prepare the warship *Tycho*,' said Mephiston. 'Gather your men. You will go forth and seek out this criminal.'

'And when I find him?'

'You will recover the sacred blood,' Dante gave him a long, level stare, 'and you will wipe his blighted existence from the stars.'

ABOUT THE AUTHOR

James Swallow's stories from the dark worlds of Warhammer 40,000 include the Horus Heresy novel *The Flight of the Eisenstein, Faith & Fire*, the Blood Angels books *Deus Encarmine* and *Deus Sanguinius*, as well as short fiction for *Inferno!* and *What Price Victory*. Among his other works are *Jade Dragon, The Butterfly Effect*, the *Sundowners* series of 'steampunk' Westerns and fiction in the worlds of Star Trek, Doctor Who, Stargate and 2000AD, as well as a number of anthologies.

His non-fiction features *Dark Eye: The Films of David Fincher* and books on scriptwriting and genre television. Swallow's other credits include writing for Star Trek Voyager, scripts for videogames and audio dramas. He lives in London, and is currently working on his next book.

BY THE BLOOD OF SANGUINIUS!

WARHAMMER
40,000

THE BLOOD ANGELS
OMNIBUS

contains
the novels
Deus Encarmine and
Deus Sanguinius

'War-torn tales of loyalty and honour' SFX

JAMES SWALLOW

ISBN 978-1-84416-559-9

BY GRAHAM MCNEILL

WARHAMMER 40,000

THE ULTRAMARINES
OMNIBUS

buy these
titles or read
free extracts at
www.blacklibrary.com

'Great characters, truck loads of intrigue and an amazing sense of pace.' **Enigma**

GRAHAM McNEILL
NIGHTBRINGER • WARRIORS OF ULTRAMAR • DEAD SKY BLACK SUN

ISBN 978-1-84416-403-5

THE ULTRAMARINES ARE BACK!

WARHAMMER 40,000

The Ultramarines return in an electrifying new novel

THE KILLING GROUND

GRAHAM McNEILL

ISBN 978-1-84416-562-9